PERFECT TEMPTATION

PERFECT FIT BOOK 4

KB ALAN

Copyright © 2021 by KB Alan

Edited by Kelli Collins
Cover Art by Syneca

ISBN-13: 978-1-955124-12-6 (Paperback)

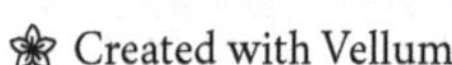 Created with Vellum

This book is dedicated to those who got us through the year 2020. The essential workers who kept the grocery stores running, and stocked. The medical professionals who went above and beyond, just by showing up, but then did so much more. The teachers and parents who had to adapt and revise and rework constantly to try and keep things going for their kids. The factory workers who had to keep showing up while others of us were able to stay home and safe. And the protestors who risked their health and safety to fight for a better us, because Black Lives Matter every single day. I am so thankful for all of you.

Special thanks to Vivienne Westlake for coming up with the title and helping me talk through what the heck I was writing xoxo

ABOUT THIS BOOK

Perfect Temptation

A kinky comment that lands on unexpectedly understanding ears leads Natalie to the surprising realization that her best friend's brother's best friend is into BDSM. Which means Noah is not the guy for her. She tried that lifestyle while in college and it didn't end well.

Noah eases the story of Natalie's past from her, and all his Domly instincts flare to life. He wants to help her figure out if she's right to close the door on her submissive needs, or embrace them and finally find the happiness she deserves. His plan to mentor her so she can decide would be going just fine if she weren't *so. Damn. Tempting.*

Note: This particular series can be read in any order. While they are numbered to be in chronological order, the references/cameos in each book are minor and there is no downside to reading them in any order you choose.

CHAPTER ONE

Natalie forced herself to keep taking deep breaths. It was the only way to prevent bursting into tears. It had been a horrible day, which led to this even more horrible night, but it was almost over. She'd screwed up, but if she just got through this punishment, it would be done, then her Master would forgive her and they could move forward.

Master D jerked on the chain between her bound wrists, bringing her closer to his side. She hadn't realized she'd drifted, her body leaning away from him, her feet shuffling in place as she waited to find out what the final stage of her punishment would be. It would suck, that much she knew. Of course it would; it was meant to. Wouldn't be much of a punishment if it didn't.

And she deserved to be punished. She'd betrayed Master D's trust, as well as that of her best friend, Felicity.

Her breath shuddered as she remembered how angry Master D had been when she'd screwed up. Felicity hadn't been angry, just disappointed. Truthfully, Natalie was still having a hard time wrapping her mind around *how* exactly she'd messed up, but at this point, it didn't much matter. The betrayal was clear to David—Master D—clear to Felicity, and to Felicity's Dom, Michael. But they'd all promised that if she took her punishment tonight, they'd forgive her and move on.

David had told her she could regain his trust by doing as he asked, without hesitation or question. It had been heavily implied, and quickly proven, that he was going to ask her to do things she'd told him she wasn't comfortable with. That was the price of regaining her Master's trust, so here she was in the club, wearing only a G-string. Sure, there were other people fully naked, so she wasn't making a total fool of herself. It was a BDSM club, after all. But she'd only been exploring her sexuality in this way for a few months, and David knew she wasn't ready for this level of nakedness.

But she hadn't balked, even though she'd felt like throwing up when exiting the changing room. She'd worried she'd be cold, but instead she felt like she was too hot, a sheen of sweat covering her, and she was positive her face had been red the entire time they'd been there.

She'd cried when Master David hung the sign around her neck, first showing her the bold lettering that spelled out *Bad Girl* in a huge font. The sign sat below her breasts and invited everyone's attention. Felicity had smirked, then winked at Natalie, as if this were all a game, or a scene from one of the books she and her best friend loved, instead of her burning reality.

For just a second, Natalie had hated Felicity. Then shame had washed through her hard and fast, enough that she'd swayed on her feet and David had been forced to jerk her into the position he'd indicated on the small platform.

This was only happening because she'd betrayed their trust, the two people—outside of her family—who were most important to her, and she was mad at Felicity for giving her a look? What the hell kind of friend was she? She'd forced her head up to meet Master D's gaze, just for a second, just long enough to show him that she was ready to submit, that she would make him proud.

David offered a paddle to Michael, who handed it to Felicity.

"I'll tell you when to stop," Master D told her.

Natalie swallowed hard. Pain was not her thing, though a well-executed spanking could certainly be enjoyable. But she'd never received more than a few swats for an infraction, and she had the distinct impression there were a lot more than that in store for her now.

She squared her shoulders, determined to make Master D proud.

Felicity's first strike was really freaking painful. It was too high, and the edge of the paddle uncomfortably close to her spine. Natalie heard her friend giggle as the girl's Master showed her where to aim. The next strike was less painful, but still stronger than Nat expected.

She swallowed back a gasp, and looked for Master D to be sure he was pleased with her. He'd moved a few steps away, talking to a man she didn't recognize. He wasn't even watching her.

Tears started to slide down her cheeks, and she hated it because she knew she'd get a snotty nose and there was nothing she could do about it.

Behind her, she heard Felicity say she was going to switch arms, as the other was already tired. The next blow was less powerful, but the edge dug into her and she couldn't hold back a cry.

David glanced over, then returned his attention to the other man.

Giggling, Felicity handed the paddle to Michael and came around to Natalie's front. "I guess we should let the experts do their thing," she said cheerfully. "I'll just watch."

Natalie closed her eyes, her body absorbing the hits from the paddle, her brain fighting to reach a place of peace. Because she had to keep forcing her annoyance at her friend, and her Dom, away. Which shamed her even more than the actions that had gotten her into so much trouble.

She had no idea how many times she'd been paddled when David returned to the scene. He smiled sweetly at her as he wiped her tears and handed her a tissue for her nose.

"Almost there, sweets. I'm proud of you for doing what I commanded, even though I know you didn't want to. One more thing and we'll call it done, go home, and we don't need to think about this ever again. You'll remember to trust your Master, won't you?"

"Yes, Master D," she managed, trying to sniffle back more snot.

"You've said you don't want anyone else touching you, but who controls your orgasms?"

"You, Sir."

"And I can use whatever means I want," he said.

Since it wasn't a question, she didn't respond, but a heavy feeling was settling in her chest, threatening to squeeze her throat closed.

They'd been very careful to discuss her limits. They'd gone over the club's limits sheet together many times, to talk about what she was open to and what she wasn't. What she was curious about and what she was willing to try, if he really wanted to, even though she wasn't interested. She'd trusted him to keep to her limits, and he always had.

Well, until tonight, asking her to wear so little into the club. But she could have said no. He'd made that clear. He would have walked away, but she could have said no.

She couldn't feel her fingers as he gripped her hand and led her to the man he'd been talking to. *This is fine*, she admonished herself. The whole reason for this was because she hadn't trusted him. He'd tested her, with Felicity's help, and she'd failed. It made sense that his punishment tonight would include another test of her trust in her Master. He wouldn't really disregard her hard limits.

The man grinned at her and patted his leather-clad leg. "Come to Daddy."

Natalie's feet stopped moving of their own accord. When David pulled on the chain between her wrists, she stood her ground firmly enough that he almost lost his footing and had to backtrack.

"Natalie," he said, in his most stern voice. "Come here."

She swallowed. She was failing. She knew that—but couldn't *not* do it. Couldn't trust that he was just testing her, and that this would all turn out fine if she did as he commanded.

"No," she whispered, though she wasn't sure she actually produced sound.

It didn't matter, because he saw her say the word. Furry overtook his expression.

"Last chance. You know why you're here. You're already on shaky ground. Hesitate one more second and we're done. You're not mine if you can't trust me to take care of you."

She looked into his eyes, tried to find her faith that he would, in fact, take care of her. She felt like she was floating outside her body, except for the fiery heat in her ass. She'd let him shame her, convince her that her action last night—done in love of a friend—was wrong and a failure of her devotion to him. She'd let him order her to walk out into the club in practically nothing, when he knew that terrified her.

He'd encouraged his friends to beat her ass, then hadn't even bothered to watch how stoically she'd endured it. And now...*what?* He expected her to sit on this stranger's lap, this stranger who called himself Daddy, and let him touch her?

Or maybe not...maybe it was a test, and he would stop her at the last second.

Fuck. That. Shit.

"Unclip me," she said, her voice calm, though sounding like it came from someone else.

"You do *not* get another chance at this," David told her. His cheeks were flushed and she wasn't sure if he was mad she was defying him, embarrassed she was doing it in front of others, or upset at the thought of her walking away.

"Unclip me," she repeated. "I'm going to go get dressed."

"What the hell are you doing, Natalie? Don't be ridiculous." Felicity sounded personally offended. "You're almost done. Hell, he's even going to give you an orgasm." She gestured to the stranger like it was no big deal.

"Dandelion." Natalie ignored Felicity and stared into David's eyes as she said the safe word he'd assigned to her. "Unclip me. Now. Or I call for a monitor."

The red in his cheeks intensified and he jerked her to him, not supporting her when she stumbled. He unclipped the cuffs and pushed her away.

Strong hands gripped her shoulders, steadying her. "You okay, there? You folks need a hand?"

Natalie was certain, from the strained look on David's face, that she was being supported by one of the club's dungeon monitors. The very reason she and Felicity had chosen this place was because they had a reputation for being strict on safety. If she told the monitor that David was ignoring her safe word, he might get banned. But he hadn't ignored her. She was free.

"I'm fine. I'm done. Thank you." She twisted free of his hands, gave David one last look to see if he would apologize, not surprised to realize he wasn't even close to feeling sorry. She turned and headed to the changing room.

CHAPTER TWO

Five years later

Natalie could never say exactly how or when she'd been adopted by her best friend's family. It had snuck up on her, and before she knew it, *bam*, she was considered part of the Weber-Crawford clan.

When she'd graduated college and moved to Boston, she'd made friends, but not close ones. She'd still been feeling burned by what had happened with Felicity and David. It had been difficult living with her roommate after that night, but she'd toughed it out for the eight weeks, including finals, before they'd graduated college and gone their separate ways.

She could admit now that she'd probably been a bit standoffish to those she'd met that first year in a new city. She'd chosen to spend most of her income on a studio apartment, rather than look for a roommate. And she'd been friendly with her new coworkers, but not inviting, especially since she didn't have any money to socialize, until she got her first raise.

Then she'd met Annalise her second year. That had been in June. By Thanksgiving, it was already expected that she would spend it with the family, and that she'd bring her Chess pie, which had become one of Joe Weber's favorites. Natalie adored Annalise's father. And her mother, Ophelia Crawford-Weber. Well, most of the Webers and Crawfords, to be honest. They were a big, messy group, and they didn't hesitate to pull Natalie in and treat her like she'd always been there.

Annalise was outgoing and beautiful. Her wild curls, thick and nearly black, a stark contrast to Natalie's own sleek blonde bob. Where Natalie was quiet and enjoyed her sedate office job, Annalise was bold and thrived as a waitress in a restaurant that was always hopping.

Her older brother, Alec, had similar features to Annalise, though he kept his hair short. Some of the stories of his college years were a bit wild, but he'd met and married Sonya a couple of years ago, and now they were expecting a baby.

Which was why Natalie was here, at Sonya's mother's house. Rosa had planned the baby shower, but then she'd been hospitalized with heart trouble several weeks ago. Ophelia, Annalise, and Natalie had promised to make Rosa's plans a reality. So far the party was going well. People were mingling and enjoying some appetizers after having finished playing one of the games.

Natalie looked around for Sonya's sister, Tammy. This was going to be the first grandchild on Sonya's side of the family, and apparently that didn't please Tammy. At all. She was older than Sonya, and they didn't have the best relationship. Sonya had told Natalie and Annalise that last she'd heard, Tammy didn't want to think about having kids until she was thirty, but somehow the fact that Annalise was choosing a different timeline for herself was an insult to her sister.

Seeing a pinched expression on Sonya's face as she walked away from her sister, Natalie exchanged looks with Annalise. The two of them had made it their mission to keep an eye out for just such an issue. Annalise was on the far side of the room, talking to Rosa. She met Natalie's gaze, though, clearly having seen the same thing.

Natalie jerked her head toward the hallway to indicate she'd follow Sonya and check on her.

She rounded the corner and jerked to a stop as she saw Alec with Sonya. He was holding the back of her neck with one hand, and both of her wrists with the other, his gaze intent on his wife's.

Natalie drew in a sharp but silent breath. It was clear to her that Alec's presence—and likely his hold—was calming Sonya down. Her cheeks were flushed but Natalie watched as her shoulders relaxed and she drew in a deep breath. Alec murmured something that Natalie couldn't hear—didn't try to hear. She thought about stepping away, but Alec straightened and glanced to her. She had the distinct impression that he'd known the second she'd rounded the corner.

"Are you okay, Sonya? I have a glass of red wine ready to spill on Tammy, just say the word. You know she won't stick around with a stain on her pretty dress."

Sonya managed a small smile and opened her mouth to respond. Natalie didn't give her a chance.

"Actually, you don't even have to say the word. Plausible deniability and all that. Just, you know, give me a wink."

Natalie focused all of her attention on Sonya's eyelids, and the other woman laughed, without winking.

"I'm fine. I just needed a minute so I wouldn't say something mean to her."

Alec snorted.

"Tell me again why it's okay for her to say mean things to you, but not okay for you to do the same?" Natalie asked, honestly wondering.

"Because I'm a better person than she is, and because my mother is two weeks out of the hospital and can't have any stress right now."

Natalie grimaced. "Fine. Whatever." She looked at Alec. "Aren't you supposed to be out golfing with Joe and Sonya's dad?"

He raised an eyebrow at her, and she couldn't help it. A little shiver pulsed through her at the air of command that she'd swear she'd never felt from him before. Not until she'd seen him holding his wife that way. And the way Sonya had reacted.

She held up her hands. "Hey, I was just asking. No judgements. I wouldn't want to go whack a ball around the grass on a day like today, either." The previous day had been gorgeous, but June gloom had descended that morning, so she hadn't minded being stuck inside for the shower.

"Dad got called in for an emergency surgery," Sonya told her. "I told Alec that he and Joe could still go, but they didn't seem too interested. I think Alec came inside to sneak a peek at the desserts."

And check on his wife, Natalie figured.

"I better get back out there," Sonya said, her hand rubbing a small circle over her big baby belly.

"Let Nat use the red wine on Tammy if that bitch says one more word," Alec said. It sounded an awful lot like a command to Natalie, and she wasn't surprised in the least when Sonya's eyes dropped and she gave a little nod. He kissed her forehead and patted her butt as she headed down the hall, her laughter floating back to them.

Natalie smiled and turned to follow, but Alec cleared his throat. "Do you have any questions for me?"

She knew what he meant. Questions about what she'd seen. If she'd known nothing about BDSM, the scene she'd stumbled upon might have seemed a bit odd, though not very. But he'd picked up on the fact that she'd recognized that the hold hadn't been accidental. While her brain was trying to decide if she should act like she had no idea what he was talking about, her mouth opened up and said, "No, Sir." She winced. "Damn it."

He was grinning now. "Hmm. I think you've been keeping secrets, little Natalie."

"Ha! Me? I was at your wedding, and I had no idea you were…" She waved her hand down the hallway.

"Well, if I'd known you wanted to come to our *other* ceremony, we would have invited you."

He meant a collaring ceremony. She wrinkled her nose. While

she'd seen some happy, committed couples—and multiples—at the club, she'd been soured on the idea of committing to a Dom.

He leaned his shoulder against the wall and studied her. She had to force herself not to squirm. This was Alec. She'd known him for a few years now and considered him a friend. A pseudo-brother. Nothing had changed. Not really, anyway.

"Tell me."

Her mouth actually opened to do just that, before she slammed it closed and glared at him.

He laughed.

"Look, I might have dabbled a bit in college, but it's not a thing for me now. It wasn't right for me." He frowned, and she rushed on. "But, I mean, I'm cool with it. No judging other people. I just wasn't made for that."

She forced herself to stop babbling.

He straightened and put his hand on her shoulder, squeezing gently. "Sounds like there's a story there. If you need to tell me, I'm here. Or Sonya. You can talk to us." He watched her for a second, then kissed her forehead and headed out the back way.

Natalie leaned against the wall, feeling like she'd gone a round or two with a boxer. If David had possessed half of Alec's Dom energy, she'd probably have gone through with what he'd asked of her. The thought did not sit well.

Putting it out of her mind, she went back into the room in time to help Annalise maneuver into place beside Sonya, so that Tammy wouldn't be in charge of recording what gifts came from which guests.

By the end of the party, she really had forgotten the incident, and was exhausted from helping to make sure that Sonya's mom didn't realize the extent to which her oldest daughter was a bitch to her youngest daughter. Rosa had retired to her bedroom for rest, glowing with pleasure at how well the party had gone. Sonya was blissfully happy, and Tammy had just been handed the garbage bag by Annalise's mother, with a nod toward the cans out back.

Natalie managed not to laugh until the door was closed, then turned it into a cough when Ophelia raised an eyebrow at her. But she didn't miss the smirk on the woman's face as she turned away.

She helped cart presents to Sonya and Alec's house, along with Annalise and her cousin Ivey. Ivey had to run, but Natalie and Annalise accepted Alec's offer to order in pizza.

After eating, she curled up in an armchair with Missy P, Sonya's cat. The beautiful white Persian was purring away under Natalie's attentive strokes as Annalise and Alec argued about which independent pizza restaurant was the best.

"You're telling me you didn't like that?" Alec asked, pointing to his sister's very empty plate.

"No, just that it would have been better if you'd gone to my place."

"Your place is slow and we'd still be waiting to eat if I'd called them."

"Maybe, but it would have been ten times better."

"Ten times?" His raised eyebrow clearly indicating he expected her to tell the truth.

"Okay. Fine. Twice as good, though, for sure."

"I disagree, and anyway, I was hungry. Sonya was hungry. Natalie was hungry. *You* told me you were starving when I asked if you wanted to stay for pizza."

"That's not the point." Annalise's pout was clearly that of a youngest sibling.

"Well, it's *my* point, and my house, so that's what matters."

Annalise rolled her eyes but dropped the subject.

Alec turned his attention to Natalie. "Missy P likes you."

She usually spent her time with the siblings at their parents' house, where big events were hosted. Alec and Sonya had bought this place last year, and Natalie had come to the barbecue housewarming, but the cat had been safely locked away in a back bedroom for the event.

"She's a sweetheart. What's her name from?"

Alec snorted, and Sonya backhanded him lightly on the chest.

"At our last apartment building, our neighbor was an older lady who had to move into an assisted living facility. She couldn't handle the stairs anymore, and needed someone to check in on her once a day to make sure she had her meals. Her niece helped her get into the place, but wasn't able to take the cat, unfortunately. Mrs. Egebe named her Misses Princess, but she seems okay with the shortened version."

As if she knew they were talking about her, Missy P stretched and resettled herself in Natalie's lap.

"Are you still living in that tiny one-bedroom apartment?" Sonya asked.

"It's loud and has no air conditioning," Annalise complained. "I still don't know why you wouldn't move in with me and my roommate. We could have afforded a nice three-bedroom apartment if we'd gone in together. One *with* air conditioning and a heater that works all the time instead of most of the time."

"Because I like you being my best friend, and I wasn't going to risk that by being roommates. Didn't you admit to me that several of your college friends had lost their friendships by moving in together?"

"Yeah, but didn't I tell you that wouldn't happen with us?"

"You did. You were also dating Dilbert at the time, and I thought it was best that he have your unreserved attention."

"You're such a bitch," Annalise said, but she was laughing as she did so. "And that wasn't his name, as you well know."

"Anyway," Sonya drawled, bringing their attention back to her. "Maybe you wouldn't mind a long weekend away from your apartment if you could stay in a lovely house, *with* air conditioning, a nice backyard, a cat companion, a full fridge, a nice wine selection, and a quiet neighborhood?"

Natalie frowned. "I thought you canceled your trip?"

The couple had planned to go the month before, but then Sonya's mom had suffered a heart attack, so they'd postponed it. Then, she knew, Alec had gotten concerned about the baby being due in a month.

"She convinced me that Cape Cod was not, in fact, thousands of miles away, and that even if her water broke, we'd still have time to make it to our hospital, but if for some reason we couldn't, there are several hospitals between here and there. But mostly she promised me that she wouldn't go into labor on our trip and that if she did, I could name the baby whatever I want."

Natalie and Annalise burst into laughter. Natalie especially appreciated that both Alec and Sonya looked smug, as if they'd each won whatever battle had been fought over the weekend getaway to the beach.

"You don't have a cat sitter lined up?" she asked. "When do you leave?"

Sonya rubbed her belly. "Luke said he'd come, but it's not like he really wants to. He just works close enough that it wouldn't be an imposition. But I thought you might actually enjoy it. We leave Friday morning and come home Tuesday afternoon."

It was hard to remember what kind of cousin Luke was, exactly. Natalie was pretty sure he was a Weber, not a Crawford, but it didn't much matter. She'd love the opportunity to have a quiet little weekend getaway herself, and told them so.

Alec walked Annalise to her car while Sonya showed Natalie where the cat food was.

"Luke's great, totally reliable, but I was a tiny bit worried that he'd…well, notice things…and wonder," Sonya said as she walked Natalie to the litter box. "I hope you don't mind, but it occurred to me you'd be a little safer in that respect." She shot a slightly nervous glance at Natalie. "When we were driving home, Alec mentioned you were, um, maybe familiar enough with some of the things we do to be, um…comfortable with me mentioning it."

Natalie gave her a quick hug. "You can talk freely to me. I wasn't involved in the lifestyle for long, but enough that I won't be shocked if you have an odd stockpile of handcuff keys on your key rack."

Sonya giggled. "I was more thinking Luke would wonder why the plant hooks in the ceiling are super heavy-duty, why there are Velcro straps under the couch cushions, and why the door to the basement is locked."

Natalie laughed and waggled her eyebrows.

"Honestly, he probably wouldn't have noticed a thing, but it made me twitchy to worry about it. Thank you for taking those nerves away."

"My pleasure. Missy P's a cutie pie and I'll enjoy my own little vacation. Maybe I'll even take Monday off, as well."

"You should," Alec said, joining them. "There are steaks in the freezer, wine in the cabinet, and a jetted tub in the master bathroom that I'm pretty sure is the reason Sonya insisted we buy this house."

Sonya snorted. "Right. It had nothing to do with the finished basement, the private back yard, or the built-in grill."

"I'm simply here to give you all the things your heart desires, my love. Especially when it involves jets."

BY THE TIME she left work on Friday, Natalie was definitely thinking about those jets. She'd only taken a quick lunch to check on Missy P, and had followed Sonya's suggestion to pull a package of steaks out of the freezer. The rest of the day had been spent working her butt off so she'd feel no guilt in taking Monday off, with a little bit of time devoted to thinking about the jetted tub, a nice bottle of wine, and blissful quiet.

Okay, so she'd also spent a few minutes here and there watching videos online about how to use a giant gas barbecue without screwing it up, blowing up the house, or turning a steak into shoe leather.

She pulled into the driveway, which had a car that hadn't been there when she'd come at lunch. Glimpsing a familiar figure in the doorway, she gathered her purse and water bottle. Noah Tucker was Alec's best friend. They'd met a couple of times, but she had no idea why he might be at the house when Alec wasn't there.

He'd turned away from the door and was waiting for her, phone in one hand, bundle of rope in the other. He'd grown a short, light beard since she'd last seen him, and it suited him. His dark hair was just long enough to give it that slightly messy look that made her want to push her fingers through it. His white skin wasn't as tan as she remembered, and she deduced he wasn't spending as much time in the sun as he used to. Or maybe he was just better with sunscreen now.

"Natalie. I was just about to text Alec," he told her. "No one's home."

"Hi Noah. They're in Cape Cod."

He frowned. "Alec told me they were leaving on the twelfth. Which is tomorrow, last time I checked."

"Once again, the fact that Alec's job does not revolve around a calendar bites someone else in the ass. They left this morning."

He laughed, and her tummy did a little fluttery thing.

"I was dropping off some rope he asked for. Mind if I leave it with you? Are you cat sitting?"

He held up the purple bundle and her mouth ran away from her. She happened to know that purple was Sonya's favorite color, and could well imagine what the rope might be used for. "Oh, yeah, every household needs a good supply of soft, strong rope."

Oh, shit.

Ever since the baby shower on Sunday, she'd been thinking back to her BDSM phase, as she mostly thought of it. She felt her cheeks flame and bit her lip, but hoped that he would take it as the perfectly innocent comment it should sound like…if you weren't the type of person who thought about rope bondage.

She forced herself to look up and found that his amber eyes had gone a bit wide.

Then a grin slowly stretched across his face as her cheeks got hotter and hotter. As a friend of Alec's, maybe he knew exactly what she'd meant.

Mortified, she turned her back to him and fumbled the keys out of her purse to open the door. And, *of course*, dropped the damn things.

"I've got it," he told her, bending down, body close to hers as he scooped up the keys from in front of her feet, leaned around her to fit them into the lock, and shoved the door open.

Damn the man for being so attractive. He was a good few inches taller than her, and she could feel the strength he commanded even though he was barely brushing against her.

They went inside and she dumped her purse and bottle on the table and picked up Missy P, who was sitting with her back to the door, pretending indifference to the fact that it had taken them so long to come inside and see to her needs.

Indifference turned to purrs as soon as Natalie gave the Persian the attention she so clearly deserved. Noah set the keys and rope down on the table, then moved in close enough to give the cat a good head scratch. Natalie tried not to breathe in the scent of him. A heady combination of flowers and dirt and shampoo. Mango, maybe?

They'd met at Alec and Sonya's engagement party four years ago, but only in a cursory way. She'd still been a somewhat new addition to the Weber-Crawford clan events, and could admit she'd been intimidated by his good looks and easy confidence. She'd watched the way he'd danced with his girlfriend at the wedding and had definitely fantasized about being in his arms.

But she'd still been raw over the whole Dom David thing, and had shoved him into the "no go" box for good. Not that it had been an issue. He'd had a girlfriend and hadn't even glanced her way. But her thought process hadn't really been about him; it had been about her and where she was at.

Her phone gave an obnoxious alert, and she carefully pulled it out without disturbing the cat. Which meant that the screen was visible to Noah, as well as her, showing a reminder she'd set to open the bottle of wine so it could breathe before dinner.

"Uh, Sonya said I should try a particular red she likes with steaks." She motioned over to the plate on the counter, where the meat had defrosted.

"Two steaks?" he asked. "Are you having company?"

"No, they had them frozen in pairs. I figured if I do a good job and enjoy the first, it won't suck to have a second over the weekend. And if I fuck up the first, it won't suck to have another *chance* over the weekend." She was babbling. But he was standing so *close*.

"First time making steaks?"

"On a grill. I've done the stovetop thing, but wasn't super successful. I even got an instant-read thermometer, but it still wasn't great. Anyway, this should be fine. I watched some videos. Chances of catching things on fire seem minimal."

He laughed. "I've used his grill. Definitely minimal."

"Would you like to stay for dinner?" she asked. "I have some broccoli I was going to roast to go with the steaks and wine."

He watched her for a second, gave the cat one last pat, then stepped back a bit. "I was going to indulge in a frozen pizza at home, alone, but I think I can choke down a steak with company instead. I can handle the grill, if you'd like. Or walk you through it."

CHAPTER THREE

Noah wasn't the least surprised when Natalie told him she wanted to work the grill. She went off to change out of her office clothes while he opened the wine that Sonya had suggested. He was a frequent guest at this house, so he knew where the bottle opener and glasses were.

She padded out in shorts and bare feet, hair pulled into a stubby ponytail, and wearing a shirt that followed her curves very nicely. It was a beautiful day outside, and he'd opened the sliding doors to the patio. A warm breeze teased her hair, and he wanted to see how good of a grip that tiny ponytail would give him. She'd had longer hair when they'd first met, long enough that he'd have been able to wrap it around his fist a couple of times. But the blunt bob she'd switched to a couple of years ago suited her. When not pulled back, it swung just above her shoulders.

As she patted the steaks dry with a paper towel, he tried to decide if her remark about the rope he'd brought had been innocent or knowing. Could go either way...but her blush made him suspect she went *his* way. Something he'd never considered.

He'd met her a couple of times over the years, but he'd been in a relationship at the beginning, and she'd become firmly entrenched in his best friend's family, and that had seemed like a no-go. But he'd been curious enough about her to learn she hadn't been in any serious relationships since he'd known her. And the one guy she'd dated long enough for Alec to meet had been a dud, according to his friend.

For just a second, he wondered if Alec had screwed up today's date on purpose, to force a one-on-one meeting like this. But Alec's casual relationship with the calendar was well known, and his friend was too good a Dom to play games like this with his friend, let alone someone he considered family.

They chatted easily about gas and flames and charcoal as she familiarized herself with the grill. She didn't need his help, but would look up at him to confirm what she said when she wasn't as sure as she sounded. He liked that. A lot. It was ridiculous, it wasn't like it took a great deal of intellect to master the art of barbecuing, but it was very close to her looking to him for approval...and he liked it.

"Sorry about the dirt," he said when the lid was down and they only needed to wait for the grill to do its job. "I was swinging by here on my way home, so I'm still in work clothes." His hands were clean, but his boots were muddy and his jeans weren't much better. He'd have to check the tile floor inside to make sure he hadn't made a mess.

She waived his apology away with the tongs. "You work at a garden center, right?"

"That's right. Now that I'm the manager, I don't always get into the dirt, but I still enjoy it and tend to make that my Friday activity."

"I have such a brown thumb. I have two plants I've managed not to kill over the years, and I just concentrate on keeping them alive and don't push my luck."

She opened the grill a little earlier than she needed to by his estimation, stuck the thermometer into a steak, frowned, and put the lid back down.

"It's something you can learn if you want to, we're always happy to help educate. But it certainly doesn't need to be everyone's passion."

"I figure if I ever manage to buy a house with a yard, I'll worry about it then. Of course, I might be eighty at that point, unless I decide to leave Boston."

He laughed. "No kidding. If I hadn't been able to use the money my parents saved for me for college as a down payment, I'd still be in an apartment, and have to take over this space to get my fix. Luckily, they didn't mind me using it for the house instead of a degree."

"I bet you have a great yard."

"I absolutely do."

She gave him a huge smile and moved to check the steaks again, just as he was about to suggest she do so.

Missy P came out to join them after finishing her dinner, twining around their legs until Noah picked her up.

"Sonya told me she was fine to come out into the yard, but it makes me nervous."

"In my experience, she likes being queen of her little world and has zero interest or curiosity about the rest of it." The hairy white beast had flopped into his arms like a jellyfish and was purring up a storm.

"That's good."

The timer for the oven beeped, so she put the tongs down and went inside to retrieve the roasted broccoli. Soon the steaks were done and they were cutting into their first bites. He waited, watching as she closed her eyes and savored the meat.

When she'd swallowed, she opened her eyes and beamed at him in triumph. "Damn, that's good!"

He laughed and tried his own bite. Delicious.

They ate in silence for a bit, the crispy veggie a perfect companion to the juicy meat. When she'd consumed most of her glass of wine, he decided it was time.

"Let me ask you a question."

The instant scowl on her face suggested that he was right in thinking the rope comment hadn't been purely innocent.

He laughed. "That tells me a lot, right there."

Her mouth opened into an O that had his dick twitching. "How…? What?"

"It tells me you've been wondering if I was going to ask, or let it go, and you wouldn't be wondering that if it had just been a random remark."

She tried to pull of an air of innocence. "I don't know what you mean."

He stopped smiling at that, and let his full Dom self bleed into his words. "Please don't do that. Tell me you won't discuss it, or tell me to mind my own business, but don't lie to me."

She flushed scarlet and dropped her eyes to the table. He waited, watched as she took in a deep breath, and squared her shoulders. She lifted her gaze to his. "You're right. I'm sorry. I know what you meant. I know what the rope is for. But I'm not involved in that kind of thing, obviously, so it was easier to pretend I was clueless. Stupid, though. I'm sorry."

He waited only a second before nodding and smiling. "Do you want to talk about it?"

She went back to her meal. "There's nothing to talk about."

"Okay. Tell me about how you ended up in Boston. It sounds like you plan on staying, even though you might be eighty before you can buy a house?"

Her shoulders relaxed, and she took a sip of her wine. "I grew up in Atlanta, and when I graduated college, the insurance company I was interning for had a position available here. It's a nationwide company, so I could definitely transfer somewhere with lower cost of living, but I like being here. I like my office, my friends, the Webers and Crawfords."

"No friends and family in Atlanta calling you back?"

"My mom and grandparents are there, and I want to visit them more, but I don't need to live there. I've finally gotten them hooked on video calls."

"And you like your job?"

She smiled. "I do. I mean, it's certainly not a passion kind of thing, like you probably have, and I know everyone loves to hate on the insurance industry, for good cause. But I feel like I'm able to help people navigate their way through it, and crazy as it sounds, I enjoy the admin side of things. If I do x, y, and z, I can expect result a, b, or c. If I feel like I need to push for a certain result, I know the steps to take for that. And, best of all, at the end of the day, the job is done. I don't spend a lot of time thinking about it once I've clocked out."

"And then what do you do? For fun?" He hadn't meant it to be a leading question. He'd been hoping she'd circle back around to their earlier conversation on her own. If she didn't, well, then she obviously wasn't ready for that. If she did, he was definitely interested in what she had to say. But her expression now showed she *had* been thinking about it, and had applied it to his question.

He held up a hand. "I just meant how do you spend your time? Hobbies?"

She sighed. "I knit. A lot. And I sell some of what I knit."

"Okay, yeah. I remember Sonya being excited to see the baby blanket you made. Why do you sound mad about it?"

"I'm not. I'm annoyed with myself. I mean, we're adults, right? We can talk about things…like this…without—"

She broke off when he started to laugh, and glared at him.

"Apparently not, since you can't even say the words. What are you trying for, sweetheart? I'll help. Is it sex you want to be able to talk about without saying it? BDSM?"

She pouted, which wasn't something he normally found attractive, but suddenly found adorable. Especially when she started nibbling on her lower lip.

Having finished her meal, she shoved the plate aside and buried her head in her arms on the table. "I'm so embarrassed."

"I'm sorry, I shouldn't have teased. Although, I'm still confused how asking about knitting turned into a conversation that may, or may not, be about sex and BDSM."

She rolled her head back and forth. "It's not you. I'm twenty-seven freaking years old."

"Well, to be fair, we don't really know each other very well. Would you have reacted this way if it was Alec asking you about this?"

With a deep sigh, she raised her head. "Probably worse. He's kind of like a brother to me."

"You don't have to talk about it now, although if you leave me in suspense about how knitting and sex go together in your head, I might hate you a little bit."

She laughed at that, and leaned back. He was relieved. He was trying very hard to achieve a balance between encouraging her to talk with a bit of teasing, and not making her uncomfortable, which he absolutely did not want to do. Well, not too much, anyway. But his curiosity was definitely piqued. Both as a man who found her very attractive, and as a Dom who worried she had some past trauma she needed to deal with.

"You don't have to look so worried," she told him. "It's not anything bad, I'm just not used to talking about it."

"Glad to hear it." And surprised that she'd read him that well.

"I experimented a bit in college. My roommate and I went to a club, met some Doms, had fun for a while, but then it turned out that I wasn't really good at the whole submissive thing, and so I stopped."

She probably didn't realize she was hiding when she took the glass and sipped slowly at it, peeking at him from over the rim. But he knew. And it wasn't that she was uncomfortable with the sex talk, not really. He was pretty sure that it was the fact there was a lot more to the story than she'd admitted.

"Fair enough. It's not for everyone. But I'm glad nothing bad happened?" He made the last part just a bit of a question.

"Yeah. I mean, not really. I just realized that what a Dom expected of me, and what I expected of me—and him—were not great matches."

He cocked his head, trying to appear curious, as opposed to

letting her see the protective instinct to attack someone who had hurt her that was trying to burst free. "If it wasn't a big deal, will you tell me? I'm always curious to know how people fit—or don't—into the lifestyle."

The sun had gone down and the outdoor lights that Alec had set to timers came on, bathing her in a warm glow. He normally would have refilled her glass, which she was still holding even though it was empty, but he didn't want alcohol to be the reason she trusted him with her story.

"I'll take the dishes in," he suggested, giving her time to decide. He stacked their plates and held his hand out for her glass.

She handed it to him, then wrapped her arms around herself, though the air was still quite warm.

Oh yeah, he was going to get this story out of her, that was no longer a question. He motioned her over to the outdoor sofa. "Get comfortable, Nat. I'll handle these."

———

Natalie was thinking so hard, she barely acknowledged that Noah had taken the dishes into the house. She did as he'd suggested, heading over to the comfortable seating area her friends had set up. Now that she knew—or at least, strongly suspected—that Noah, like Alec, was into BDSM, she could stop thinking of him as a potential guy she might hook up with, and relax with him.

Maybe tell him about what had happened, get an outsider's opinion on the events. It would be interesting to know what he thought. While she was firm in the knowledge that she wasn't made for that lifestyle, she'd also come to strongly suspect that David had acted like an asshole. It would be nice to know that wasn't just her being embarrassed over failing.

But, if that was true...then where did that leave her? She'd stopped reading *those* books. Her favorite books. Because it had been too confusing to try to separate the fantasy of the books to what her reality had been. She knew she didn't want to go there again, so really, reading them now shouldn't be any different than reading a good vampire romance, *right?*

So, okay then. This was her chance to get over the experience, finally, and really move forward. It wasn't as though she'd been in stasis for five years, but she could admit that she hadn't really given most of the guys she'd dated a real shot. Partly because she hadn't been interested in them enough to try, but that was her fault, as well. She'd avoided anyone she thought might have D/s tendencies, even the slightest bit.

Noah came back, shutting the door now that the bugs were out. He'd changed into basketball shorts and taken his muddy boots off. He had a fireplace lighter with him, using it to light the bug candles on the little coffee table in front of her. She'd curled up on one end of the outdoor sofa, Missy P sprawled across her lap, tail swishing back and forth.

He sat down on the other end of the sofa, turned toward her, elbows braced on his knees, and gave her a very serious look that made her glad she'd decided he was off her potential guys list. "So. How about those Red Sox?"

It took her a whole second to realize what he'd said, and then she burst out laughing. His grin was quick and did things to her nether regions that it shouldn't, considering she'd safely locked him away into the friend zone.

"It's okay. I've worked my way around to being interested in an outsider's perspective on what happened. Or, an insider's perspective. Whatever. You know what I mean."

"Absolutely. Someone who wasn't involved, but has the necessary history and background to judge what happened."

"Right." She bit her lip. "But, I mean, we've danced around it a bit. *Do* you have the history and background?"

"Smart girl, well done." He nodded. "Yes, I've been active in the BDSM scene for ten years. I frequently take on monitoring and mentoring duties at Apex, the club I use here in town. You would be very smart to confirm all that, and look into the club, its reputation, and my reputation, if we were playing. I'm glad you asked. Even a personal recommendation from someone like Alec or Sonya wouldn't be enough for you, because you don't know their play style."

She let out a breath. "Okay. So, you know, I've already come to terms with the fact that I didn't handle things well, which is why I know I'm not designed for that kind of play, or lifestyle, so you don't have to worry about telling me. But it's kind of a long story. If you can let me get the whole thing out before you judge…" She wasn't sure how to finish that.

"I shouldn't have said judge," he said, sounding careful. "I'll give you my opinion on your story, but it's not about judging you. And yes, I'll let you get the whole thing out."

Great, now she had him handling her with kid gloves. While she didn't really know him, she was confident he wasn't an asshole. And she could take it. She *wanted* to know what he thought, now that she'd worked herself up to it.

"Okay. So, my roommate in college was Felicity. She and I became best friends in sophomore year and moved into an apartment off campus for junior and senior years. We're both big readers, and we got into these BDSM romance books."

"You said it!"

She laughed, enjoying his attempt to relax her. "Yeah, fine. I can say BDSM. And sex."

"Good girl."

She tried to pretend the shiver was due to the evening air cooling down, but she wasn't that good of a liar, even to herself. Swallowing, she forced her attention to the story, and not the guy sitting only one seat cushion away.

"Right, so we started talking about these books, and wondering how much was real and how much was just romance novel fantasy. And then she searched online and we joined a forum. We did a lot of reading and wondering, then we worked up the nerve go to an open-house event at a club. We'd checked it out as best we could and felt it was safe."

She glanced at him, and he nodded, but didn't say anything.

"We met a guy named Michael, and he and Felicity hit it off pretty well. He said he really wanted to introduce me to his friend David. One thing led to another, and pretty soon the two of them were together, and David and I were together. They were aware we were new to the whole scene, so they took us out on dates, but also eased us into the sub thing."

She paused when Missy P stood and stretched, then made her way from Natalie's lap to Noah's. Couldn't blame the cat, she decided.

"We were together for six months, went to the club several times, David and I scened together at his apartment a couple of times."

"You felt good about it? Comfortable?"

She hesitated, trying to recall her feelings at that stage. "Yes and no. I'd had a two-year relationship in high school, and dated a few times in college, but nothing serious. Looking back, I was having a hard time deciding if I liked David the guy I was dating, or Master D, and the reconciliation between the two. Plus the things we were doing were all so new and exciting, but it was also kind of embarrassing to call a guy 'Master D' and 'Sir.' It might just be knowing now what I didn't know then, but it was like I wasn't quite getting what I wanted from either of them, but combined, it was enough to make me think it was working."

"That makes sense."

"Does it? I've really never deconstructed this whole thing, to be honest. It all ended right before finals, so I threw myself into that and graduating, getting the job, moving to a whole new state, a whole new way of life in the north, and just...never really fully processed."

He nodded. "It does."

"Okay. So, we'd been together six months. I came home from my internship one day and Felicity was crying. She said that she was super stressed about finals and sure she was going to fail and her parents wouldn't pay for another year of college, or support her, and she would have to break up with Michael, and on and on.

Honestly, I thought it was pretty weird because she was a fine student and hadn't had any concerns about her grades, as far as I'd known, all year. She bitched about assignments or teachers now and then, but nothing like this. She had her head buried in her hands and was just sobbing—and then she told me she wanted to kill herself and just be done with it."

She'd forced that last bit out in one long sentence and now needed a breath. Her stomach had knotted up as she remembered the scene in their apartment all those years ago. A glance at Noah found that he was watching her patiently, no reaction to what she'd said.

Taking another breath, she focused her eyes on the candle and tried to tell the story as factually as she could. She wanted his real opinion, not something colored by her emotions.

"I put my arms around her and promised her she'd be fine, that everything would be fine. That I was positive she wouldn't fail anything, but even if she did, it wouldn't be the end of the world, her parents weren't going to stop loving her. All of that until she stopped crying. I said maybe we should go to the hospital and talk to a doctor. She shook it off, said she was fine, that I'd made her feel better. I told her we could go to the counseling center on campus in the morning, but she brushed me off and started making dinner... like nothing had happened."

She startled when Missy P's furry head bumped her arm, and found that she'd hunched forward toward the table. She sat back and the cat circled her lap four times, then dropped down. The warm, furry weight brought Natalie back to the present. She'd been so out of her element that night, terrified she would do the wrong thing, say the wrong thing. And so confused, because it was completely out of left field.

Another glance at Noah proved he was still watching, waiting patiently for her to continue.

"I didn't sleep that night. I was so afraid she would do something, even though she acted normal through dinner and told me everything was fine when I asked before she went to bed. I sat on the couch all night, until she got up, took a shower, and went to class. I skipped my morning class and went to Michael's house. And I told him what she'd said."

It felt like a lead weight was sitting in her stomach. She remembered having a hard time saying the words to her friend's Dom, but feeling so relieved that someone else would be able to help her figure it out, make sure they took the right steps to help Felicity.

She'd fucked up so badly. The shame of it burned like acid up her throat. It took more effort than she liked to force herself to face Noah. To see his reaction.

No change. He had the same patient expression.

She swallowed down the burning sensation and bit her lip. Missy P made a little trilling sound and Natalie resumed petting her.

"Michael told me to go to David's and wait for him, and tell him what had happened. About both the previous night, and then about going to see Michael. I—I was confused. I didn't realize yet what I'd done. I was so upset and tired, I did head over to David's, but before I got there, I realized he was at work and didn't get off until five, and I was still worried about Felicity, and I couldn't really afford to miss more classes, so I went back to campus instead. Which was pretty much a waste, since I couldn't focus, even though I texted back and forth with Felicity a couple of times to make sure she was okay.

"When I got to our apartment, Felicity was studying, like normal, but she looked at me like I was crazy, asked me if I wasn't supposed to be at David's. I asked her if she wanted to go to the counseling center before they closed, but she just shook her head at me like I was an idiot and told me to go to David's before I got into 'more trouble.'"

She managed a wry smile in Noah's direction. "At that point, I was too dumb and tired to even know what she meant, and so confused, so I just did what she said and left."

He still showed no visible reaction, but she had no doubt that she had his full attention.

"Hold on for one minute," he said, and headed into the house. He quickly returned with two glasses of ice water and set one in front of her.

Suddenly her throat felt like sandpaper. The ice rattled in the glass as she brought it to her lips, but she felt better after taking a long drink.

CHAPTER FOUR

Noah hadn't gone into this conversation with a lot of expectations. But he had absolutely *not* expected to have trouble keeping to his side of the sofa. And yet, here he was. Bringing Natalie the water had helped. A little. But the urge to pick her up and cuddle her into his lap, to share his warmth and strength while she recounted the events of her past, was almost overwhelming. Luckily, as a Dom, he'd worked hard on his patience and control.

"Thanks," she said, lowering the nearly empty glass.

"You're welcome."

He waited in silence as she took a couple more breaths, then started speaking again.

"I waited for David on his front porch. I remember thinking I really, really needed a hug." She shook her head. "Like I said, at that point, I didn't even realize I'd screwed up."

Making sure she couldn't see, he gripped the throw pillow next to him in a tight fist. He was determined not to interrupt her narrative. In his admittedly unschooled opinion, it seemed important to let her tell it as she remembered it, without interrupting to make corrections.

"But when I saw his face, I started to realize I'd missed something. He stormed up the steps and into the house and slammed the door behind me. I started to say something. I have no idea what. But he pointed to the floor and told me to kneel and wait for him."

She finished the water in her glass without looking at him. The cat had disappeared when he brought the drink, and Natalie had brought her feet up to the edge of the cushion, her arms wrapped around them.

"We'd always talked about any scene before starting. Negotiations at first, just like Felicity and I researched about. Toward the end there, we didn't really negotiate every scene, but they were always preplanned, and we'd talk about it some. I was so surprised, I just stood there for a minute, and he kind of turned red and just kept pointing at the floor. So I kneeled and waited."

He could easily picture a younger version of the Natalie he'd first met. Longer hair, a little too skinny. Innocent and trusting. Tired, scared and confused. He twisted his fist. He might have to buy his friends a new pillow.

"Finally he stood in front of me, hands on his hips, and told me it had been a test. He'd asked Felicity to tell me she was suicidal, as a test of my submission to him. And I failed. Spectacularly."

She startled when he nudged the second glass of water into her line of sight. Her miserable smile of thanks was too much. He needed her to know that he was on her side.

"How so?"

She looked at him in question from over the rim of the glass.

"How did you fail this test?"

Frowning, she studied him, but he kept his face impassive. With a sigh, she cradled the glass in her hands and returned her focus to the coffee table. "I was supposed to go to Master D. Preferably call him that night, or at worst, go to him in the morning. By not doing that, and by going to Michael instead, I showed that I didn't trust Master D. And it was a betrayal of my relationship with Felicity."

"I don't get it."

She looked up at him sharply.

"How was talking to her Dom a betrayal, but talking to *your* Dom wouldn't have been? Not that I'm saying it was, one way or the other, I'm just trying to understand the logic."

"Because…wait…I'm trying to remember how David said it." Her forehead wrinkled as she thought back. "Actually, it's all kind of a blur, to be honest. He was shouting and I was tired. But it basically boiled down to the fact that I should have come to him, and I would have been rewarded for showing my trust. But since I didn't, he needed to punish me. And since Felicity and Michael were involved, they would need to be part of the punishment, so we were going to the club as soon as we got changed. I wasn't allowed to speak, and if I did everything he told me to, when it was over, I'd be forgiven and we could move on."

He couldn't help it. He let his confusion show on his face.

"Sorry, I'm not relaying it very well."

"I don't think that's the issue at all."

She blinked at that, then shook her head. "Let me finish."

"Okay. But let's go inside."

He wanted to give her another minute and get more water. Plus the bugs were getting annoying.

She settled into the corner of the couch and he took the big armchair that sat diagonal. Missy P hopped up behind him and made herself comfortable behind his head.

"So, we went to the club. One of the things that we'd been working on was my being comfortable with my body, in public. When Felicity and I first went, we wore sexy clothes, but nothing less than you'd wear to go dancing. He'd gotten me to the point where I'd wear a corset and tiny shorts. It was something he really wanted to keep progressing with until I was willing to be naked in the club, but he'd been relatively patient about it."

Her breath hitched in and out. "But he said part of my punishment was to wear only a G-string. He had it ready for me. He said if I didn't trust him enough to do this, that there was no point in moving forward together."

"So you did," he said, when she didn't continue.

She nodded. "I did. He put a sign around my neck that told everyone I was a bad girl." Her voice shook, but she firmed it up. "He tied me to a pole and Felicity and Michael paddled me. That was their part of the punishment. While they were doing that, David was talking to someone I didn't recognize. Then he came over and released me. Said there was one last thing, and then the punishment would be over."

He doubted she was aware that she'd gone stiff. Holding herself ready, as though she was about to receive a blow. She'd flinched when she'd mentioned the paddle, and he wanted to ask her questions, but she'd gone silent and didn't seem to know how to proceed.

Fuck it.

"Natalie." He waited until she looked up, which took a few seconds. "I'm going to pick you up."

She stared at him, uncomprehending.

He stood up. "I'm going to pick you up," he repeated.

There was no reaction from her, so he slowly reached over and slid an arm under her legs. He picked her up and sat back down in the chair, cradling her. She was stiff for a full minute, though she didn't protest. Then she melted into him, and he took a deep breath.

"Are you okay?" he asked.

"I'm sorry."

"For what?"

"I—I'm not sure."

"You have nothing to apologize for."

"Oh."

"Are you okay staying here for the rest of your story?"

"I—yes. Thank you."

"No, thank *you.*"

She frowned, but didn't question him. Instead, she pulled in a deep breath and started talking again.

"I should backtrack. When Felicity and I were doing research, we learned all about how you should tell anyone you're sceneing with if you have trauma or physical or emotional issues that might impact a scene. And we picked the club we did partly because we saw they had a good limits sheet. We went over that thing for two weeks together, before we ever went to the club. A lot of stuff we had to look up online to even figure out what they were. We debated which items were a hard no, which things we might be interested in exploring, and what we were fine with. There were a bunch of the first, a *lot* of the second, and we were scared there were way too few of the last, on our first trip."

Missy P had leapt off the chair when he stood, and now she jumped into Natalie's lap and immediately settled in for pets.

"One of the reasons we liked David and Michael was that they really took the time to go over the sheets with us, too. They asked a lot of questions about our choices and even though it was horribly embarrassing, it felt very adult and smart and healthy."

She pulled her top lip between her teeth, and he resisted pulling it back out again. It took her a few minutes to continue, so he braced himself for what was coming.

"I had a thing, from my childhood. I'd told Felicity about it, and I made reference to it on my limits sheet, and I had a long conversation with Master D about it. I'd gone to therapy for it when I was in high school and my freshman year of college. I'd stopped, because it was fine, but in this context it needed to be known. See, when I was eight, my cousin Holly—my mom's sister's daughter—would come and stay with us a lot of weekends, because her parents had irregular work schedules. When she wasn't in school, and they were both at work, she'd come to us. Which she and I thought was great. She was ten."

Her fingers were gentle on Missy P, but her voice was tight.

"When I was nine, Holly started acting funny. When I was ten, she told me she was tired of playing the games with my dad and wanted it to stop. He'd been molesting her."

He tightened his hold on her, and she patted his arm. "It's okay. It was really awful, of course. I told her we should tell her mom, and we did. Then we told my mom. My mom filed for divorce...then my uncle shot my dad."

"Wow."

"Yeah. My uncle freaked out and left, and my dad called an ambulance. He didn't want to tell them why my uncle would do that, so he said he'd done it himself, by accident. They didn't think it was fatal, but he ended up getting an infection and dying about a week later."

"My mom and I moved in with my grandparents. Changed our last name back to theirs. The police never knew it was my uncle who shot my dad. My aunt and uncle moved away with Holly. My grandparents put me through college. They were great."

"You lost the father you thought you had, and your cousin. I'm sorry."

"Thanks. I would hear from my grandparents about how Holly and my aunt and uncle were doing. They all had therapy and seemed to be okay, last update I had."

"That's…good."

"Yeah. Anyway, I told David about it, and he understood. One time when we were playing at the club, there was a couple nearby doing their thing, and she was calling him Daddy. Master D made no big deal of it, he just maneuvered us farther away so that I couldn't hear them, or even see them, and we continued."

She kissed the top of the cat's head, then gently nudged her off the chair. She fisted her fingers in his shirt and took a deep breath.

"So, that night. When he led me over to the stranger. The last thing I expected was for the man to say 'come to Daddy'."

"Fucking hell."

"I'm sure I was supposed to trust David. That it was a test, not a punishment. I've thought about it a lot, over the years. What would have happened next if I hadn't said my safe word and left. That he would have praised me, said all was forgiven, and we would have been done. With the punishment, I mean. But…I don't really care. I don't regret leaving. I regret being in the position in the first place, but not leaving."

"Good."

She stilled at that. Looked up to him.

"You did the right thing. I'm proud of you. For being strong enough back then, and for telling me now."

Her whole body shuddered. "Oh."

"Your Dom was a twat."

She gasped. Then giggled. Then burst into tears.

———

NATALIE WASN'T sure how long she cried in Noah's arms. She was only sure that he didn't rush her and didn't seem to be annoyed with her. He murmured reassurances into her ear and ran his hand up and down her arm in a constant caress. It was soothing, and eventually she wound down.

Finally, she sighed and unwrapped her fingers from where they'd melded with his shirt.

"Thanks," she said. She tried to brush out the wrinkles she'd left, but it was impossible.

"No thanks necessary. I should tell you, I've changed my mind. I will absolutely be making judgements about what happened."

He said it so matter-of-factly, while also being so calm and soothing, that she wasn't the least bit worried about it.

"Would you prefer I start from the beginning? Or the end?"

"I think I'd like alphabetical." She had no idea where that weird quip had come from, considering she was too exhausted from sharing to really be thinking clearly.

It took a whole twenty seconds, but then he burst out laughing. Shaking her with the motion.

"Actually, I don't need to start anywhere, unless you have specific questions. Everything you said, after the part where you and Felicity carefully researched what you were getting into, was pure bullshit. I'm sorry that happened to you. I'm sorry one or both of those asshats thought it would be a great idea to convince your friend to do something so stupid and horrible. I'm sorry she decided it was a good idea to go along with it. From that point forward, everything the three of them did was *wrong*, and everything you did was right.

Period. And once you got to the club, it wasn't just wrong, it was abusive. Actually, probably before that, too. But if I think about it too hard right now, I'll get pissed off, and that's not what you need. By the way, what's David's last name?"

She huffed out an almost laugh. "None of your business. Maybe I'll go see a therapist again. Mine in Atlanta helped me so much, but I never really thought about seeing someone for this. I was too busy moving states and getting my new life figured out." She frowned. "Might be hard to find someone who understands what I'm talking about, though."

"I'll text you a link. There's a list of therapists who've been vetted by the local kink community."

"Thanks."

He didn't say anything after that, just kept holding her. He didn't seem in a big hurry to move, either.

"I do have a question, now that I think of it," Noah said after a while.

She was so comfortable, she didn't even tense up. "What's that?"

"What does any of that have to do with knitting baby blankets?"

Once again, she found herself laughing. He had a wry smile, but waited for her to explain.

"Ah, right. Well, when I moved up here, that's what I did with my time, rather than reading kinky romance novels or going to the club or missing my best friend. Grandma had taught me the basics, so I went all-in on it as a hobby to the point I started selling some of my stuff online."

"Ah, I see. And you really just put all of this behind you? I don't mean that particular incident, or those idiots, but your…needs?"

On the one hand, it was hard to believe she was having this conversation with anyone, let alone Noah freaking Tucker. But on the other hand, he made it so easy and comfortable.

"For a long time, yes. After my last boyfriend, I did wonder if I should start thinking along those lines again. But it was too painful to even think about exploring. And the idea of finding a safe place, people I trusted, was just…a lot." She wasn't going to admit it out loud, but her fantasies had definitely started edging in that direction the last year or so. Her vibrator had burned out and when she was exploring the online shops for a replacement, she'd strayed into the BDSM department and lost an hour as she looked at all the offerings.

Then she'd shut it all down and gone to the mall to get a massager, instead.

She glanced at the clock. "Holy crap, it's nearly nine. I've kept you here all evening." She climbed out of his lap. Even though the room was warm, as they hadn't turned on the air conditioning, she missed his heat.

"I promise you it wasn't a problem." He offered her a grin. "The meal was delicious. I'm sorry you had to bring that all back up, but I'm hoping it was actually a good thing for you."

She nodded. "Yeah, it probably was. Thank you so much for helping me through it."

"You know, sometimes unloading something like that can sneak back up on you. I'm happy to spend the night in case you need to talk later. I can sleep in the guest room."

She started to say no automatically, but then she thought about it. *Really* thought about it. "I appreciate your offer, but I do think I'm okay. I'm so used to being alone, I think I'll process better if I have the night to myself."

"All right, if you're sure." He stood and handed her his phone. "Add yourself there and I'll text you the link to the forum with the therapy recs. Then you'll have my number if you need to call or text." He made her meet his gaze, made sure she was paying attention. "Promise me you'll call or text if you get overwhelmed, or just need to talk."

"I will. I promise." She put her info into his phone and handed it back.

When he glanced down, he immediately grinned. "Your last name is really Handel?"

"Yes?"

"The Handel rose is one of my favorite climbing roses. I recommend it to customers all the time. They take a little bit of work and effort, but it's mostly about finding the right spot for them and letting them flourish. Then they'll climb, make big, fragrant blooms, white that shades to light pink, then dark pink all along the edges. Beautiful."

"Oh," she exhaled. Somehow she'd started holding her breath as he was speaking. *Wow.* You had to appreciate a man who loved his work.

He dropped a kiss on her cheek while she stood there kind of stupefied. "Don't forget, call me if you need to. You promised."

"Okay." She followed him to the door and locked it behind him, then fanned her face.

She wasn't sure how long she stood there before Missy P complained that she wasn't getting any attention. Pushing away from the door, she moved to the kitchen to see what needed to be put away.

Nothing. In the brief times he'd left her outside, he'd rinsed the dishes and loaded them into the dishwasher. The bottle of wine had a stopper in it and was sitting on the counter. She grabbed it up and hunted down another wine glass, then studied the pantry. Finding a bag of pistachios, she smiled. Perfect.

The bathroom in the owner's suite wasn't large, but it was extremely inviting. The jetted tub was opposite the vanity, with the toilet in one corner and a decent-size shower in the other. The subway tiles were several shades of slate blue, one of which matched the vanity, and nicely complemented the off-white tile floor. The tub surround was wide enough to house a plant that Sonya had promised Natalie didn't need to water, and a trio of candles that she'd been encouraged to use.

She set her glass of wine and a small bowl of the pistachios on the ledge, and started the water running. It didn't take long to choose a soothing playlist on her phone, grab her ereader, shed her clothes and climb into the nearly full tub. The water felt wonderful and she sighed in satisfaction.

The jets started up with a quieter rumble than she'd expected.

She took a sip of her wine and gave some thought to what she wanted to read. The romance she wasn't quite halfway through had seemed just fine this morning. But now…she was tempted to go into her archives and find some of her old spicier reads.

Maybe she needed to rethink her decision to ignore all thoughts kinky. But the books hadn't just been fantasy. They'd made her *want*.

She ate a couple of nuts and sipped her wine, forcing herself to admit that the last five years of ignoring those wants hadn't gotten her anywhere. Her relationships hadn't been great.

Then again, plenty of people didn't find *the one* right after college. She had loads of single friends and acquaintances. Even if she was meant to be in the lifestyle, that was no guarantee she'd have found the right guy in the past few years, either. *But.* She had to admit, looking back, it didn't feel so much like she'd hooked up with the wrong guys, as she'd been faking it all, even to herself. Damn it.

She really should go see a therapist. She would, she promised herself. In the meantime, the question was, should she re-attempt to explore the kink? The idea of doing it alone was unsettling. Annalise wasn't someone she could turn to for this. And that felt weird and almost dishonest.

Enough introspection for one night, she deserved to relax. Without thinking about it too much, she grabbed up her reader and searched for the author who'd been her and Felicity's favorite, back in college. Maybe the stories, and the ideas, would seem trite to her now, as an adult, and she could laugh at herself and move on.

She scanned the covers. Oh yeah. That one had been her favorite. Curious to see how it would hold up, she selected the book and leaned back, super glad she'd gotten the waterproof reader last year. She maneuvered so that the jets were on her shoulder muscles, and started reading.

By the end of the second chapter, she'd finished the wine and nuts and was completely caught up in the story. By the middle of the third chapter, she was reading one-handed so her other hand was free to circle around her nipples, then pinch and pull, one and then the other.

When the Dom in the story strapped his new submissive to the spanking bench and teased her into mindless begging, Natalie finally put the book aside and slid down so she could aim one of the jets at her core.

She braced her hands on the sides, and imagined being told to keep them there. She splayed her knees and lifted her hips, angling so the stream of water played along her pussy lips, up and down, before slowly making her clit the target. She gasped when the water connected, and again, that voice in her head ordered her not to move.

Tilting her head back, she imagined she could feel a collar around her throat, feel a warm breath against her temple as the orders were whispered into her ear. The blood pumping through her body centered on her clit, and she had to grit her teeth not to move away from the stream.

Too much, too much… Ahhh!

She came with a jerk of her hips that pulled the water away from its target, her legs collapsing from the strain of holding her in place. She gulped in air and let her hands drop to her sides.

Well. Maybe she should open the door she'd closed all those years ago, after all.

Her phone beeped with an incoming text. She glanced over and saw a message from Noah, with the link he'd mentioned.

Her already flushed face heated again, as if he might be aware of what she'd just done. And, now that she thought about it…had that voice in her head, giving her the commands, been his?

She dried off her hands and picked up the phone to shoot him a thank you text. Poor guy. He'd just been dropping something off for a friend, and now he was stuck topping her in her fantasies.

She giggled and turned the jets off. Lying back in the warm, still water, she remembered the safety of being held in his arms. At the time, she'd been focused in her head. But some part of her had been aware of how giving and caring he'd been, how secure she'd felt in his arms.

Maybe, when Alec and Sonya got home, she'd offer to cook Sonya dinner if her friend would come over and talk things out with her. But the baby would be here soon, and the new parents would have a lot more on their minds than helping her decide if she wanted to dip her toes into the kink world again.

She sat up with a reluctant splash. The water had cooled and she was going to prune. When she climbed into bed a short while later, she picked the book back up. Only this time, the hero's face and voice were very familiar, regardless of how the author had described him.

CHAPTER FIVE

Noah realized his dominant protective instincts were in a bit of overdrive after what had happened with Natalie on Friday. Being aware of that didn't mean he was going to ignore his need to check in on her, though.

He'd worked on Saturday, then gone to Apex. The BDSM club was the one he'd settled on after trying out several. Luckily, it was one of the closer ones, as well. He'd have been willing to drive for quality, but he was pleased he didn't need to. Unusually, last night he hadn't quite been able to relax into the vibe. He'd watched several scenes, been approached by a couple of willing subs, but hadn't been in the mood to work with anyone.

He'd been worried about Natalie being alone after such an intense experience. He'd feel the same about any sub he'd helped through a difficult moment. The fact that her smiling face, as she'd taken the first bite of her steak, kept flashing across his vision meant nothing more than that he'd enjoyed their dinner. Her tear-stained face as she'd rested in his arms was just a pull on his protective instincts. Totally natural.

And therefore it made perfect sense to come see her on Sunday, to make sure she was doing okay, so that he could put those instincts to rest.

When everything was ready, he called her. And, okay, he could admit that he mostly bowled her over, not giving her a chance to say no. Within fifteen minutes, he was pulling into Alec's driveway and she was standing at the front door, watching him approach.

"So, you have the day off and therefore you're going to spend it doing the thing you do all day at work?" she asked as he grabbed the shovel and fertilizer from the back of his truck.

"Remember, I don't get to do a lot of this at work anymore. Do you mind grabbing the pot from the passenger seat?"

She didn't look convinced, but did as he asked and pulled out the dahlia plant. Right now it was just green leaves, so she didn't appear too impressed. "You said this is to celebrate the baby?"

He bit back a laugh at her attempt to sound enthusiastic over his gift. He'd started the pot several weeks ago, so that it would bloom around the baby's due date. He'd planned to bring it over and plant it for Alec and Sonya when they were at the hospital, but this would work just as well.

"Here, I'll show you," he told her as he put the shovel and fertilizer down in the backyard. He pulled out his phone and brought up a picture of what the flowers would look like in just a few weeks.

She gasped. "Oh, wow, is that really what color they'll be? I swear, it's a perfect match for the blanket I made." She handed his phone back to him and rushed into the house, returning quickly with a blanket. It was more lacey than he'd expected a knit blanket to be, and clearly took a lot of skill and effort.

"Gorgeous," he told her, appreciating the way her lovely blue eyes lit. "No wonder you're able to sell these, that's really beautiful. And yes, the color in the picture is a pretty good match, and very close to this. Poor Alec, maybe we should have asked him what *his* favorite color is."

She laughed. "I did. He said the color of his wife's eyes, and batted his lashes at her. She gave him the last bite of cake she was eating at the time, so I'm pretty sure he had ulterior motives in his answer."

Noah laughed. "Sounds about right. What's your favorite color?"

"Orange." She gestured to the plant. "Would you like some help with this?" Her face said she was offering only out of politeness, not curiosity.

"Thanks, but no, unless you're wanting to learn. Probably better if you keep out of the dirt. I wouldn't want whatever you're working on now to get messed up. If that's what you were doing?"

She blushed, which intrigued him. "Uh, yeah, I was knitting while listening to an audio book."

He slanted a look at her while he started in with the shovel. He'd already figured out where the dahlia would go, and checked the soil, so he didn't need to focus completely on what he was doing. "Good book?"

The blush definitely intensified.

He remembered that she'd said she and her roommate had started their initial curiosity about BDSM by reading books. *Well, well, well.*

"Yeah, it's a good one. From an author I really enjoy, but I hadn't read her last few books."

"That's always a treat."

"I better get this blanket back to safety," she murmured, and sped back into the house.

It was pleasant but mindless work getting the plant into the ground. He lifted his face up to the sun. Yes, a good spot for the flowers, they liked their sun, too. He hosed off his hands and the shovel, dumped the half-full fertilizer into the now empty pot, and carted everything to his truck through the side gate, rather than through the house.

When he made it back to the yard, Natalie was standing by with a glass of water, which she held out to him.

He drained the glass. "Thank you, just what I needed. You look a little red. Should we get back into the air conditioning?" He was such an ass. He knew damn well her flushed cheeks weren't due to the sun. But she turned and led him into the house without objecting.

He spotted knitting needles sticking out of a green bundle of yarn, up on a bookshelf that was at head height, and he realized that maybe knitting and cat sitting didn't go hand in hand. The cat in question was curled up in a shaft of sunlight, on the floor by the window.

"How was yesterday?" he asked, taking a seat on the couch without asking.

"It was a nice day. One of my coworkers lives nearby, and we went for a bike ride. Sonya's bike is a little too tall for me, but we didn't go far, so I managed. It was such a pretty day, and we went early, before the heat was too bad. It was nice to come back to air-conditioning."

"I bet."

"It might be time to upgrade my apartment. I hate moving, though."

"It always sucks," he agreed. "But if you'll be happier when it's done, it's probably worth the effort."

"Yeah, I'll have to look into it. This kitchen is twice as big as mine, which inspired me to actually cook dinner again, so I spent half the day petting Missy P while exploring recipe videos and blogs. I went to the market, made dinner, and the cat graciously allowed me to do some knitting before deciding it was time she claimed my lap, so we watched a movie. It was a great day."

"I'm glad. What did you make for dinner?"

"Lasagna. I pretty much filled the dishwasher, another reason to do it here. I would have had to clean everything by hand at home. I'll be eating leftover for days, though." She checked her watch and beamed. "It's nearly noon. Want some lunch?"

He grinned. "I could eat some lasagna. To help you out with that leftovers issue, of course. To be a good friend."

She rolled her eyes. "It's good to have friends who are there for you when you need them."

"Exactly."

When they were nearly finished with the generous portions she'd served up, including a fresh salad, he got more specific with his earlier question. "So yesterday was good. No issues from bringing up your past?"

"No." She waved her fork at him, dismissing the idea. "No. Not really."

He narrowed his eyes at her, and she sighed.

"No issues, I mean that. Nothing bad. It's just…got me thinking. Was I right to walk away from the whole concept of being submissive? At the time, it seemed clear to me that since I didn't really even understand what happened, but felt so ashamed and guilty, that it was best to just stick to, quote, unquote, normal relationships. So I did."

"And were those satisfying?"

She waggled her head. "Eh. Not really, but I blamed the guys, or us just not being a good fit. I didn't blame the lack of submission."

"But now you're rethinking things."

"Yeah, I guess. I read one of my old favorite books, and, well…" She blushed.

"You can tell me."

"You shouldn't have to deal with all this. You're not my therapist. Or boyfriend."

"I'm your friend."

She just looked at him, and he had to laugh. Okay, she wasn't a pushover. "Fine, we were more acquaintances than friends. But personally, I think Friday night tipped us firmly into the friend camp. If you don't want that, tell me, and I'll back off. But I enjoyed spending time with you, and I'm enjoying it now. I don't see why we can't be friends."

She studied his face, and seemed to be satisfied with what she found there. The relief he felt that she was going to talk to him was a surprise.

"All right. So, what I was thinking was that I orgasmed harder after reading that book than I did the entire time I was with my last boyfriend."

"Because you were in the right headspace," he guessed.

"Maybe. Probably. But maybe it's just that the author is really good and the visuals were super-hot. Maybe it's just fantasy. And as I've already learned, the fantasy does not always translate to reality. Besides, I've gotten off while reading vampire romances, too, and I'm not looking for someone to turn me into an undead creature of the night."

"Are you bothered by the idea of being submissive?" He had a vague idea that most of the charm of vampire romances was the alpha hero taking care of his human—for now—lover, who was always in some kind of trouble, but decided not to mention that. Especially since he hadn't actually read any.

She frowned. "No. Not really. More by the idea that I could go chasing after that ideal scenario, and just be constantly disappointed by guys who don't measure up, in scenes that will never fulfill me for real, and maybe getting hurt along the way, like I did in the past. I know for sure I'm not a masochist, so putting myself in harm's way like that seems like a bad idea."

"And by harm's way, you don't mean whips and chains, but the chance of being abused, like your ex did."

"Exactly."

"Makes sense."

Clearly startled by his agreement, she stared at him.

"It's smart to be wary. Last time you did everything right—research, open communication with the top, best friend at your side—and you still got hurt."

"Right." She bit her lip. "I guess I just have to decide if the potential goal is worth the possible pain."

"Part of the calculation could include that this time, you have a couple of sources of information and support, with more experience than you had last time. I think I know Sonya well enough to be sure that she wouldn't mind talking to you about any questions you might have. Alec, too, if you were comfortable with that. And I'll remind you that I consider myself a mentor in the scene, so in addition to being your friend, I'm happy to be one of your trusted resources."

Deciding to let her think on that for a few minutes, he pushed his chair back and grabbed both of their empty plates. "This was delicious, thank you for sharing."

She blinked, and stood to follow him into the kitchen. He rinsed and swiped the plates and she put them into the washer.

"You know, you've fed me dinner and lunch now. Only fair for me to return the favor. How about we go out to eat tonight? There's that Lebanese restaurant not far from here. We can walk over. It will be relatively cool by the time we walk back."

"Oh. That would be nice. I suppose having lasagna three meals in a row would be a bad idea. Maybe I'll freeze the rest."

He grinned. "Good idea. I'll be back around six." He planted a kiss on her cheek and was out the door before she had a chance to change her mind.

NATALIE WANTED to talk to her best friend, but she wasn't sure what she wanted to say. They normally talked every day or two, and she'd sent a couple texts—pictures of Missy P, of the lasagna—but how could she explain that ninety percent of her thoughts since Friday night had been about sex? Kinky sex? Especially without pulling Alec, Sonya and Noah into the conversation?

In the years they'd been friends, they had, of course, discussed boyfriends and sex. But Natalie hadn't ever felt she was lying, even by omission, because she'd put kinky thoughts out of her head and insisted to herself that she needed vanilla. So that's what their conversations had been about.

She hated that there was something that felt so heavy in her head, she couldn't share it with Annalise, at least not yet. She still needed to wrap her head around it a bit. If it was something she was going to push aside and go back to ignoring, then it wouldn't matter. But that was getting increasingly difficult to imagine.

It wasn't that she was suddenly obsessed with sex or anything.

Or at least, not exactly. But as she listened to the audiobook she'd downloaded, it got harder and harder to pretend that something hadn't been lacking in her romantic life these last several years.

Aside from all that, the fact that she and Noah were going to dinner was absolutely the kind of thing she would normally be talking to her best friend about. Even though it wasn't a date. At least, she was pretty sure it wasn't a date. She just had no idea what it actually was.

She *had* told Annalise that Noah had come by the house, and she'd given him one of her steaks. She'd just left out the part where she'd spent a great deal of their time talking about her past and crying in his arms. Luckily, they'd talked all through dinner before he'd asked her to share her story, so there'd been plenty to babble about to Annalise without going *there*.

Actually, now that she thought about it, she was kind of surprised Annalise hadn't pushed, or suggested, that Natalie try and go after Noah. That exchange had been before Noah had shown up this afternoon, and made plans for dinner, so not mentioning it wasn't weird. Yet. But she was going to have to figure her shit out. Soon.

She fed Missy P and gave her a nice long petting session before going to change. Crap. She should have gone home to get more clothes. The restaurant he'd mentioned was nice, so she couldn't wear shorts. The dark blue, wide-leg capri pants she'd worn to work on Friday would have to do. Luckily, one of her other tops would go nicely with it, so she wasn't actually wearing the outfit he'd already seen him in.

Makeup was the next debate. Since this wasn't a date, she didn't want to go full out. She did light mascara and a lip gloss, and a quick swipe of neutral shadow.

He knocked on the door as she was considering carrying a purse. The pants had a button pocket on the back, so she slid her driver's license and credit card in there, secured it, grabbed her sunglasses and keys and opened the door.

How had she already forgotten how handsome he was? He'd

looked so good, so in his element, in the backyard working with the plant that afternoon. Now he wore chinos and a short-sleeve, button-down top that seemed to have…she looked closer…tiny little bowler hats all over it.

"Hello again," he said. "You look lovely."

"Thanks, you clean up quite well. I like your shirt."

"I like your sandals."

She looked down at her shoes. The sandals were the kind that laced up and wrapped around her ankles several times. Kind of bondage like. She could only shake her head and laugh.

It was a pleasant walk to the restaurant, not as warm as Saturday had been, with a light breeze. It meant a lot of people were out and about, which she loved to see.

She adored Boston. Not that she hadn't liked Atlanta, but growing up there made it different. She'd chosen Boston. Well, okay, she'd chosen the job, but there were a lot of places she could transfer to if she wanted. She probably should, if she wanted to buy a house. But she really liked her city.

"Have you always lived here?" she asked Noah.

"No, I moved here when I was twenty-one. From Oregon. I love it, though, and this is one of my favorite neighborhoods."

They chatted their way to the restaurant, where they had a fifteen-minute wait to be seated. Natalie grabbed a menu, getting hungrier as they looked at the delicious options. Once they were seated, they ordered feta fritters and a dip assortment while they figured out their main meals.

The appetizers came quickly, and were extremely tasty. He grinned at the way she moaned around the first fritter, but she couldn't help herself, it was damn good.

"How did you get into the nursery business?" she asked him, hoping to focus his attention on something else.

He snorted. "Mostly because I really hate screwing up."

"Something we have in common, then, although I suppose it's true of most people."

He nodded. "When I was twelve, my dad gave me the job of

mowing the lawn. He told me that if I wanted to, he would let me use the mower to offer my services to the neighbors, and he would front the cost of gas for a month, and I could keep all the profits." He took a pull on his drink. "My dad is a financial advisor," he added, his eyes twinkling. "Now retired and living in Arizona."

She laughed. "I love it."

"My allowance at the time was only five dollars a week, and I'd just developed a budding comic book obsession *and* a love for seeing movies at the theater, so it seemed like a great idea, and I took him up on it."

"Nice. Sounds good so far."

"I was able to get two houses to commit to my doing their lawns twice a month, and one who said they'd give me a call whenever they needed me. That went on for about six months. Then I added a new customer and she said she'd pay me an extra ten dollars if I would also weed her flower bed. Of course, I said sure."

"Uh oh."

"Yeah, I had no idea what I was doing. Don't know why she thought I would, to be honest. She was furious when she saw what I'd ripped out."

"And you decided you wouldn't be making a weeding mistake again."

"Yep. Hopped online and went down the gardening rabbit hole. I bought some replacement plants for her and put them in, researched how to take care of them, and told her no charge until the next season."

"And a passion was born."

"I enjoy the art of it, and the science of it."

She nodded. "Okay, I can see that. That's a pretty cool way to think of it, really. But you didn't go into landscaping."

"I found I like this side of things much better. Helping people make what they like grow, bringing their visions to life, yes. Designing for them, not so much."

His farro and her chicken arrived, and they both declared them winners, and shared a bit from each dish.

She was comfortable enough to ask a question that had been gnawing at her. "So, now I'm curious, and you can absolutely tell me it's not up for discussion. I'm wondering how you got started with…" She looked around. The restaurant was crowded, but conversation were loud and no one was paying them the least bit of attention. "BDSM."

He smiled that grin that caused the corners of his eyes to wrinkle and made her a little melty inside. "You said it again."

The approval in his voice was even better than the smile.

"I don't mind. At the first nursery I worked at, while I was in college, one of the women was amazing. I couldn't figure out why I was drawn to her, but not *interested* in her. We became friends, and one night she asked me if I'd ever done anything kinky."

He passed another bite of his food over to her without pausing.

"Of course, I immediately assumed she was hitting on me, and tried to let her down gently. She just laughed me off and explained that she wasn't interested in me that way. She said she'd wondered if I was like her. A dominant."

"Oh, wow, that must have been an eye-opening conversation."

"It was. She was great. We're still friends, but she fell in love with a man and woman in New York, and moved out there to be with them."

"But in the meantime, you'd learned some stuff about yourself."

"Yes, we had a lot of talks, and I read some books, watched some movies, jumped online. It was great having her to point me toward the better sources, and the clubs she'd already vetted."

"What was your first experience like?"

"Gilda introduced me to a friend of hers, an experienced sub, who let me top her a few times. She was great, too. And then I let another Dom do a couple of scenes with me, so I would know what it was like from the other side. Gilda offered to do it, but I thought it would be more beneficial to have a man top me."

She knew her eyes had grown big on that last part, and even though she felt naive, she couldn't suppress her shock.

He laughed at her, gently. "What, you don't think I could handle it?"

A giggle escaped her. "It's not even just you, I'm having a hard time imagining anyone who wants to be a Dom, who has that mindset, being willing to submit."

"It's not that unusual. A good Dom absolutely knows that the *submissive* is in charge the whole time. Their willingness to hand over the reins, for as long as they choose, is what makes the whole dynamic work. Their strength in submitting is kind of awe-inspiring to us."

She had to blink at that. Honestly, maybe it was self-centered of her, but she hadn't spent a lot of time thinking about it from the other side. No, that wasn't true; in the books she read, there were certainly scenes from the Doms' perspectives, and some of them had been similar to what Noah was saying, but she'd never pulled that idea into reality, and wondered if that was how any Dom she'd met felt.

"What was David like, before he screwed up so badly?" Noah asked, mirroring her thoughts.

She thought back. "He was…instructional. Like I said, we had a lot of conversations about limits and negotiations. But he was…" She pursed her lips, trying to settle on the right word. "Arrogant. Which I thought was a good thing at the time, but looking back, I'm not impressed."

"Confidence is a good thing. Arrogance is a little more questionable."

"Like the confidence to let another man top you, when you aren't submissive."

"Like that. Confidence in a sub is attractive, but it has a different vibe to it."

She nodded, but slowly. She was going to have to give that some thought. All of this. Speaking of which. "I went through the list of kink-friendly therapists, and I'm going to call one on Monday."

"Well done, I'm proud of you."

CHAPTER SIX

As Noah watched Natalie finish off her meal, he had to caution himself. She wasn't his sub. She wasn't his girlfriend. She was his friend, and he'd offered himself to her as a trusted source. A mentor. Taking that away just because he liked the way she looked, the way she acted, the way she responded to him, wasn't cool.

Besides, the last few years, he had only played with experienced partners. Natalie didn't even know if she wanted to be in the lifestyle, though he was pretty sure she wasn't going to just walk away. There was too much curiosity and yearning in her voice when she spoke about it.

She needed a safe way to explore the idea, and come to terms with either putting it firmly in her past or making it part of her future. The smart thing would probably be to help her find someone trustworthy to do that exploration with. Then, *if* she decided to continue, and *if* she was interested, they could consider sceneing together.

But...that just didn't feel right.

"How much thought have you given to playing? Or not?" he asked. "Or are you waiting to hash it out with the therapist, and putting it out of your mind for now?"

She blew out a breath. "A lot of thought. When I'm not listening to my books and getting horny."

He laughed. "I may have to give these books a try."

"I think you'd be pleasantly surprised how engaging they can be."

He waggled his eyebrows, and she laughed.

"I think it's one of those things that once it's in your mind, it's hard to just walk away without giving it a try. Part of me is convinced that if I try it now, as a more confident, sexually aware adult, that I'll think it's kind of fun, but not really be interested in the whole lifestyle thing." She started to lift her water glass, then froze. "I'm sorry, was that rude? I don't mean to be insulting to anyone who *does* want it."

"No. I promise, you can talk about these things with me without me getting defensive and upset."

"Right. Sorry." She shook her head and laughed. "Anyway, that's where I'm at now. Wondering if it's kind of like when I was absolutely convinced that I needed an Apple Watch. That this one thing would transform my life. It would tell me when to get up and when to drink water and when my appointments were coming, remind me all the things my phone was reminding me, but I would actually use them more because it was right there on my wrist. I don't even remember all the things I was sure would change with my life." She sighed.

"I can't help but notice that you aren't wearing a watch of any kind."

"Yeah. I loved it for like six months. Then I would wear it without using it as hardly anything more than a watch for six months. Then I got annoyed with the whole charging aspect, and just...forgot to wear it most days. Then I forgot about it entirely."

"New toy syndrome. You think submitting will be like that? A phase?"

"Kind of. Like, part of me hopes it will magically fix my lackluster dating life, my so-so sex life, bring renewed energy and spirit to my everyday life, blah, blah, blah, and part of me knows that's not really how it works."

"Ah, I see. And I agree to a certain extent. But, if you've been forcing yourself into a certain kind of dating life, into looking for a certain kind of partner, when really you need something else entirely, then finding that something else *can* be transformative."

"True. But it's a little more investment to try it out than buying a fancy piece of electronics."

She had a point, and it got him thinking. "You need a relatively relaxed, no-commitment, no-strings test."

Frowning, she nodded.

"I have a friend with a cabin about an hour from here. If you want, if you think you can trust me for this, we can go to the cabin and spend the weekend in D/s mode. Try different things, explore what works for you and what doesn't. And if you decide this isn't your future, then at least you'll know."

She bit her lip. The waiter chose that moment to bring the bill, and Noah took it from him. Natalie reached into her pocket, but he shook his head.

"My invitation. My treat."

"Thank you."

The waiter quickly returned and they began the walk back to Alec's house. He kept quiet, letting her think as much as she needed. If she started another conversation, he'd let it go. For now.

"It's a very generous, and tempting, offer," she finally said.

"But?"

"No but. I think I'd like to take you up on it. And appreciate you offering. I'm trying to figure out how to warn you that I might not be very good at any of the things you'd want to do, without making you mad."

He stopped, and she walked another step before turning back to him. The sidewalk was still busy. The sun was setting and the golden-hour light wrapped her in a warm glow. He wanted to ease his hand to the nape of her neck, hold her steady, and kiss her gently. But that wasn't what he was trying to offer her, so he resisted.

"Smart thinking," he told her. "If you agree to this, do you know what your job will be?"

"Um. Trust you to try different things to see what does, or doesn't, work for me?"

He pulled her to a stone wall that surrounded someone's yard. It was hip height, so they sat down.

"We'll use the limits sheet from the club, like you did before. We'll talk about all of it. That will be before we go. But once we're there, your only job will be to stop me if I do something that makes you uncomfortable or that you don't like. Beyond that, you leave it to me."

She frowned.

"It will be one hundred percent my job to make sure things are good. Not yours."

Now her nose wrinkled. "I don't think you can just decide I'll be good at a blow job, for example."

"You don't think so?" He leaned in, put his lips right on her ear, one hand resting on her thigh. "If I tell you to open up and take me, I could just leave you to do as you please. Or maybe I'll use your hair to hold your head right where I want it. I'll tell you to lick the head for exactly how long I want you to lick me. I'll tell you to suck when I want you to suck, to swallow when I want you to swallow. If I tell you to hum, or to hold your breath, or to scrape me with your teeth, won't you do exactly that?"

Her hand gripped his forearm and she swallowed audibly.

"Y-yes."

"Then do you agree that the only thing you need to be good at is listening to me?"

"Um. Maybe?" Her voice was kind of a squeak.

"Then it will be my job to convince you."

He stood up and pulled her to her feet, tucked her close to his side and picked up the pace back to the house. Her eyes were dilated and she kept glancing at him, but didn't say anything. When they were safely inside the house, door locked behind them, he sat on the edge of the couch.

"Come here, Nat."

She was standing near the door, holding Missy P. Her lip disappeared between her teeth as she watched him, but she set the cat down and moved to stand between his legs, where he indicated.

He saw that she was about to kneel, assuming that's what he wanted, so he put his hand on her hip. "Don't move."

She froze.

He studied her. Taking his time, making his perusal, and his appreciation, obvious. Then he worked the straps on her sandals free. "Lift this foot." He pulled the shoe free, then repeated with her other foot. "Put your hands on my shoulders and kneel down. Watch my eyes."

She dropped gracefully to her knees, her gaze on his.

"Very good. Will you let me kiss you?" he asked.

Surprise flitted across her face. "Yes, please."

He smiled. He put his hand where it had been itching to go all night, his fingers at her nape, his thumb on her jaw. He leaned down, and when she started to lean forward, he squeezed his hand. She stopped and her lips parted. He rubbed his nose along hers, then along her cheekbone and into her hairline, breathing deeply.

"Put your hands behind your back, interlace your fingers."

Her breath caught, and she immediately complied.

He sucked her earlobe into his mouth, then gave it a little nibble. Kissing his way along her jawline, he reached her lips and gently took her bottom lip between his teeth.

She whimpered.

He released her lip and licked the spot, soothing it as air puffed out at him. "Don't move," he told her, then slid his tongue into her mouth.

Her mostly breathless whine pleased him very much.

Tasting her, exploring her, he took his time, enjoying what she gave. What he took. After a few minutes, he pulled away. Her eyes were closed, her face flushed. "Put your hands on my knees."

It took her a second, and her hands were a little shaky as they landed on his legs. Then her fingers dug in, securing herself to him.

He didn't sip and he wasn't gentle. He invaded. Taking, and with the taking, giving. His fingers at her neck tightened. He slanted her head a little and went deeper. She moaned and he considered taking more. Touching more. Pushing.

With an internal sigh of regret, he eased back, gentled. He brushed her cheek with his thumb, sucked her tongue in for one last caress, then kissed the corner of her mouth and moved back.

She stayed where she was, lips swollen and wet, eyes closed. When they finally blinked open, he smiled. "Do you think you can trust me to make things good for both of us?" he asked.

Slowly, her head went up and down, her gaze never leaving his.

"Excellent."

Her fingers relaxed on his legs, the tiny bite of her nails disappearing as she came back to herself.

"I don't know if that was mean, or really nice," she finally said.

He barked out a laugh. "Sometimes things can be both at the same time." He helped her to her feet and encouraged her to sit down next to him. "Do you have any questions?"

"Would I be an idiot to go off to a cabin in the woods with a self-proclaimed Dom who I've only been casually acquainted with for several years?"

"When you put it like that, yes. But we're not in a hurry. Are you comfortable talking with Sonya and Alec? Maybe you'll want to visit the club, see the vibe and culture there, that we're part of. Talk to some of the submissives, even some of my play partners. We'll go when you're ready."

***

NATALIE WAS READY RIGHT NOW. She badly wanted to ask Noah if he'd take her into the bedroom. That kiss had gotten her hotter and wetter than her last boyfriend had ever managed.

But she was trying not to be an idiot, and really didn't want to make the same mistake twice. She could be certain that Noah wasn't going to take her off into the woods and murder her. And she was fairly confident that he wouldn't abuse or mindfuck her, but could she be certain? No. Of course, she supposed you could never be one hundred percent certain of that kind of thing, but she needed to do some due diligence.

She glanced over at Noah and found he was watching her with a half-smile. "I think your brain is going a hundred miles an hour."

"About that, yeah. You've given me a lot to think about. Also, Annalise is coming over for lunch tomorrow. If I talk to her about this stuff, which I probably will, do you want me to leave your name out of it?"

He rubbed his hand over the back of his neck. "Oh. I should have thought to mention this. She knows."

Natalie's mouth dropped open and she stared at him. "What?" she managed.

"Right. Alec had a very careful conversation with her several years ago. Before he met Sonya. He wanted to be sure that if anything happened to him, she would know to talk to me so we could clear out his, um, *belongings* before his parents found stuff at his apartment."

"Oh. Okay. That's good. That will make this a lot easier."

Then the truth suddenly hit her. *That's* why Annalise hadn't gotten all excited when Natalie'd said she and Alec had dinner together. Annalise hadn't figured Noah would be interested in vanilla Natalie, that their dinner really had been just between friends.

"Yes, be as open with her as you feel comfortable. But..." He winced, and paused.

"What?"

"We don't know what you want for your future. I'm happy, and honored, to help you figure out if you want to proceed or not." He paused again.

"But you're not my boyfriend," she guessed.

"But I'm not your boyfriend. Or your Dom, not really. It's more like a mentorship, to help you figure out if you want to go forward with exploring these things. It can be...easy—very easy—to get emotionally caught up in something like that, let your heart get involved. Especially when the only play you've done before has been while developing a boyfriend relationship at the same time as a D/s relationship."

He aimed his gaze at her, his voice serious.

"If we agree to a weekend, I'll be your Dom for that time period, but anything beyond will be discussed after that. It's nothing to do with you or how desirable you are." He glanced down at his lap, and she could see that at least some part of him was excited after their kiss. "You'll need to really think about, and decide if you want sex to be a part of the weekend. We can absolutely explore your submission without it."

That was definitely something she should think about. Except, she really didn't need much effort to decide. But he was right; it would be hard to keep her heart out of the equation if they went there. "I don't want you to do anything you're not comfortable with, either."

He grinned. "I promise you that I am, uh…up for it, either way."

She snorted.

"But," he continued, "I'd rather not set Annalise up for thinking things are more than they are."

Natalie nodded. "That makes sense." She couldn't fault him for that, and even had to agree. The twinge she'd felt disappeared and she reminded herself that he didn't have to do any of this. Sure, he probably felt a bit of Domly responsibility toward her, but it absolutely wouldn't have been difficult for him to set her up with some people at the club he trusted to help her figure things out, and bow out of the equation. He didn't need to help. He didn't *have* to kiss her. Or invite her to play for the weekend. He wanted to do those things. With her. And that was exactly what she needed.

With a reminder to call or text him if she needed, and a promise to email her the Apex limits sheet so she could start thinking about it, Noah headed out. Natalie and Missy P moved to the backyard. She lay down on the sofa, the cat stretched across her stomach, and thought about what she wanted. What she needed? Maybe.

When the temperature had dropped, she went back inside and filled the tub. She didn't bother with the wine this time. Or her book. She had that kiss. The words Noah had used. The way he'd spoken. His hand holding her still, his desire holding her steady. She completely understood his wanting her to think twice about whether they would include sex in their weekend, but there was just no way she was going to deny herself the hotness that was Noah, given half a chance.

She lit the candles, and turned out the lights, but it didn't really matter, because she closed her eyes the second she slid down into the water. Noah's face wasn't hard to conjure into her mind. Nor was the memory of that kiss, the way she'd felt both calm and intensely excited from his hold on her. She lifted her hips into the jet's stream, gasping as she found her mark.

Imagining the press of his fingers around her wrists, holding her in place, but also magically being able to tease her breasts. His breath on her neck, his lips, his tongue, anywhere and everywhere. She aimed the pulse of water into her core, her legs straining to keep her positioned just so, then slowly maneuvered until the stream was directly on her clit. She gave a short scream as the sensations overwhelmed her. Her butt dropped back down to the tub and she lay still and panting in the swirling water.

A noise had her slowly rolling her head toward the door. Missy P had apparently come to check on her. The cat gave a little *mrrrp* and moved back out of the doorway, apparently satisfied her food provider had not perished. She would have laughed, but she didn't yet possess the energy.

CHAPTER SEVEN

Natalie knew it was kind of ridiculous to be nervous about having Annalise over. The chances of her best friend turning her back on her were slim. She knew Annalise. Trusted her. But, well, it wasn't like she didn't have some history with best friends turning on her, though she supposed Felicity would argue the point about who had turned on whom.

Annalise arrived with salads from one of their favorite restaurants.

"Wow, this sweater is fantastic, is it a commission?" Annalise grabbed the nearly finished piece from where Natalie had stashed it out of Missy P's reach on the bookshelves. Her friend was well versed by now in how to care for projects still on the needles. She rubbed her cheek on the softness, then carefully returned it to its place.

"Yes, a coworker's sister." She made a mental note of which pattern it was to consider for Annalise's Christmas present.

"I'm so excited for the baby. Have you heard anything from them? I've been careful not to bug them."

"I sent a couple pics of Missy P and Sonya told me they're having a great time."

They sat at the table, inside with the air-conditioning, since the heat had rocketed up again. Annalise eyed her as they started in on their salads. "You look...I don't know. What's going on?"

Her friend knew her too well. "Well, actually I do want to talk about something. Um, how do I start?"

Annalise raised her eyebrows.

"Okay. So. When Noah came by, we had a conversation that brought up something from my past that I've been ignoring since I moved here. I contacted a couple of therapists today, to see if I can find a good fit and start talking to someone."

"Oh, Nat, is it about your father? What do you need from me?"

Damn, she loved her friend. The warmth of that filled her up and pushed away her nerves. Mostly.

"Thanks, hun. No, nothing to do with him, this is from college. Um, right...I'll just say it. When I was in college, my best friend and I decided to explore the world of BDSM. We read a lot of books, fiction and nonfiction, we did a lot of research online, and eventually we went to a club and hooked up with a couple of guys. Doms."

Annalise stopped her fork halfway to her mouth, dressing dripping off the salad. "Wow, seriously?"

"Yeah. Eat your salad," she added with a laugh.

"Hmph." Annalise did as she was told, but waggled her eyebrows.

"It...worked for me. For us. Our Doms were both patient with guiding us. Or at least, that's what I thought. We hadn't gotten too heavy into things when my Dom, my boyfriend, decided he wanted to test my trust in him. He used my best friend and her boyfriend, so they were all in it together. It was...well, it was fucked up. I blamed myself, figured I just wasn't as suited to what we were doing as I'd thought, since I was so completely *not* suited to what he—they —had done. I walked away. Ran, kind of. I finished my finals without hardly speaking a word to Felicity, who was also my roommate. I moved here, and I put it all away."

Except for the occasional fantasies with her vibrator. She hadn't even let herself have much fun with her personal toys, though, keeping to a massager and a boring vibrator. What a waste, she realized.

"I felt like they'd betrayed me. They felt like *they'd* been betrayed. It wasn't great, and I just...pretended like it never happened and stopped reading those kinds of books, or looking for the kind of guy who might be even the slightest bit interested in that kind of thing."

Her eyes went wide. "Oh. Enter Noah." And then her eyes lit with excitement. "Oh! You guys would be so great—"

Natalie lifted a hand to stop her. "Hold on. Don't get ahead of yourself."

Annalise pouted. She pushed her empty dish aside and waited while Natalie took another bite. Her fingers drummed on the table and Natalie smiled while chewing.

"Right, so I happened to make a comment, that you would have just thought was a little funny, but he recognized as being...well, a certain kind of dirty. And then I *saw* that he recognized that, and we started talking...and I told him all about what happened."

She pushed her own dish aside and felt her eyes get a little wet. "And Noah told me that I was right, and my boyfriend had been an asshole."

"Well, duh." The indignation in Annalise's voice was loud and clear.

"I mean, it's not totally unbelievable that I could have been wrong," Natalie said with a fake pout. "And if I wasn't, then it means I was wrong to walk away and pretend that kind of thing wasn't important to me."

"Psh. It was the right decision at the right time, and I don't see any reason to look backwards for a bunch of should'ves and could'ves. The more pressing point is, did you jump Noah's bones?"

Natalie looked up as if asking for guidance from a higher power. "My best friend. A one-track mind. A dirty one-track mind."

"I mean, isn't that the track we were on?" Annalise shrugged. "Besides, he's hella hot."

Natalie sighed. "He is. But he's offering to help me out, decide if, and how, I want to move forward with this…lifestyle. He's doing me a favor, letting me work it out with someone I know and trust, and I'm not going to return the favor by pretending it's more than that. He's like, an expert in the field. A mentor."

Annalise narrowed her eyes. "It *could* be more than that."

"Maybe. Maybe not. But whether it goes that way or not, *you* can't push him or give him any shit. That wouldn't be a very fair reward for helping me out."

"Fine." It was more of a sigh than a promise, but Natalie figured it was good enough. "Now, tell me all the good stuff."

NATALIE HAD MANAGED to redirect her conversation with Annalise without, in fact, going into specifics of "all the good stuff". Either about her time in college or with Noah. There had been a little pouting, but then the two of them had gone shopping for the baby and all had been right in Annalise's world. This was to be her first niece or nephew, and she was extremely excited.

By the end of the week, Natalie had connected with a few therapists and picked one. She'd had her first session the following week, and was so glad. Although nothing was quite like the moment when Noah had called her ex a twat, the validation of having done the right things, made good, healthy decisions for herself, and that she wasn't being a fool to risk exploring things with Noah, was an amazing relief.

Of course, Mandy, her therapist, had asked her how she felt about him.

She'd been forced to admit that she was very attracted to him, and would be sad if he shook her hand and walked away after considering his "job" done, but she didn't want to miss the opportunity, either. She was willing to take the chance, after taking none for so many years.

She'd waited for her therapist to chide her for that, but no. Mandy had agreed with her that some risks were worth the heartbreak. They'd gone over the Apex limits sheet together before she'd sent it to Noah. And then *they* had gone over it together, on the phone. They'd worked out a plan to go to his friend's cabin for the Fourth of July. Apparently the owners of the place were more interested in fireworks at the beach, so it would be empty, giving them the three-day weekend to work with.

Now it was Friday, and Noah was due to pick her up at her apartment at any time. He'd told her he might not leave work exactly on time, so not to worry if he was late. She was click-clacking away on her new knitting project, but had already messed up twice. Giving that up for now, she put the project into her travel bag and went to stand at the window.

She'd had a long talk with Sonya, who had told her that she and Alec would be more than happy to take Natalie to the club with them, with her under their wing, until she was comfortable on her own. She'd considered it. Considered absolving Noah of his position of responsibility toward her, so that they could explore playing together more as equals.

But when she imagined walking into a club, back into *the scene of the crime*, as it were, she got hot and lightheaded, and not in the good way. Maybe it was foolish, but she trusted Noah to help her see if she could find a place of comfort in the role of submissive without being on display at the club, where anyone could witness her anxieties. Besides, with the baby coming, it would probably be ages before Sonya was up for a trip to Apex.

Her therapist had told her there were other options, as well, but hadn't argued when Natalie explained that this felt the safest. Part of Natalie wondered if it was because she liked Noah and he was hot. But mostly she figured it was because she liked him, he was hot, and he'd made her feel safe and secure and understood. Plus, she had checked, and he *did* have a reputation for being a patient teacher and a good Dom.

When she saw him walking down the sidewalk, she was surprised. She'd expected him to pull up on the street below and double park while waiting for her to come down. Instead, she got to watch his easy confidence as those long legs brought him closer to her. He glanced up and found her watching him as he approached. The grin he blasted her made her a bit weak in the knees, and she had to remind herself that this wasn't about starting a relationship.

By the time she grabbed her stuff and opened the door, he was at the top of the stairs. With a smile, she handed him her overnight bag when he held out his hand. Then one of the two grocery bags she carried, when he motioned for more. His car was only around the block, and they quickly stowed her things in the back. When he got in, instead of turning the car on, he turned to her.

"Here's the plan. It's normally a little more than an hour to the cabin in New Hampshire. Probably a bit longer with traffic today. For this weekend, I'm considering this car an extension of the cabin, and the cabin to be on scene at all times, unless one of us specifically says otherwise. Which means in the car, you'll be wearing my collar. If we need to stop for something, we'll negotiate you taking it off."

She blinked. Okay, they were definitely starting. A very nice little shiver ran through her.

"When you're wearing the collar, you will call me Sir," he added.

She swallowed. It had been five years, but it didn't feel weird to say it. Not now, not with Noah. "Yes, Sir."

His lips only turned up the tiniest bit, but his pleasure at her immediate response was clear.

He reached behind her and brought out a single gorgeous rose. It was very fragrant—she realized she'd been catching subtle hints of it since getting in the car. The petals started off white, turned to blush, with a fiery pink edge.

"Oh, is it *my* rose?"

"It is. This is a Handel rose. Be careful, I left the thorns on. I thought it was apropos."

She took it gently and brought it to her nose for a good sniff. Lovely. It had a tiny vial of water at the end of it, so she hoped it would last for a while.

She finally remembered herself. "Thank you, Sir."

"Since this weekend is about deciding what you like, what works for you, I don't want to use just a safe word and have you enduring what doesn't work for you, just because you can. We'll do a scale of one to five. One means great, keep going, five is full stop. 'Full stop and then we talk'; not 'full stop and I throw you in the car and drive you back to town'."

She considered that. "Okay. So four would be this isn't great can we talk about what's happening. Three would be…keep doing what you're doing, I guess, but I'm not convinced."

"Or, this isn't the most comfortable, but I can take it."

"Got it. Sir."

His lips quirked. "Then that's enough for us to get going, we can talk more on the drive." He reached into the cup holder and pulled out a thin cord choker that was sage green. "This has a magnetic clasp, so it can be taken off very easily."

She swallowed as he reached around her, the click of the magnets coming together louder than she expected. It was incredibly light, and yet she was hyper aware of it.

"Okay?" he asked, his voice quiet, his expression watchful.

She nodded.

He raised his eyebrows.

"Yes, Sir. Thank you."

"All right. From now until I get us out of the city, no speaking unless I specifically ask you a question, or you need to say four or five. If you have a question or there's something you need before then, you can put your hand on my thigh and I'll let you know if you can speak."

"Yes, Sir."

He brushed his lips over hers, straightened in his seat, and turned on the car.

Traffic was heavy, and there were a number of times that she almost said something, just out of reflex. A comment about the bumper sticker on the car in front of them, or to ask how his workday had been. She was just used to filling empty time with easy chatter.

His driving was competent and sure, so she didn't think his

request for silence had anything to do with navigating the city on a holiday afternoon. She found herself moving her neck, just slightly, so that she'd feel the tiny collar against her skin more firmly.

It was about twenty minutes before they reached the interstate, and he glanced over at her.

"Okay, we'll talk about the cabin now. Mostly you're going to answer me if I ask you something directly, but if you have a question, you may say, 'Sir, I'd like to ask a question'. Do you understand?"

"Yes, Sir."

"First question. How did it feel having your speech restricted like that?"

Oh. Well. That wasn't the kind of question she'd thought he'd ask, but she supposed she should have expected it. She pulled her lips between her teeth, thinking.

"I don't mind comfortable silences, and it *was* comfortable, I didn't feel like a child being told to sit and be quiet. I kept wanting to chatter, but mostly out of habit. I guess it seemed weird because it made me kind of feel like we're in a scene, but being almost out in public makes that super strange."

He nodded. "The cabin is on a half-acre of land, at the edge of a pond. It's big enough that you can use kayaks and canoes, even electric motors, but no motorboats allowed. What that means for us is that you can make a fair bit of noise, but there's the possibility there will be people on the water not too far from the house. Just something to keep in mind."

She tried to imagine making enough noise that someone could hear her outside of the house and beyond. At the club, she'd seen some screamers in action, but had never been one herself, so she just nodded.

"You were curious about forced nakedness in private, but hesitant in public, so you can keep your clothes on from the car to the cabin, but you'll stop directly inside and take off your clothes. You'll use the bathroom, then return to the front door and kneel and wait for your next instructions."

The city was well behind them now, and trees lined the expressway. It was a clear day, only a few wisps of white clouds dotting the blue sky. She'd been so shy, back in college. Unless she and David were actively having sex, she'd worn panties. Now she was used to being naked with men when they were about to have, having, or had just had sex, so she'd indicated some curiosity. The idea of actually stripping down to nothing without being in the mood was very odd.

"Yes, Sir."

"As we've discussed, we're going to try a few things, so don't be worried about stopping something you don't like. However, I do expect you to give everything a fair shot."

She nodded her understanding and kept quiet as the car ate up the miles into New Hampshire.

"Sir, can I ask you a question?"

"You can."

"What are things that you like to do the best?"

"Maybe we'll talk about that some other time, but not this weekend."

Damn. She hated the idea that he might do something that she liked, but he didn't.

He chuckled. "You'll remember that limit sheets are for Doms, too, not just subs."

She narrowed her eyes at that. "Wait. I sent you mine, but you didn't send me yours."

"You didn't ask."

A huff escaped her before she reined herself in. "Sir, would it be possible to see your limits sheet?"

"Yes, you can check the glove box. But, I'll warn you. I've modified it for just this weekend by listing the hard limits only. Everything else is something I'm willing to explore with you to some extent. You're going to have to trust me that I want to do this with you. Don't spend time wondering which things I prefer and which things I'm just doing to get through it."

She nibbled on her lip. That was exactly what she was going to be wondering, she was pretty sure. Pulling the list out, she quickly saw that his only hard limits were things like branding, face slapping, golden showers and piercing. A lot of what she'd put as hard limits were on his list, but not everything.

"I—Sir, may I ask a question?"

"You may."

"I don't want this to be a chore for you." She realized it wasn't actually a question, but he didn't seem to mind.

"Nat. Do I look coerced to you? Have I given you the impression that I'm easily led into doing things that I've no interest in doing?"

"No, Sir."

"We'll have breaks," he said. "It's not going to be full-time experimentation. Some of what we try will be intense, so you can narrow things down on that limits list a bit."

He'd told her that before, but it was good to hear again. And she made a mental note to ask him about his own sheet when they left the cabin.

"Did you eat lunch?" he asked, when they'd both been quiet for a while.

"Yes, Sir." She'd asked if she could bring food for them for the weekend, and he'd surprised her by hashing out a few recipes and snacks they both liked, and splitting the shopping with her. He'd taken the cold items, since he had a cooler, and she'd gotten the rest.

"There are a lot of items on the list that you marked maybe and curious to. We can't get to everything, obviously, so I'm going to try and mix things that I'm guessing you'll like, and things I'm guessing you won't care for, to help you narrow those down a bit."

He'd told her that, as well. And that it would help her focus her direction on what kind of Dom to look for in the future. She didn't like thinking about that. About playing with someone other than him. But she needed to remember that this wasn't about seeing if they were compatible. This was all for her, to help her get some direction for her future.

CHAPTER EIGHT

Noah had given a lot of thought to the weekend at the cabin. Natalie's limit list was full of "maybe" and "curious" answers, a bunch of "hard no" answers, and a few "definite yes" and "let's try" options to round things out. The problem he'd started to have was that he felt like he was pretty sure which things she would actually like, and which she wouldn't. Which was ridiculous, because they'd never played together and barely knew each other.

But he couldn't shake the feeling, and so he'd been careful to keep that in mind when selecting which items from the list they would be trying. He'd liked putting his collar on her, even though it was a cheap one he'd picked up at the costume jewelry store. It was boring, but on her graceful neck, it looked like it belonged.

He'd been to this cabin several times with his uncle. They'd spent a couple of weekends fishing, and had a great bachelor party another time. So he knew where he was going and what he would find. Thankfully, the cabin had a washer and dryer. They should find the bedding clean and stowed in the closet, and basics like spices, condiments, paper towels and toilet paper, unless the previous guests had been assholes.

Before they left, they would do the wash and make a list of

anything that was running low, so he could pass that on to Cedric, the owner. Or, if Natalie needed a break from the cabin, they'd go to the store and do a big stock-up.

When he pulled into the long driveway, he slowed down. It was a dirt road and it had been a rainy spring, so they bumped and plodded over the ruts until they reached the cabin. Then he turned to her.

"Did you bring a journal?"

"Yes, Sir."

The excitement and nerves were so clear on her face, he almost had to smile. "I want you to write down your feelings about the trip here so far. I won't be reading your journal, so you can say anything you want. When you're done, come straight into the house. The door will be unlocked. You remember your instructions from there?"

"Yes, Sir."

"All right. Don't rush it. We have all weekend. It's more important that you make your notes than that we start five minutes earlier or twenty minutes later. Give me the rose, I'll take it inside."

"Yes, Sir."

He resisted the temptation to kiss her, and simply nodded his approval. He got out of the car and took her bag and her grocery sacks into the house. When he came back out, her head was down, her lip stuck between her teeth. He got his own bags from the trunk, then returned for the cooler.

The car door shut as he carried the cooler inside. The door opened onto a large room, with a small dining table and tiny kitchen at the far right side. The rest of the room was taken up with two couches, one of which opened up into a bed. One wall was almost entirely windows, facing the pond.

At the far end of the main room was a short hallway, with the bathroom off to the side and the bedroom at the end. The cabin was plenty big enough for two people, though it had been a bit tight for the bachelor party.

He didn't react when the front door opened and closed.

Leaving the cooler on the kitchen counter, he took a seat at the dining room table and watched as she undressed. She kept her head tilted down, so that her hair swung in front of her face. He suspected it was so that she could pretend he wasn't watching her. Watching as she revealed lithe legs and larger-than-he'd-realized breasts. His fingers twitched with desire to touch her. But he could be patient.

She'd been folding each item and setting it on the little bench next to the door, and he bit back a grin as she eased her panties down and slid them into the middle of the pile of clothes. Then she fast walked to the bathroom, not looking his way.

He'd taken her bag and most of his into the bedroom, and now he took what he needed from the toy bag he'd left behind. Setting it aside, he opened his laptop. He started a new email, but gave Natalie his full attention as she scurried back to the door and knelt. He hadn't given any specific instructions on how she was to present herself.

She lowered herself to the floor and sat back on her heels, toes curled under, hands on her thighs, head bowed. He checked the clock, and went to her after a few minutes. Time to get started.

"Very good, Nat. I'm proud of you, I know that wasn't super comfortable."

Her head stayed bowed, so he used a finger to lift her chin. "Eyes on me, now." Her eyes were a bit wider than normal, and she wasn't the least bit aroused that he could see. "We're going to try a slightly different kneeling posture, all right?"

She blinked. "Yes, Sir."

"Put your feet flat on the floor, let your toes relax."

She made the adjustment with a little sigh.

"Hands at the small of your back. You can grip one wrist, if you like, or hold your hands. Try to keep your shoulders back, but if they get tired, that's all right. There, that's very pretty."

He tucked her hair behind her ears, on both sides. It was silky smooth and he remembered that it smelled good. If she were his, he'd have fun playing with different shampoo scents, maybe accustom her to a particular flavor while submitting to him. But she wasn't his, and that wasn't his purpose here.

"Keep your head up so you can see me if I indicate I want you to do something. If I'm sitting and you're kneeling next to me, you can rest your head on my leg. Now, we're just missing one thing."

He lifted the collar he'd bought for her so she could see it. The fake leather was a deep orange, three-quarters of an inch wide. It had a D-ring on each end that stopped just short of each other. A small padlock connected the two rings. He pulled out a key and opened the lock. "This one is a real collar, it won't come off with a little tug. Okay?"

She swallowed and her eyes brightened. "Yes, Sir."

He pulled the magnetic collar off and wrapped the new one around her neck, centering the two rings. He threaded the lock through them and clicked it shut, then checked the fit. The collar lay along her neck, but he could fit two fingers under it. The little lock rested just above the hollow of her throat. Perfect.

"Would you like to see?" he asked.

"Oh, yes, please!"

He opened the camera on his phone and set it to selfie mode, then turned it for her to see. Her arm was halfway to his phone before she caught herself.

"Sorry, Sir."

"Good catch. For now, I'm going to give you one freebie on every new rule I give you that you break. That was your freebie for breaking position. If you do it again, it'll count as a strike against you when we get around to some spanking or paddling. Back to where we were. You can take a picture, or not, your choice. If you do take a picture, you can decide if you want to text it to yourself. You just can't delete it from my phone."

She took the phone from him with one hand, the fingers of her other hand lightly exploring the pleather, before dropping away. He heard the click of the camera and waited as she texted the photo. She handed the phone back to him and put her hands back into position. He saw that the picture showed only between her chin and her cleavage.

"Thank you, Sir, it's beautiful."

"It's beautiful on you, and you've done great so far. Now, you're going to put away the food we brought. No speaking. I don't care where you put anything, I'm sure you can figure it out just as well as I can."

"Yes, Sir."

"I'll help you up." He'd been kneeling in front of her the whole conversation, of course, but he was used to kneeling while working. Not all the time, but enough that the short stretch hadn't bothered him. He stood and offered her a hand, which she took, though the fire in her cheeks had returned. She'd just remembered she was naked, and he managed not to grin, though he absolutely appreciated the view.

He walked to the little dining table, turned the chair closest to the kitchen around and sat, propping his ankle on his knee. This put him about two feet from the tiny room as she walked into it, with his intention to just sit and watch very clear. She cleared her throat, but said nothing and kept her hands down, though her fingers danced against her thighs.

She went to the cooler on the counter and glanced his way. He nodded at her, and she took a deep breath and tried to focus. The corner of her lip disappeared between her teeth. As she pulled a few items out and moved to the fridge, he let himself enjoy the view. He suspected that she usually wore a bra to hold in her generous breasts, even when lounging at home.

At first, she tried to hold her belly in, but that gave way as she got to work. When she bent over to put the cheese and milk in the fridge, he received a lovely view of her ass, which would look much lovelier when he'd had a chance to pink it up a bit.

It appeared she was pretending he didn't exist, which didn't surprise him. And she was hustling, which tempted him to remind her that when her task was done, she wasn't suddenly going to be allowed clothes, but he kept his mouth shut.

When she finished, she turned toward him and hesitated. He gave it a second, willing to give an instruction, but curious to see what she'd do without one. She walked to him, lip a little red from the worrying she'd give it, and dropped to her knees in front of him, assuming the position he'd given her.

"Very nice, pet." He put his hand on her head and slid it down to her neck.

Her eyebrows furrowed.

"Not a fan of the nickname? Or is it the touch?"

"I—the nickname, Sir. I guess I would be worried that a nickname would sneak into regular life by accident and be embarrassing to explain. But since this is just a weekend, it's fine. I don't mind."

"Hm." He'd left his hand on her neck, but now ran it over to cup her shoulder, give it a little squeeze. Nothing sexual, just a grounding. He picked up the rose that he'd set on the table and held it up to her cheek, ran it softly over her lips and down her throat. Twirled it there for a moment, then moved it to her nipple, brushing it over and over as the little nub stiffened and deepened in color.

"What about petal?" he asked. "You have all the different shades of pink, like your rose does."

She blushed. "Yes, Sir. Thank you, Sir."

He put the rose back and picked up a simple black Velcro restraint. "Left hand."

Her breathing increased, her breasts rising and falling in a way that enticed him. He was very much looking forward to some playtime that included her breasts. She held out her left hand and he wrapped the cuff securely, but not tight. They had a thick neoprene lining that would keep her comfortable, while secure.

"Switch."

She pulled her left hand back as she brought her right forward, and he repeated the process. This one had a quick link on it to attach to the other cuff when he was ready. She watched him as he worked, securing the cuff and testing the fit.

"Stand up, hands on my shoulders. Left foot on the chair." There was enough space between his knees for her to place her foot on the seat between his thighs. He quickly secured one ankle, then the other, and stood. The last item he'd left on the table was a thin leash. It had a very small clasp, nothing that would bother her against her throat or damage the small lock that closed her collar. Still, her eyes were huge as he snapped it on.

"Hands and knees, you'll crawl with me. Don't let the leash get taut, it should be slack at all times."

He could see that she wasn't at all sure about this, but she didn't hesitate. She dropped to her hands and knees and waited for him to move. They crossed from the small dining area next to the kitchen, through the main room of the cabin and into the bedroom. It wasn't more than twenty feet, but he suspected she found every one of them to be annoying.

"Stand at the head of the bed, there." She crawled the couple of feet to the queen bed, then stood. Her breathing was fast again, but he was pretty sure it was from indignation, not arousal. But assumptions were bad, so he'd best check. He walked up into her space and ran his hand from between her breasts, down her stomach—which flinched under his touch—to her center. He'd told her to shave herself completely last night, more to give her something concrete to do to prepare herself than for his personal preference. Her skin was smooth and soft, as ordered. He cupped her with his palm, not attempting to open her full lips. Dry.

The bed had four wooden posts. Simple iron headboard and footboard that made geometric shapes between the posts gave him plenty of options for bondage. He took the leash off, threaded it through the headboard, putting the clasp end through the handle and pulling tight. He reattached it to her collar. There wasn't much give, but as along as she stayed next to the post, the leash didn't pull.

"Hands behind your back, Petal." He clipped the cuffs together and surveyed his handiwork. Now she was getting aroused again.

He brushed a soft kiss over her lips, then turned away. It didn't take long to get the sheets from the closet and make the bed, brushing against her as he tugged them into place in her corner. The little line between her eyes was the only sign of her displeasure.

When he dropped the pillow while trying to get it into the case, her arms jerked, but she stayed quiet. He fluffed the pillows and arranged them against the headboard and nodded. He took a set of towels from the closet and moved them to the bathroom, then grabbed her journal and pen, which she'd set with her clothes next to the front door. When he returned, she was watching the doorway, waiting for him.

Natalie thought it took a while for Noah to return to the bedroom, but had to admit it had probably only been a minute. He had her journal, which he set on the bed. He came and unlocked her wrists.

"Up on the bed."

He held her elbow and made sure she was able to sit without the leash pulling at her collar. Then he handed her the journal. "I know it's only been an hour, but I want you to update your thoughts."

"Yes, Sir."

She opened the book. He stretched out on the bed next to her and got on his phone. At first she wasn't sure what to say, but tried to think what had happened since the last entry.

Walking into the house, stripping. *Gah*, the stripping had been difficult. They'd talked about it, so she knew he'd likely make it a requirement at some point, but she'd sort of thought they'd ease into it. Holy hell, it had been scary to stand in front of him like that. The warm appreciation and approval in his gaze had helped. A little. But then he'd put the real collar on her, one he'd clearly gotten just for her. Or, at least, she assumed orange wasn't his usual color, and it was her favorite, which she'd told him.

It had brought back some memories. She'd been so freaking excited when David had first put a collar on her. She and Felicity had preened together in the mirror. Looking back, she felt so young, and trying to compare David to Noah was just a joke. David had worked hard to be a Dom. Which, to be fair, maybe Noah had too, at that age.

Now, it seemed effortless. It took only a look from him to make her feel under his control. A touch brought her calm and excitement at once. The collaring had made her forget about being naked in front of him. For a minute. But walking to the kitchen had been nerve-wracking. And then the bastard had just sat there, *watching* her!

The idea of doing service to a Dom was something they'd talked about, and something she'd assumed she'd be attracted to. Putting their food away should have made her happy. But it had been irritating and hadn't made her feel any sense of peace or satisfaction, like she'd thought it would. Okay, well, there'd been a tiny bit of satisfaction at the appreciation in his gaze, but it hadn't been strong enough to make her stop wishing she could put on a bra and panties, at the least.

Of course, that had quickly morphed to excitement, again, when he'd wrapped the cuffs around her wrists and ankles. Now things were getting started! Only to have the weird feeling of him attaching the leash grow into...what? What had she felt, crawling behind him to the bedroom? It wasn't shame, exactly. It definitely wasn't excitement. A little irritation, for sure. Humiliation? Her knees had hurt, her boobs hadn't felt great. She'd been thankful the floor appeared to be quite clean.

Then he'd made her stand there, unable to move, while *he'd* made up the bed. That had been almost worse than the kitchen episode. Wasn't it supposed to be her doing the work? But she'd stood there wrapped in his bonds, leashed to his bed, under his control. So... yeah, she was a mass of confusion right at the moment, which was what she tried to convey in the journal.

She noted how hearing him call her petal made her melt, both from the personal aspect of his selecting the name, and the knowledge that he'd heard her uncertainty, understood it, and come up with an alternative that they both liked. She breathed deeply, feeling the collar at her neck. It wasn't big, but it was much more substantial than the little deal he'd had her wear in the car. It made her feel like his hand was on her.

It surprised her how easy it was to fall into the rhythm of calling him Sir. All those years ago, it was something she'd had to work at. She was a tiny bit worried she'd screw up and call him that at a family event. It just seemed so natural while they were in scene. She'd have to see if it slipped out when they weren't playing.

"How are you doing, Petal?"

She blinked her way out of her thoughts and looked over at Noah. Then looked down at the journal and realized she hadn't written anything for a few minutes. She closed it up and set it and the pen aside.

"All done, Sir. Thank you."

"What number are you at?"

It took her a second to think what he meant and then to decide on a number. Yeah, what they'd done so far hadn't revved her up, but that wasn't the point. And sure, she'd still love some clothes, but maybe being naked would mean they could get to some of the sexy stuff soon. "One, Sir."

"All right. Do you need a break?"

"No, Sir. Thank you."

He checked his watch. "I think you can go ahead and make us dinner. The chicken thighs, rice and roasted squash you talked about sound good to me. How about you?"

"Yes, Sir." The baked chicken was something she'd made a hundred times and could do without thinking too hard, so it sounded great to her.

"All right." His grin suggested he'd read her mind.

He rolled off the bed and picked up a bag that she hadn't seen. He put it on the bed and rummaged through it, glancing at her, then back into the bag. He tossed a bottle of lube to her side and showed her an anal plug. It wasn't big, she was relieved to see.

He came around to her side of the bed and helped her to stand. "Wait here," he ordered with a wink, since it wasn't like she could go anywhere.

He was gone less than a minute, returning with her rose. With his gaze on her, he touched the rose to her forehead, then down her nose, pausing so she could inhale its scent again. Then he teased the velvety-soft petals along her lips, under her chin and down her throat.

The bloom circled her breasts, played along the valley for a minute, then he pressed the stem into the sensitive tissue. She gasped. Not from pain, exactly. Although the sharpness was increasing. But these were Noah's thorns, from her rose, and she closed her eyes to better experience the sensation.

Which is how she missed being ready for him to take one of her nipples into his mouth, sucking gently, caressing with his tongue, all while the thorns pressed into her and the scent of rose embraced her.

"Give me a number, Petal."

"One, Sir."

He chuckled, was still doing so as he pulled her other nipple in for the same treatment. He adjusted the stem, marking new territory. His free hand drifted down to her core, teased her pussy just barely, moving some of her wetness around.

When he let go, her nipples were hard points that stabbed toward him, begging for more. He got up from the bed and held out a hand. "Stand here. I don't want to see that leash pulling."

She watched as he pulled the bag toward him and removed some leather straps. When he took the key to her collar from his pocket, she had to suppress a whimper. She'd grown used to it so quickly and didn't want him to take it off yet.

His eyes crinkled, suggesting he was aware of her pout, but he didn't say anything. He laid the lock and collar on the bed, and picked up the black leather straps. The first piece went around her neck, buckling into place. It was wider than the previous collar, probably an inch, maybe even a little more. From the center of the collar dropped a strap of leather that lay along her cleavage, then another circle that buckled around her back, forming a harness just underneath her breasts.

He stepped back, fingered the fit, then adjusted the buckle to shorten the vertical piece. She wasn't sure she was going to like this. Already, she could feel her breasts sagging over the strap. Surely this would be much more attractive on a woman with perky breasts. Hers were too big to be contained this way. She felt…floppy.

He fluffed her boobs, plumping them and squeezing a bit, then pressed the red spots where the thorns had poked at her. Under his slightly calloused fingertips, her sensitivity seemed to grow.

Stepping back, he studied her. "Gorgeous."

The sincerity in his voice went a long way toward making her feel better, though she wondered what she actually looked like. He didn't give her much time to worry about it.

"Bend over so your cheek is flat on the mattress."

She did as she was told, her nose an inch from the leash he'd discarded. He ran his hand along her back. "How are your shoulders feeling?"

"Fine, Sir." She hadn't thought about them. Now that he mentioned it, she was aware of a tiny bit of strain, but not much.

He picked up the lube and squirted a generous portion between her butt cheeks, then slowly—very, very slowly—worked it along her rim. His finger edged into the opening. "Relax for me." His other hand picked up the rose and trailed it along her back, teased her nose, slid along her arm. All the while, his finger pressed slowly forward, aided by the slick gel.

Taking a deep breath, she did as he asked, consciously relaxing those muscles. Accepting him inside her. He slid in to the first knuckle. "That's my girl," he crooned. He left the rose on her back and moved his free hand to her core, sliding a finger easily into her wetness. The pinch at her ass was about the same as what the thorns had given her breasts, so she relaxed even more. He rewarded her with another finger in her pussy.

Working his finger in and out of her rear, he loosened her up some more, then pulled free. More cool lube, then she felt the hard, and yet soft, of the plug.

"Keep breathing. You're doing great. What's your number?"

"One, Sir."

He brought his fingers, slick with her wetness, to her clit, and circled and tweaked it while he pushed the plug in past the first knob. She was breathing hard now, wishing she could move her hips to direct his fingers. Another knob popped past her resistance. She'd noticed three on the little devils.

He leaned over and sucked a mouthful of her ass cheek between his teeth. She gave a startled squeak and the plug was fully seated. He licked and soothed the spot on her cheek, then kissed her tailbone and wiggled the beast inside her a bit. She'd seen it. Sitting on the bed, it hadn't looked big at all. Barely wider than his thick finger. Inside, it felt like a flashlight. Okay, not really, but *damn*.

It wasn't uncomfortable, so much as…just weird. Foreign.

"Up you go, Petal."

He used a hand on her arm to help her stand, which totally changed the feeling of the object inside her. Her instincts were to push it back out again.

"I'm not going to give you a harness, you should be able to hold that in yourself for a little while. If you push it out, you're just going to have to wash it and I'll put it in again. Don't move."

She heard him go into the bathroom and wash his hands, while she tried not to squirm. He came back in and studied her. "Ready to make dinner?"

Oh, yeah, she'd already forgotten about that. "Yes, Sir."

He led the way to the kitchen and she was glad she got to walk, instead of crawl, but it felt *so weird*. She stood in the kitchen and he unhooked the cuffs, then massaged her shoulders as she brought her hands forward. He gave her a little slap on the ass. "Get cookin', woman."

She slanted a look at him, but focused on what she needed to do.

C H A P T E R   N I N E

Noah set up his laptop on the opposite side of the table this time, so he could keep an eye on Nat, but it wouldn't appear that he was just watching the show. She'd walk a few steps, squeeze her butt cheeks a bit, continue on her way. Her tits were flushed and her forehead was a little damp. He smiled at his computer screen, though he wasn't really trying to get anything done.

She was looking for a pot, and she bit her lip as she debated bending over or squatting when she found it in the lower cabinet. She tried squatting down, then popped back up, one hand braced on the edge of the counter.

"Need help, subbie?"

"I don't think so, Sir."

"Let me know if you do."

"Thank you, Sir."

She bent over and retrieved the pan, and continued on. The refrigerator made a noise, the ice in the dispenser tumbling, and she jerked and froze.

"Sir, may I…push the plug?"

He grinned. "You may."

She reseated the plug, washed her hands, and resumed cooking.

When the chicken and squash were baking and the rice was simmering, she turned to look at him.

"How much time do we have?" he asked.

"Twenty minutes. I set the timer."

He nodded. He gestured to the chair across from him, which was still facing the kitchen. "Take a seat, hands behind the chair." When she'd complied, he snapped the cuffs together again. "I'll be right back."

He went into the bedroom and studied the nipple clamps he'd brought. He may have gone a little overboard, but he'd been dreaming about seeing her breasts, and being able to decorate them. Making a selection, he returned to the kitchen.

"Hook your feet around the chair legs."

She didn't hesitate, her eyes trained on him. Soon, they'd take a break. Eat dinner. Decompress. But first, he'd adorn her magnificent tits.

Her nipples were still puckered, though not enough. He went to his knees in front of her and nuzzled the smooth flesh of her breasts, licked the little red spots from the thorns, inhaled the scent of Natalie and leather. He licked her pebbled areola, then he pulled her nipple into his mouth, pulsing it gently with his tongue.

When it was firm, he let it go and looked. Deep purplish red, glistening with his saliva. He checked her face. She looked like she needed to be fucked.

"Do you like when I play with your breasts?" he asked.

She sighed. "Yes, Sir."

"That's lucky, then, because I'm very fond of them." He held up the nipple clamps. They were shaped like crowns, blunted prongs that would dig into her flesh, and a strong magnet that would hold the crown in place, pinching her nipple. He'd tested the magnets, and they weren't super strong. Enough that they would stay on, for sure, and she would feel the pressure, but not actual pain.

He showed her the crown. "Pretty, right?"

"Yes, Sir."

He pushed the prongs into her skin and inserted one side of the magnet, then the other, watching her face carefully. No sign of pain. He cupped the breast in his hand while he took her other nipple into his mouth and prepared it. When the second clamp was secured, he dropped back to his heels and studied her.

Fucking gorgeous. He wished he could take a picture. Her flushed skin surrounded by the leather harness, her beautifully crowned nipples, the need for more in her eyes. He decided to share the pleasure of what he was seeing. Rising, he put a hand under her arm.

"Up you go."

He led her into the bathroom and turned her to face the mirror. His hands on her shoulders, he let her take in the beauty that she was.

Her eyes went wide.

"Even better than I'd imagined," he said. "And I was imagining you looking pretty fucking amazing."

"Wow."

He smiled. "I'm going to fuck your tits before we leave this cabin," he promised.

Her mouth opened into a little O.

"You've done so well today. Do you think you deserve to come?" He slid one hand down to cup it between her legs.

"Yes, Sir. I mean, I don't know, Sir. But I would like to, please."

He smiled at her reflection, nuzzled her ear. "Nicely said, Petal."

Sliding two fingers into her welcoming heat, he eased the heal of his hand against her clit, increasing the pressure as her eyelids went to half-mast and her head fell back to his shoulder.

Her hands scrabbled, latching onto his shirt. He nudged her butt with his thigh, so that she'd feel the plug. A tiny grunt escaped her.

"Can you come for me like this?" he asked. "You look incredible. My leather wrapped around your amazing breasts, holding your throat. Wearing my plug, my clamps holding your nipples tight, your cunt clutching my fingers like you don't want to let me go."

She muscles spasmed around his fingers and he ground harder against her clit. "I—I—I think so, Sir."

"I want to watch your juices run down your thigh and hear you scream loud enough that I'll be glad we didn't open any windows."

Her breath was hitching now. He looked down and watched as he added a third finger. Her toes were curled under her, her grip on his shirt tightened.

He drew his fingers from her, which caused her to whine, which turned to a panting shriek as he pinched her clit, then fucked her hard with his fingers. She ground herself against his palm before going rigid in his arms, coming with a long cry. He kept his fingers inside her, moving slowly, his palm still. Her toes uncurled and her fingers relaxed. The plug dropped to the floor with a thuddy little bounce.

She opened her eyes at that, a worried look on her face.

"I was going to help with that, but it was next on the agenda."

Her tired smile of relief was pure sweetness. He took out two fingers, and hooked the other to find her G-spot. Her eyes went wide with shock and she came again, squirting into his hand.

"Oh, shit," she breathed.

"Nicely done." He kissed her temple.

She blinked at him. He pulled free from her and used both hands to separate the nipple clamps. A tiny gasp was all she managed, but he soothed her nipples, for longer than was probably necessary. When he was sure she could stand on her own, he washed his hands and dried them, then unhooked and removed her cuffs. He handed her the butt plug and nodded to the cleanser he'd left next to the sink.

"You wash this while I do the rest."

She did as he asked, and he removed the ankle cuffs and unbuckled the chest harness. When her throat was naked, he dropped a kiss on it. She was drying her hands when the buzzer sounded from the kitchen.

"We're breaking the scene now, all right? Go ahead and put on your robe," he told her. "I'll get the rice."

Her eyes were still a little dazed when she made it back into the kitchen. He stopped fluffing the rice and went to her and rubbed his hands up and down her arms. "If you set the table, I'll get the chicken."

"Okay."

Soon they were at the table. He was starving.

"This is great," he told her when he'd demolished half of it. The chicken was baked to crispy perfection, the vegetables roasted with Italian seasoning, and the rice simple and fluffy.

She smiled and looked up at him. "Thanks. Wow. This is kind of weird."

He nodded. "Tell me."

"No, it's fine, it's good."

"No, really. Tell me. I want to know what you're thinking."

"Oh." She took another bite. "I guess...it's not what I was expecting."

"You were thinking I'd keep you tied up the whole time?"

"Maybe ninety percent of the time," she admitted.

"It will come, I promise. This part is really more mental. There are a couple more variations of waiting on your Dom that I want to try, and then we can move on. But consider what we've done and how much it can depend on your mindset. I'm guessing you had a different mindset while putting the groceries away than you did while cooking. But both were the same ask. Your top asked you to do a thing for him, while he did something else."

She frowned over a bit of squash, then nodded.

"You could have spent the time you put away the groceries thinking happy thoughts about accomplishing this for me—for us—while also giving me the pleasure of viewing my property in a way that I enjoy. But I'm guessing that's not what you were thinking."

Now her eyes went a little wide.

He reached out and put a hand on your arm. "That was *not* criticism. You did nothing wrong." He gave her arm a squeeze and let go. "Keep in mind that I'm the one teaching here, so if I expect you to do something, I'll tell you. I can't tell you how to feel, or think, but I could have coached you into the right headspace, or at least enough that you knew what to try for."

Another thoughtful frown.

"For some, the most important part of their submission is the quiet time. Or the service. Doing their top's laundry when they're not even home to watch, cleaning the kitchen while naked, sitting at their feet at the end of the day. For some, it's a gift to their top. For some, it's like meditation. Or any combination. Tonight you're going to get naked, serve me a beer, and sit naked at my feet while I read. Tomorrow, we'll do one more thing. That's not to say this will show you all the varieties of this kind of service. There are as many varieties as there are relationships between people."

"Okay. Right. And when you learn meditation you have to work up to it, so just because you can't do it for long now, doesn't mean you can't build that ability."

"Exactly. Plus, consider that if the point of sitting at your Dom's feet is to focus on your devotion to him or her—or, I should say them. You have my permission to point out to me when my language isn't inclusive." It was something he was trying to retrain his brain on, and it was harder than he'd assumed.

"Good point. Please do the same with me."

"If you're to focus on your devotion to this person, on what pleases them and how simply doing as they've asked is one of those things, then it would stand to reason that it would be much easier to do that once you've gotten to know that person. The point here is that things will change and evolve with you, and with your relationship. Something you hate this weekend might end up being your favorite thing with the right person. This is more to open your mind to the possibilities than to create hard limits that you never reexamine. And to give context to things that are just a list on a limits sheet right now."

"That makes sense." She nodded as she leaned back in her chair, her plate empty.

He figured it was time to let her brain rest from all things BDSM. "If you're up to it, we can go take a walk outside, before the sun sets."

"It's a great cabin. You said your friend owns it?"

"My uncle's brother, actually. But also, my friend."

Her nose scrunched up. "Wouldn't that be your uncle?"

He polished off his last bite of chicken and drank the last of his water. "My uncle Paul was my mother's brother. He married my uncle Leon when I was ten, so I just considered them both my uncles. Uncle Leon's brother Cedric owns the cabin."

"Gotcha. Was?"

He nodded. "Uncle Paul got Leukemia. I came out to help them when things got bad, about seven years ago. He passed away a year later. And I stayed. I spend the holidays with Uncle Leon and his family."

"Oh, I'm sorry about Paul. That must have been difficult, coming out here to do that."

"Thanks." He picked up his plate and hers, and headed into the kitchen while she grabbed their glasses and napkins. "When I graduated high school, I wasn't really thrilled with the idea of going to college. Sitting in a classroom all day wasn't my thing. I'd built up the mowing into a small landscaping business. My parents were great about not pressuring me into school, though they would have preferred it. But I was still at loose ends and when Paul told us he was sick, I was the one in the best position to come help. Leon's family is great, and Paul was close to them, but they were all working or had little kids. They couldn't give up their jobs like I could. It made sense. I was glad to spend that time with him."

There was no dishwasher, something Cedric moaned about but probably wouldn't change anytime soon. Noah started washing while Natalie put away the butter and soy sauce and grabbed a towel to dry.

"It sounds like you have a lot of family," she said as they worked together.

"I do. I wish you had that, as well."

She turned and shot him a beaming smile. "But I do. Annalise and her family have made it clear to me that I'm not a guest. I'm not a friend. I'm one of them." She shrugged. "Do I miss my aunt and uncle and cousin and wish we could be part of their lives? Absolutely. But I won't be alone when my grandparents pass. I've been slowly hinting to my mom that she should move up here when she retires."

He didn't let the fact that his hand was wet and sudsy stop him from putting his hand on her cheek to hold her still for a kiss.

THE EMOTION in Noah's eyes when he leaned in to kiss her completely distracted her from the fact that his hand was wet. He pulled back from the kiss and used the towel in her hand to wipe her cheek dry.

"I'm glad," he told her, then turned back to the last of the dishes.

"I am, too. Sometimes I think about the fact that the first time I met Annalise, and she invited me over, I actually said no. Just being shy. But she pushed, and I went, and it was so easy after that."

He hung the towel up to dry. "She's a good person, and you two make a great team. Why don't you put on some clothes, and we'll take that walk."

The way he said it, like she'd just been lazing around the house all day instead of the fact that she'd been following his orders...she stuck her tongue out at him. He pretended to snap a bite at her and she laughed and turned away.

It almost felt strange putting on her clothes. She checked her watch. It was only a little after seven. She'd been there less than four hours. Bizarre. He held his hand out to her when she joined him on the porch, and they walked to the water first.

"It's not a big pond, I think only about half a mile long. Cedric loves to fly fish. His wife likes to swim and snorkel."

The air was thick and humid, which suddenly made her realize that the cabin had been very comfortable. Not hot, but not too cool on her naked skin, either. She'd been so nervous when she'd first gone in and stripped that she hadn't thought about it.

"How did you make sure the air-conditioning was on the right setting before we got here?" she asked.

"They've got it set up to a smart thermostat. I used my phone when I got to your place, before I came upstairs."

She could see two canoes slowly making their way past, along the far shore. It looked like a woman and a teenager. "I love the extra sunlight this time of year. It's when I start to do things like join a book club or go to the gym to start swimming laps, or decide that I should take a foreign language class. But then when I'm coming home from work in the dark, I just want to curl up on my couch and hibernate."

He nodded. "Let's walk." He tugged her hand and started back toward the cabin. "My job is very defined by the seasons, obviously. And I enjoy certain aspects of all of them. But I definitely feel like I get more out of the day in the summer than the winter. Which is weird, it's the same number of hours."

"Exactly!" She shot him a grin, then almost stumbled. He was smiling *that* smile again. With the little crinkles next to his eyes. He was too freaking sexy for her sanity. She looked down, as if to be sure of her footing. They'd left the path that led between the cabin and the pond, and he was leading her into the woods. Within only a few feet, she felt like they were in their own little world. She couldn't see the water, where people might be, couldn't hear the road.

He pointed. "Way over there, that break just downhill, that's the closest neighbor."

It was like he was reading her mind again. She still hadn't decided if that was a good thing or a bad thing. "I need to get out of the city more often," she said.

"Nature feeds the soul. Then again, so does an abundance of restaurants."

Her laughter had several birds taking flight.

They kept going until they reached a tree that was wider than she was. He pointed up. A rough tree house was nestled into the branches. They moved around to the other side, where a ladder had been built alongside a rope with knots every foot or so.

"Originally it was just the rope, but we put the ladder in a few years ago."

"How fun. Can we go up?"

"Sure."

"I honestly don't think I've ever been in a real tree house." She climbed up first, using the ladder. When she reached the top, she used the rope to help pull herself over. The space was about six feet square, bigger than she'd expected.

Four collapsed camp chairs were leaning against one wall, and a shelf had been built into another. There was a window with a beautiful view of the pond. "This is pretty cool."

"It's a little silly, since we were adults when Cedric decided to build it. Why do you need a tree house when you have a perfectly good lake house? But his kids will have kids eventually, and they'll get a kick out of it. For now, we come out here once in a while when it's not too hot."

"I think it's great," she reiterated. She considered using the rope to go down, but decided she had enough physical adventures coming up for the weekend, no need to waste herself when there was a perfectly good ladder she could use. She backed down and waited for him to do the same.

"Let's head back, the sun will be setting soon and it will get dark fast."

He pointed out some interesting plants to her on the way back, and even some tracks that they pretended to have a clue what they could be for. She settled on beaver, having no idea if that was even possible, and he was equally insistent they were fox tracks.

They sat on the Adirondack chairs on the porch and watched the sun sink behind the trees. When the light was nearly gone, he turned to her. "Are you ready to play?"

It was hard to imagine *not* being ready to play, when Noah was the one doing the asking. Then again, she'd enjoyed this interlude of dinner and a walk, just as Natalie and Noah.

She held her hand out to him in answer. His gaze was full of approval and he stood, pulling her from the chair. When he closed the door behind her, he took her head in his hands and dropped a kiss on her forehead.

"Strip, grab me a beer, and meet me at the couch."

"Yes, Sir."

It was still hard to take her clothes off. Hadn't she just been thinking it was weird to put them *on*? The couch was perpendicular to the door, so she could see Noah settle into a seat, without looking directly at him. Which meant he could see her, as well. She was determined to do as he'd asked, no hesitation. She managed it, though it took force of will when she reached her underwear. As she walked to the kitchen, she had the bizarre feeling of thinking she was *too* naked, but not because of her lack of underclothes. It was that she hadn't had to do anything he'd asked of her, since she got into his car, without his collar around her neck.

It was a bit disquieting how important that felt already.

She grabbed the beer and remembered to use the church key that was attached to the fridge with a magnet, before bringing it to him. He had an ereader in his lap, and she made a mental note to ask him what he was reading, next time they were back to just being them.

"Thank you, Petal." He took it from her and set it on the table next to him. "Kneel here in front of me." He'd put one of the throw pillows in front of the couch. He pulled her collar and the lock from next to his leg, where she hadn't seen it. A little bit of peace flowed through her as she dropped to her knees and kept her head high so he could wrap the orange band around her and secure it closed with a little snick.

"Now, you'll sit here, back to the couch. Or, if you prefer, you can do one of those yoga poses where you bend over your thighs and rest your head on the ground. But using the pillow."

"Yes, Sir."

She moved the pillow out of her way and sat down cross-legged next to him. "Sir, may I ask a question?"

"You may."

"Earlier, you told me that if I was kneeling next to you, I could rest my head on your leg. Is that still okay, if I'm sitting down?"

"It is."

"Thank you, Sir."

She adjusted so that his thigh was a perfect pillow, and took a deep breath, thinking about what he'd told her about mindset. She heard him pick up the bottle, set it back down again. Her only instruction was to please him by sitting still and staying quiet.

Doms were weird. Why was that pleasing?

She didn't startle when his hand touched her head, because she'd been hyperaware of his movements. As he smoothed his hand over her hair, she concentrated on the simple pleasure. It was interesting to think of the differences between Dom and sub. She'd never wondered if she might be a top. She supposed there might be some scenario, somewhere, in which she could imagine being a switch. But not by inclination. Although if anyone had asked her what she'd like to be, that would have been her pick. Best of both worlds, right?

She shifted her butt without moving her head or disturbing Sir's hand as he continued to sift his fingers through her strands, then smooth it down. Occasionally he moved to cup her shoulder and caress her arm, which was nice, too.

But what kind of books did he like? She figured him for thrillers. But maybe he was reading a gardening book? Or horror? No, sci-fi, she decided, and wished she'd kept the pillow under her butt.

Her mind wandered and circled in a way she would readily admit was not the least bit meditative.

"How are you doing, Petal? Give me a number."

Oof. That was tough. She was fine, really. Just sort of bored and not sure if it was okay for her to adjust her sitting position. But certainly nothing that she couldn't endure to make him happy.

"Two, Sir," she finally decided after a minute.

He didn't answer, just resumed petting her hair.

She woke up with a start when Noah barked out her name. She had no idea when she'd fallen asleep. She sat up straight and tried to blink her brain clear.

CHAPTER TEN

Noah hadn't expected to leave Natalie at his feet for too long. He'd just wanted to give her a taste and have her think through what she did and didn't like about serving in this fashion.

He also hadn't expected her to fall asleep and start gently snoring on his leg.

He gave her fifteen minutes to rest up a bit, then schooled his voice so his amusement wasn't evident. On the one hand, it was cute. On the other hand, it gave him an opportunity to punish her. She hadn't given him a chance for that yet, and he wanted to see what worked, and didn't work, for her in that arena.

"Natalie."

She jerked upright and looked slowly around herself.

"Was sleeping on the very small list of things I asked you to do for the next little while?"

She turned to look at him.

"No, Sir." Her lip disappeared between her teeth and her gaze dropped to the ground.

They'd discussed punishments, of course. He decided the simple, classic spanking was a good starting place.

"Do you think a punishment is in order?"

She let her lip go and sighed. "Yes, Sir?"

He managed to keep his face blank, but it was a struggle. She was so damn cute. "I think five swats over my lap."

"Yes, Sir. I'm sorry, Sir."

"Stand up."

She shoved to her feet, not particularly gracefully, but without hesitating.

He moved over so her head wouldn't be smashed into the arm of the couch and patted his thighs. She stared at his legs, but didn't move. Her head had bowed, and her hair swung free, obscuring his view of her face. He tilted so he could see her—and his heart slammed into his chest.

Her eyes had gone wide and glassy and her breath was coming in tiny pants.

He surged up and scooped her into his arms, cuddling her cold body against himself. He'd kept an eye on her temperature as she'd sat in front of him, and she'd been fine. Sudden understanding of how stupid he'd been beat at him. He grabbed the blanket from the back of the couch and got it as much around her as he could without letting her go.

"Natalie." One arm holding her closely, he used his free hand to tip her chin so she was looking at his face. Not that she was seeing a damn thing.

"Natalie," he repeated, sharply, when she didn't respond. She blinked, and he started to breathe again. "Petal."

She blinked again and her eyes began to clear, confusion, then horror replacing the blank look. "I'm sor—"

"Uh uh," he interrupted, laying a finger across her lips. "No apologies. I fucked up. I'm the one who's sorry."

"I—I don't really know what happened."

"Tell me what you remember, but with the full understanding that you did nothing at all wrong. Are you comfortable?" He really meant "do you feel safe" but thought that would only confuse her right now.

Her eyes darted around and she moved her hand, which had

been limp against her stomach, to his shirt. Holding it in her fist, she nodded. "Yes, Sir."

"Good. Can you tell me what you remember?"

"I was sitting on the floor. It was boring, but I was trying to do like you said, think about the right mindset. And then—I guess I fell asleep. You woke me up and decided on spanking. Five times."

"How did you feel about that?"

"I wasn't excited, because I knew it wouldn't be like a good kind of spanking, but I was pretty sure I could handle five. I was wondering if you would go light, or hard, or both."

He'd been planning on both.

"And then what?"

"I'm not sure, really. I think you told me to lay across your lap so you could do the spanking and...I froze. I think. I—I want to apologize again."

"Thank you for not doing so." He couldn't believe he was smiling again, already, but she really was pretty damn cute. "I'll say it again. I don't even mind repeating myself. I'll say it as many times as you need to hear it. You didn't do anything wrong. I triggered a...let's call it a panic attack, and you were only doing what you were told to do. How, in that scenario, can you be to blame?"

She frowned. "I didn't think I'd have a problem being spanked. We talked about it, before this weekend."

"We did. You said you'd been paddled before, and bent over a spanking bench, but I didn't specifically ask you if you'd been spanked on someone's lap. On a man's lap, especially."

"Oh. My dad, you mean. You think this was about him." She shivered, and he ran his hand up and down her arm, over the blanket. "He never spanked me. At least not that I remember."

"I think it's just a...generational connotation, if that makes sense. Or societal. The father, the disciplinarian."

She frowned. "I think I'm okay now."

"Let's sit a little while longer." He had to decide if he should still punish her or not. His instinct was not, but he didn't want her to see this as a failure. And he suspected that she would, no matter what he told her.

She kept quiet for five minutes, which was fairly impressive. "You're too cozy, I'm going to fall asleep again," she warned him.

"Fair enough. I'll give you three choices on what we do next."

The little line appeared between her eyebrows again.

"One, you lay over my lap and I spank you five times. Two, you lay over the arm of the couch, and I stand behind you and spank you five times. Three, we move on to the next thing and save your five swats to add to your next punishment. If you make it to the end of the weekend with no further punishments, I'll be impressed and only give you three."

He was hoping the challenge of making it through the rest of the weekend would appeal to her. She narrowed her eyes as she studied him."

"What happens if I say your lap, but then I freeze up again?"

"I hold you like this until you snap out of it and we decide what to do next from there."

"Hm." And then she shocked him by reaching a hand up to his cheek. "I know you don't really want to, but I would appreciate if we could try your lap again."

So much for being an inscrutable Dom. He put his forehead to hers. "Then that's what we'll do."

He lifted up and unwrapped the blanket from around her, helping her to stand. "What number are you at?"

She hesitated.

"Don't fudge," he warned. "You'll get a lot worse punishment than a spanking if I think you understate it."

"Three, Sir."

"All right. I'll warn you now, if we make it as far as a spanking, I'm going hard on your ass just to feel better about not feeling good about this." He pretended to glower at her.

"What?" She laughed, as he'd hoped. "That makes no sense."

"Doesn't have to make sense. I'm the Dom."

She snorted, and, without further hesitation, draped herself over his lap, her toes stretched out behind her, her hands flat on the floor.

Instead of wrapping one hand around her waist, as he'd originally intended, to make her feel secure so she wouldn't fall off, he rested one hand on her shoulder, and swept the other down her back, over her butt, upper thighs, and back around, until she was breathing steadily again.

"What's your number?"

"Two, Sir."

His sweet girl.

He put his arm across her back, holding her down.

"What about now?"

"One, Sir."

Fuck, he was going to have to rethink his plan of not pushing her into a relationship. "Good girl, I'm proud of you."

"Thank you, Sir." The last word was a bit of a screech, as he surprised her with the first spank. Contrary to what he'd told her, he didn't go hard. More medium-light. He smoothed his palm over the globe he'd smacked, then gave it another, slightly harder. Then he caught up with her other cheek, in rapid succession. He paused, his hand resting on the first side, feeling her muscles flex and quiver under his palm. Then he gave it one last, harder smack.

He rolled her over and into his lap and checked her face. Flushed red, eyes dilated, lips parted. Gorgeous.

She reached out and took his shirt in her hand, though he didn't think she was even conscious of it. "What's your number?" he asked.

"One, Sir."

"I'll let you write in your journal in a minute, but tell me what you think about the spanking. Specifically, over the lap like that?"

"I know you could have gone harder, and I don't like getting punished, but I think it was good. I liked that you were holding me while doing it, so thank you for letting me try your lap again. I think that first reaction was just a one-off, I don't think it will be a problem again."

He kissed her nose. "All right. You can get your robe and your journal and come sit on the couch with me. If you want, you can read or knit when you're done, or we can watch TV." He reached up to unlock her collar, and she flinched back, then stilled. "No scene for a while."

"Okay." She touched her bare neck, and he checked to see if it was red or chaffed, but it looked fine.

They ended up on the couch with Natalie on one end, back against the arm, feet nearly in his lap, listening to an audiobook with her earphones in while she knit, and he read. The gentle clicking of the knitting needles was somehow soothing. Her orange satin robe did an amazing job of hiding, yet highlighting, her breasts, and he was having a hard time concentrating on his book.

In some ways, the day had gone pretty close to how he'd planned. He just hadn't foreseen finding her so damn tempting. He wanted to reach over and pull her breasts from the robe, let the fabric frame them for his viewing pleasure, but she needed a break. Even more, he wanted to slide between her legs and fill her up with his cock.

Said cock was very interested in that idea, which had Noah questioning his plans for the rest of the night. She'd only had the one orgasm, and he'd decided at dinner that she was ready to enjoy some time in the bed, but now he was worried he was making excuses so that he himself could get some relief.

When he'd originally mapped out the basic plan, he'd left sex out of the equation, figuring he would need to read her, and their encounters, to know if and when it was a good idea to include it or not. The fact that he was now questioning his instincts wasn't great. He'd been attracted to her from the beginning, but the way she'd reacted to everything he'd thrown at her today was ramping that attraction up in a big way.

He'd angled himself just slightly, so that he could see her without staring at her. He checked that she wasn't watching, and adjusted his dick. It was nearly ten, and he was pretty sure he hadn't managed to change the page on his book in more than five minutes, but he was determined to give her more of a rest. Not so much physically, but mentally.

Natalie's legs shifted. The clicking stopped and she scowled, then messed with the yarn. Finally, the clicks resumed.

He forced his attention back to the book for another half hour, then looked over to her.

"How are you feeling?"

"Horny."

As soon as the word escaped her lips, Natalie slapped a hand over her mouth.

Noah's eyes widened and then he burst out laughing. "You and me both," he finally said.

"Well it's your fault! At least I'm not alone in it, though."

"My fault you're so fucking sexy and responsive and willing and eager and giving me all sorts of ideas that make it hard to remember we have the whole weekend, and we've only been here half a day and need to take it slow?"

"Yes."

He grinned. "Fine. I'll take the blame."

She raised her nose in the air and sniffed, delicately. "Good."

She turned off her audiobook and pulled out the earbuds. He narrowed his gaze at them. "Wait," he said. "What were you listening to? Didn't you tell me some of your books were erotica?"

"Erotic romance, actually, but this wasn't that. You still get all the blame."

He heaved a big sigh. "Fine." He reached out and gripped her ankle, then slowly pulled until she was flat on her back and her feet were in his lap. And then he started to rub her feet. *Holy hell.* She'd read about such things in books, but had always figured it was mostly exaggerated, or simply an excuse for touch. He dug his thumb into her arch and her eyes rolled back into her head. How had she never gotten a real foot massage before?

She stuffed a pillow under her head so she could watch as he turned her into jelly.

"You're not ready to do another scene right now," he said out of the blue.

Apparently the look of concentration hadn't been due to focus on her feet, but to their earlier conversation.

"Especially one with sex."

She narrowed her eyes at him, and tried not to pout. He continued to rub her feet.

"However, I'm perfectly willing to be seduced. One might even say I'm primed for it."

Her mouth dropped open. That was not what she'd been expecting. At all. "Is that right?"

"The Dom has retired for the night," he clarified.

"Hm." She noticed that when he'd started on her second foot, he'd left her massaged foot in his lap. How convenient. She reached over and grabbed the pillow they'd left on the floor, stuffing it behind her so she was a little bit closer to him. "I'm not sure I'm interested in putting in that kind of work," she teased. "I've had a tiring day."

As she spoke, she rubbed the heel of the foot he wasn't holding along the bulge in his pants.

He nodded. "I can understand that." He sounded nonchalant, but his fingers spasmed on her foot. She pushed a little harder. And could feel him respond, even through his shorts.

Before she could overthink things and dwell on memories of her unsuccessful and/or unsatisfying encounters with men in the past—because, really, those men weren't *Noah*, so this didn't compare—she made her move.

She faked an exaggerated yawn, hand over her mouth, eyes wide. "Oh. Excuse me. I'm very tired, I think I'll retire now." She pulled her feet from his hands—and his crotch—and rose as gracefully as she could manage, turning her back to him.

She fiddled with the sash on her robe and let it fall away about halfway to the bedroom door.

"Oops!" she turned fully toward him, watching as she bent over and slowly retrieved the robe.

He'd already half risen from the couch, his gaze hot and focused. On her. With a little smile, she turned and resumed walking, not bothering to put the robe back on.

She didn't hear him coming until a low growl of warning sounded from right behind her. Then his hands were on her, turning her, before she was bent over his shoulder and hauled off her feet.

She shrieked and grabbed his shirt, but his arm around her legs was secure. His other hand found her butt and slapped it. They made it to the side of the bed in only a couple of steps, but he didn't set her down. Instead, the hand on her ass slid between her thighs and found her wetness.

He growled again, and flipped her onto the bed.

She scooted back and watched as he pulled his shirt off in one swift move. He unbuttoned his shorts and she barely got a glimpse of his boxers as he shoved both down. Then he crawled onto the bed, hands on either side of her as he made his way up her body.

Even though he wasn't touching her, his heat and presence surrounded her. He bent his elbows until his lips were a fraction of an inch above hers. "Nicely done, Nat."

His voice was rough with the need she felt as well, and the extra spurt of pleasure at his words only drove that need higher. But she was supposed to be seducing him, right? She lifted her head, closed the scant distance between their lips, and tasted him.

She explored the shape and texture of his lips, then slid her tongue into his mouth. One of his hands went to her breast, palming it and gently thumbing the nipple. When he gave it a tighter squeeze, she tore her mouth free and gasped.

"I want to touch you everywhere," he said.

"Me too." Reminded that she could, she hooked her hands over his shoulders, drew them along his back muscles and tried to reach his ass, but came up short. Fine, there was plenty that she *could* reach. She ran her hands up his sides, surprised when he jerked.

Wait. Was he *ticklish*? The very idea had her giggling.

"I don't care if we're in a scene or not, if you tickle me, you *will* get spanked," he warned, which caused her to laugh full out.

"Well, that certainly gives me ideas."

He pretended to scowl, but she could see he was fighting a grin. "Brat."

"I might need to re-read some books with bratty subs. Do a bit of research."

"I'm going to take away your earbuds."

Since he'd straightened his arms to talk to her, she had more room, and decided she might as well use it. She brought her hands to his chest and scratched lightly over his nipples. His eyes went hot and she licked her lips. And did it again.

He reclaimed her breast with one hand, moving to reach the other nipple with his lips. He sucked it in, hard. She gasped and arched her back, offering more of herself to him. He squeezed her breasts together and pulled both nipples in. She moaned.

"I'm going to fuck these amazing tits before we leave this cabin," he reminded her.

"O—okay," she managed to pant. "If that's what you want."

She'd never had anyone so enthralled with her boobs before. Her last boyfriend had left her bra on her during sex, which she'd found kind of insulting.

He nuzzled her cleavage, then kissed his way down to her belly button. He looked up to watch her eyes, keeping the hold steady as he took a bite of her belly. Hard enough to leave a bit of a mark, she managed to think, as he let go and ran his tongue along the offended area. She was beginning to think he had a biting fetish.

Moving lower, he widened her legs and took another bite, right on her mound. *Fuck*, why was that sexy? Again, he licked to soothe, and she pressed her thighs into his shoulders.

He sucked her clit into his mouth, and she jolted with a tiny orgasm that had him raising his eyebrows at her. Well, if he'd underestimated her need, that was his fault, not hers.

"Noah, I need more," she urged.

He grunted even as he sucked, but brought one finger to her pussy, slid it in with ease. She ground her head into the bed, her legs wrapping around his back, her hips lifting up into his hold. He took his finger from inside her and replaced his lips on her clit with the wet digit. Then he replaced his finger with his mouth, his tongue pushing into her while he rubbed at her clit.

"I—I—"

He bit her, gently, soothed, sucked, fucked his tongue into her, bit her again.

"Oh, fuck. Noah!" she wailed as she came.

He kept his fingers on her clit, giving it gentle little squeezes, as he kissed his way back up her body. When he reached her breast, he bit the side of it. Her legs spasmed against him and she felt incredibly empty.

"Please, Noah. I need you inside me."

"Mm," he hummed as he reached her lips. "Does that mean you don't want to suck me?"

Immediately, her mouth watered and she tried to sit up.

He laughed. "I'm happy to fuck you right now. Very happy."

Instead, he let her shove his shoulders until he was on his back. She scooted down and almost grabbed him up, but made herself wait. Bracing herself with one hand on his hard thigh, and the other on his abdomen, she leaned in so that her nose was pressed against his dick, and inhaled.

She wouldn't have been able to say what Noah smelled like, because it was just…Noah. Earthy and tangy and warm. She nuzzled him with her cheek and looked up to check his face, just as she gave the taught flesh a little kiss.

The hunger on his face was mesmerizing. Letting go of his thigh, she cupped his balls, gently at first, then firmly. She brought her other hand to the base of his cock, holding him steady. Then she dropped her mouth over him and took as much of him in as she could manage.

She didn't have a ton of experience with this, but the books she'd been listening to had been so enthusiastic, she'd been thinking about it. About him. About this. She used her tongue and her cheeks to get him wet, then slowly pulled free.

"Nat. Jesus."

She kissed the tip, where his fluid was gathering. Wrapping her palm around him, she worked it up and down while she lowered her mouth and took in his balls. His hips jerked under her. She kept her hand moving while she licked and sucked like he was her candy treat.

When his hand came down to her head, his fingers threading through her hair and urging her back up to his dick, she followed his request and licked her way up and down his shaft before engulfing him once again.

She made it farther down this time, concentrating on letting him reach the back of her throat. As soon as he did, she lifted up again, and did her best to fuck him hard and fast. The hand she'd wrapped around his base twisted and squeezed, and she bobbed her head, sucking and licking.

She really felt like she was getting her rhythm going when suddenly the world upended and she was on her back, with Noah's hands at her face, gentle in their hold, at the same time his hard body landed on top of her and he pushed into her in a single, hard thrust.

Wrapping her legs around his ass, she held him tight as he took her lips in a gentle kiss. Her racing heart slowed down, melting with the gentleness even as her hips tried to encourage him to move.

"So amazing," he murmured.

"Noah," she whispered.

"Natalie."

When he finally moved, it was slow, tender. He ran his thumb along her cheekbone, peppered her face with little kisses. When his pants grew heavy again, and she was about to beg him for more, he pulled free. Before she could curse, he grabbed a condom from the bag that was still on the other end of the bed and ripped the package open.

They'd done testing the previous week, and she was on birth

control, but they'd both agreed to condoms during sex. She was impressed he'd remembered, because she hadn't given it a single thought. When he re-entered her, everything changed.

Now, he fucked her. Hard and fast and amazing. She held on, picked up his rhythm, and met him thrust for thrust. When he reached a hand down between them, she knew he was close. He fingered her clit and she squeezed her eyes closed.

"Come for me, Natalie. Come now," he insisted.

There was no choice in the matter. Electric currents fired from her core, shooting out to her head and her toes and every point in between. His arm was braced next to her face, so she turned her head and bit his biceps, rather than scream.

"Fucking *fuck*," he growled, and she felt him release inside her. It seemed to last for several moments, before he brought his hand up to her face and lowered himself down onto her. Hot and slick with sweat, they lay still, catching their breaths.

Finally, he pulled free from her and flopped over onto his back.

She snuggled up into his side and fell asleep.

CHAPTER ELEVEN

Noah woke up feeling quite refreshed. He'd been surprised and amused last night when Natalie had fallen asleep at his side, before he'd even removed the condom. He'd let her rest for a little while, then urged her up and into the shower. They'd dried each other off, crawled under the covers, and crashed hard.

But it was a new day and he had all sorts of plans.

He looked down at the blonde head tucked into his shoulder. Nothing he'd imagined about this weekend had prepared him for making love to Natalie. And that had been without her wearing his collar. Now he was imagining having her in his collar, in his bonds, under his control.

His dick twitched. He sighed. There were things to be done before they reached that point, if he wanted to stick with his general plans. And, he decided, he did want to do that. His needy dick was just going to have to wait. It wasn't as though he hadn't been fully satisfied just hours ago.

Natalie's breathing changed enough that he could tell she was waking up. He checked outside. It was full light and he imagined some of the other vacationers would be hitting the water by now. Maybe he and Natalie could go for a swim when it got really warm.

Tomorrow was the Fourth of July. If he timed things just right, maybe he could make her world explode as she climaxed. The thought had him grinning.

They would leave Monday morning to try to avoid some of the holiday traffic, and so he could go relieve his assistant manager who'd agreed to work the long weekend. On the one hand it seemed incredibly far away, but on the other hand, it seemed like their time was already running short.

His stomach growled and he felt her smile against his chest. She dropped a little kiss on him, then lifted her head to look at him.

Her eyes were sleepy, but happy to see him. His dick twitched again.

"Hungry?" she asked.

He knew what she meant, but fuck if he wasn't starving for her.

"Apparently. But I was thinking we could go for a little walk before breakfast, and before the heat builds up. Then you can make me some scrambled eggs."

"That sounds perfect."

"Then that's what we'll do." He gave her butt a teasing smack. "Up and at 'em."

She blew him a raspberry, then squealed and jumped out of the bed when he pretended to growl and attack her.

They spent a few minutes in the bathroom, and he noticed that she didn't seem in a hurry to put her robe on. They got dressed together and headed out. The birds were singing up a storm. As he'd suspected, they caught sight of a couple of paddleboarders and a kayak. An older man and a young boy were in a skiff, fishing a few yards away.

He led them in the opposite direction this time, showing her their nearest neighbor on that side, then circling back up to the road, across their driveway, and around to the other side of the house. He and Gloria, Cedric's wife, had planted a bunch of perennials in a good spot on that side. He couldn't help but do a little deadheading and weeding while he showed it to her.

When they went back into the house, she looked at him questioningly. He nodded and she began to strip by the door. He went into the bedroom and brought out the chest harness and his bag of goodies. When she folded her panties and added them to the top of the pile she'd made, she turned to him and lifted her chin, ready for his collar.

Fuuuuck he really, really liked her. This was not the mentor headspace he'd planned on for the weekend. His instincts said that was fine, this was fine, but he was worried he was deluding himself just so he could have her more. But it didn't actually change the scenes he'd planned, it was only what was in his own head.

He wrapped the collar part of the harness around her throat, buckling it closed. Then the strap under her breasts. He pushed his fingers through her hair, moving it away from her face. He ran his thumbs over her eyebrows, drifted his fingers down her cheeks. Then kissed her lightly on the nose.

"Hands behind your back."

She did, pulling her shoulders back and presenting herself to him.

His touch wasn't nearly so light when he moved to her breasts. He pushed them together, over the strap of the harness, and licked and nibbled at her nipples until they were hard points. He reached into a side pocket in the bag where he'd put the nipple jewelry he'd decided he wanted to see her wear today.

Sliding the silicone loop over one nipple, he used the bead to adjust the loop until she drew in a sharp breath, then let it out a little bit. When he let go, the teardrop jewel dangling from the short, delicate chain, swung, adding weight to the pull. She pulled her lip between her teeth.

"What number are you at?" he asked.

She let go of her lip. "Two, Sir."

He placed the second clamp on her other nipple, then flicked both pendants to make them swing again. She gave a soft gasp, but didn't move.

"What number now?"

"Two, Sir."

He kissed her chin and dove back into the bag. Using the same restraints as the previous day, he wrapped her wrists and ankles, then attached the wrist cuffs together at her front. She frowned down at him.

"I thought you wanted me to make breakfast?"

He just watched her face, fascinated as the blush hit her neck, and slowly crept up her face. Then she bit her lip, and he supposed she was trying to decide if apologizing was better than keeping quiet.

"Did I order you to be quiet?

She blinked, then let out a breath of relief. "No, Sir."

"Did you address me correctly while wearing my collar."

She winced. "No, Sir."

"That's one. We'll see where we're at later. I'm hungry."

"Yes, Sir. Sorry, Sir."

Then she looked down at her bound wrists again, and frowned, but didn't ask any questions.

He pulled out the second-stage butt plug and lube. "Kneel on the ground, forearms flat, ass in the air."

She went down, one knee at a time, his hand ready in case she lost her balance. She settled into position with a little butt wiggle that he was mostly sure was truly adjusting herself, and not meant to tease him.

He took his time, running his hand along her back and butt, her skin warm and smooth. He cupped her pussy. "Relax for me. You promised to make me breakfast soon," he reminded her.

"Yes, Sir."

He eased one finger into her and scraped the nails of his other hand along her cheeks. She was wet and getting wetter. "I'm going to spank you now. Not as punishment from before, but because it will please me to feel your ass move while my fingers are inside you." He eased a second finger in. "Is that all right with you?"

"Y-Yes, Sir. Thank you, Sir."

He swatted her with the same strength he had on the last spank last night. Twice. She clenched around his fingers, a tiny whine escaping her. He picked up the lube and thumbed the cap open, squirted a healthy dollop into her crack. He swirled the plug through the gel. When he placed the tip against her puckered hole, she took a breath and relaxed, accepting the plug to the first knuckle.

"Well done, Petal. Deep breath and we'll do another. Push out," he said, when she exhaled. He seated the plug fully, gave her a couple of seconds to adjust, and then twisted and wiggled it a bit. Then he smacked her ass again.

"There now. I'll just go wash my hands, you stay right there, please."

"Yes, Sir."

When he returned, she watched him approach, eyes bright with eagerness and hunger. Probably not for the forthcoming eggs. She waited patiently while he dug into the bag again.

"Sit back on your heels now," he ordered.

He knelt in front of her. "You've done very well about not speaking when I've ordered it, so this isn't a punishment. It's one of the things you wanted to experiment with. Plus, it's sexy as hell." He held up the silicone bit gag. "You can bite down on it all you want."

Her eyes were wide and a touch apprehensive.

"Any questions?"

She swallowed. "No, Sir. Wait. Yes. What about my safe word numbers?"

He'd been going to explain, but was glad she'd asked.

"You'll see when you have it on, I'll still be able to understand you. We'll try it out."

She gave a decisive nod.

"Open up and bite down." He eased the gag between her teeth and buckled it tight enough it wouldn't move, careful not to pull at her hair.

"All right. Tell me five, four, three, two, one."

"Five, four, three, two, one," she repeated. Then she nodded at him that she understood it was still clear enough for him to hear.

"Good girl. Are you ready to make me breakfast?" He helped her stand up and she frowned down at her cuffed wrists. Well, frown might be the wrong word, with the gag in place, but the bunching of her eyebrows was clear enough.

"I don't see any reason you can't make scrambled eggs for us while wearing what I've chosen for you to wear. But, I *will* be pissed if you hurt my property." He stared into her eyes. "You. My property. You're not allowed to damage it. So if you think there's something you can't do with your wrists that close together, you will come ask for my help. If you miscalculate and hurt yourself, you *will* be punished."

She blinked, then nodded.

He jerked his head toward the kitchen. She scurried away, her brain going a million miles an hour, if he was to guess.

This time he sat at the side of the table, so he could still see her easily and watch her progress, but he wasn't simply watching the show. He used his ereader to check his email, actually managing to answer a simple one as she found a pan, carefully broke the eggs into a bowl, stirred them up, and started the toast.

The movements were mostly one-handed, though occasionally she used both, awkwardly. When she pulled out the cheese and grater, he made sure he was looking at the ereader, not the kitchen, though he could see her from the corner of his eye. It only took a minute for her to come to his side and kneel beside the chair.

"Yes, Petal?"

"Sir, can you—" She broke off, then started again, speaking more slowly so her words were clearer through the gag. "Sir, can you help me, please?"

"Of course." He smoothed a hand over her hair and waited while she stood and led the way back to the cheese grater. He held the handle at the top and she used both hands to push the block down and up, several times, until there was a small mound of cheese. She looked up at him, with a question.

"That's enough for me, but don't you want some?"

Her eyes widened and she looked back at the mound, and prepared to grate more.

"Just kidding, that's plenty."

She rolled her eyes at him and he kissed her nose. He returned to the table and she used her bound hands to rub a bit of saliva that was escaping from her lips.

She used both hands to put the skillet on the stove, then turned on the flame. He watched carefully as she poured the eggs in and let them set for a minute, then used a rubber scraper to stir them. The skillet was heavy enough that it didn't move under her careful stirring.

When the toast was buttered and the eggs were ready, she turned off the flame and used the scraper to slowly spoon the two portions onto their plates.

He got up and poured them each a glass of orange juice, and brought them to the table while she brought first his plate, then hers. Then she knelt at his side. He knew some Doms would make her wait until he'd finished eating, but cold eggs were gross and he wasn't a sadist.

He unbuckled the gag, disconnected the link between her cuffs, and nodded at the chair next to him.

When she sat, she used a napkin to clean the saliva from her lips, and worked her jaw for a minute while he forked up some eggs. They were tasty and he tucked in, as did Natalie.

"How are you feeling, Petal?"

She swallowed. "I'm good, Sir. Thank you."

"How are your nipples?"

She blinked and looked down at the little jewels hanging from her breasts. "They're okay, Sir."

"And your ass?"

"I'm worried that the plug will fall out when I stand up," she confessed.

He grinned. "That would not be a good move on your part," he warned. "Thank you for making breakfast, it's delicious," he added before she could say anything.

"You're welcome, Sir." It was a little more grumbly than her usual response and he had to work not to laugh.

They finished their plates and worked together to clean everything up. Despite her fears, she managed to keep the plug where he'd put it. When they'd finished, he put his hands on her waist and boosted her onto the counter so that her breasts were at his eye level. He widened her knees and stepped between them.

"Offer your breasts to me," he ordered.

The little line between her eyebrows appeared. She pulled her shoulders back and straightened up tall.

"Use your hands," he advised.

Understanding dawned and she cupped her breasts and presented them to him, pushing them together slightly. He pressed his nose between the cushions of flesh, breathing deeply, then turned and nibbled his offering.

"Squeeze for me," he said.

He watched her fingers dig into her skin and licked around and between them. When he'd explored both globes, he pulled back and observed. She continued to squeeze and knead, her breaths shallow.

When he reached forward, she stopped, started to drop her hands. He shook his head and her fingers dug in again. He moved the bead on one of the nipple clamps, releasing the loop from around her flesh. He replaced it with his mouth, sucking and tonguing the darkened skin, enjoying the feel of the hard nub against his tongue. He repeated the actions on her other breast, and slid his finger into her pussy. Wet heat gripped his finger and she gasped.

He thumbed her clit, working her, building her up. Her legs had wrapped around him, squeezing him tight. When he judged that she was close to coming, he released her nipple and watched her face.

"No coming," he said.

He saw his words penetrate the haze of her need. Her eyes went wide, then squeezed shut, because he hadn't pulled his finger from inside her or stopped working her clit. He eased up, leaving his finger and thumb in place, but not moving them. When her muscles relaxed a little bit, he resumed pushing his finger in and out. She whined, which brought a smile to his face.

He kissed her nipples, then her chin. Her eyes had opened back up. Cloudy with desire and need and a tiny bit of desperation that he found sexy as hell. His version of sadism, he supposed.

He bent down and tongued her clit, wrapping his arms around her butt to pull her closer to the edge of the counter. She squealed, but didn't resist him. He enjoyed teasing her for another couple of minutes until he was pretty sure she couldn't hold back any longer, then pulled back with a sigh.

With his arms still around her, he picked her up off the counter and let her legs drop down to the ground. A small thud alerted him that she'd dropped the anal plug again. His smile was, he supposed, a little bit evil.

NATALIE DIDN'T EVEN REALIZE what had happened until Noah smiled. She looked down. The little plug had fallen right out. Again. But she'd held it for longer than before. Although, this time she couldn't blame the release on her orgasm, because the bastard hadn't let her have one. Which, all right, was one of those Dom things, but *he'd* been the one pushing her to the edge!

One part of her knew that was totally the point, but the other part couldn't believe *Noah* had done this to her. For the first time, she kind of wished he'd put the gag back in so she wouldn't have to work so hard not to glare at him.

He kissed her forehead and removed the chest harness, wrist and ankle restraints. He took her face in his hands so that they were eye to eye. She was pretty sure he was perfectly clear of what she'd been thinking.

"Go clean up. Don't forget the plug. You can put the wrist and ankle cuffs in my bag, but no looking into it. Put on your robe and do your journal and then we can go swimming, if you'd like?"

"Yes—that sounds good. Ought to cool me off." She'd almost said Sir, but was glad she'd caught herself. And even more glad that he laughed.

She made quick work of the cleanup, put on her robe and curled up on the couch with her journal.

There was a lot to catch up on. The previous night hadn't seemed like a lot while they were at it, but now that she'd started writing, remembering, it seemed like so much. Her first butt plug. Making dinner. Her first Noah orgasm, and holy hell, that had been something else. And then to step away from all that and go for a walk in the woods, learn more about the man she'd known for years without knowing much about him at all.

She bit her lip. Maybe she'd ask him about that. Ask him what he'd thought about his best friend's sister's best friend. They'd only had a handful of conversations, always in a room full of other people. She'd thought he was handsome and confident and so far from what she was looking for in man. But she'd watched him dance with his girlfriend at the wedding. And she'd turned away. Had she recognized his dominant tendencies and stayed away on purpose?

Maybe.

She wrote about sitting at his feet. And falling asleep. It had just been so damn *boring*. Part of her was embarrassed. The idea was that she'd be thinking about him, about his needs and happiness. That hadn't quite worked out, which had led to the spanking. She still couldn't believe—or quite understand—the little panic attack she'd had. Nothing like that had ever happened to her before. But he'd been so good, so careful, and yet he'd taken her at her word when she'd said she wanted to continue.

And she was really glad he had. Otherwise, she might have built the spanking up to something scary in her head. Instead, it had been...interesting. Not quite fun, though she knew it could be, when punishment wasn't the point.

Her hand was getting tired. It had been a long time since she'd written things out with a pen, rather than on a computer. But she didn't hate it. It was an interesting way to gather her thoughts about what had happened. The weekend kept threatening to be over-whelming, there was just *so much*, but she didn't know if Noah was pacing himself, or he had a knack for knowing what would be enough for her. Maybe both. Because she never thought she needed a break until after he told her they were taking one.

It was comfortable in the cabin, but she knew it was hot outside and the idea of taking a swim was appealing. Noah was in the kitchen making chicken salad sandwiches and she could hear him humming, though she couldn't quite identify the tune. She watched as he added a dollop of mayonnaise, then stirred, tasted, nodded, and went for the salt and pepper.

He was so sexy. He'd always been this sexy, but she'd never imagined he'd turn his attention to her. Not like this. Of course, the idea of *this* would have freaked her out a few years ago. She needed to remind herself that he was doing this as a favor to her. Not that he didn't want to, she was absolutely convinced he was enjoying his time here as much as she was. But he was here to help her through something, to come to some decisions, not for her to fall for him.

She just needed to keep reminding herself of that. Especially when he looked up and caught her staring, and gave her that devastating grin. *Bastard.* Her lips twitched at the ridiculous thought.

"Done with that?" he asked.

"Five more minutes," she told him. She had no idea what she was going to write for five minutes, but she needed to get her thoughts under control before he put on a bathing suit and got all wet and *fuck.* She focused on the paper in front of her and began to write.

I will not fall in love with Noah Tucker. I will not fall in love with Noah Tucker. I will not fall in love with Noah Tucker.

With a sigh, she closed the book and took it into the bedroom. She'd brought a one-piece and a two-piece. He'd done a shockingly good job at convincing her he enjoyed her body no matter how little she was wearing, so she went ahead with the bikini. But she did put a coverup on. Grabbing her flip-flops and sunscreen, she found him ready to go with two towels and a bag with the food.

The heat greeted them the second they opened the door. It felt good, for now, and she liked knowing that they could cool off in the water. It was fun having their own section of the shore. There was a small dock and he told her that there was a canoe in a shed they could get, if they wanted to.

"I think I'd rather jump in. If you're sure it's safe to swim."

"It is. You said you used to be on the swim team?"

He'd asked about her swimming abilities when they'd made their plans to come out here. "Yes, all through high school. I love the water, but I don't make the effort to get to a pool very often. I tried the gym, but the best time to go and expect to get a lane was before work and that wasn't fun for me."

"Not a morning person?"

She laughed. "Not usually. You?"

"It's not my best time, no. I'm more of a night owl, I guess."

He set their towels on the dock and they kicked off their shoes and walked to its end. "Is this where you guys fish from?" she asked.

"Sometimes. Or we wade in, or bring the camp chairs to the shore. We've tried all the different areas."

She leaned back, soaking in the sun for a minute, then sighed. "I better put my sunscreen on or you won't be able to figure out what's red from sunburn or what's red from your hand. And I know you want to know," she teased.

"Smart girl. I'll be nice and help you, since it's to my benefit anyway," he teased back.

"Oh, wow. Gee, that *is* so nice. You're going to rub your hands all over my mostly naked body, as a kind gesture from a friend."

"Exactly. I'm a giver."

She pulled off her coverup and opened the lotion, pouring it into the hand he held out. She didn't flinch when the cool lotion and his warm fingers started on her shoulders. She was used to his touch now, to giving in and experiencing whatever pleasure he felt like providing. She'd come to trust him so quickly, she mused.

His hands worked every inch of her body that wasn't covered by the skimpy suit, his finger sliding under the edge to be safe, he told her. Considering he'd left her on edge not too long ago, you'd think her body would be warned to not get her hopes up. And rationally, she knew he wouldn't do anything out here, in full view of whoever might pass by. In fact, they waved to a couple who paddled by not too far out from them.

She knew, because she'd put a hard limit on it. And he would respect that. He put the lotion bottle down and sat behind her, pulling her back into his chest.

"Share it with me, now," he teased.

"I'd be happy to actually put it on you."

"This is more fun." He nibbled the top of her ear. "Except you taste like sunscreen."

"I wonder if they have edible sunscreen, like they do lube."

He laughed. "Probably not, because I'd lick it all off, and you'd still end up burned."

"Damn, I was thinking we could make a million off that idea."

"Do you want to be rich?" He rested his chin on her shoulder.

She thought about it. "I mean, I wouldn't say no, obviously, but I don't want to do the things that people generally have to do to become rich. I don't want to work that hard, give my all to some business idea. I'm putting as much as I can into my retirement accounts for now, until I feel like there's enough that they'll start making more money than I can add in myself. Then I figure I'll upgrade to a better apartment, or take some better vacations, that kind of thing."

"Interesting. Get the compounding going and then take a bit of a break."

"Right. I'll keep investing, but not as much a percentage of my salary. What about you? Would you want to be rich?"

"I've thought about trying to grow the nursery into something bigger, in the future. Opening multiple locations. Or adding in a landscaping business. Right now I'm on track to buy the nursery from the owners in five years. It's the deal we made when I became the manager. Part of my pay is toward ownership so they can retire. I've done some things to increase business, especially with online marketing, social media, that kind of thing. But I think I'm pretty happy with where it's at, for now. And I don't see myself going full mogul."

She couldn't quite reach her toes to the waterline, and it was getting hot. "Want to go in?" she asked.

He stood up and pointed. "It's more than ten feet deep over here, off the end of the dock. Then it gets shallow pretty quickly."

He winked at her and made a shallow dive into the water. His muscled back and tight ass were a lovely sight. Then he reappeared, shaking the water from his hair.

She bit her lip. *I will not fall in love with Noah Tucker.*

CHAPTER TWELVE

Noah was glad Natalie had suggested getting into the water. Because he'd been sitting behind her, reminding himself that she needed a bit of a break from the intensity of what they were doing, and ravaging her on the dock, even if it wasn't a scene, would *not* be giving her a break.

Not that he would really have done that, but the thought was giving him all sorts of ideas about what he *could* do, and it was just best that he dunk his head. Both of them.

She dove in and came up grinning. "That feels so good." Then she disappeared back under. He stayed where he was, treading water, until he heard her behind him. Turning, he found that she was about a pool's length away already. She waved and dove back under. He was surprised she had this much energy, he thought, as he floated on his back.

She made it back to him quickly, and floated at his side.

"I forgot how different it is from a pool. And I'm trying really hard not to think about worms and fish and other things."

"Better than chlorine," he said.

"Hmm."

Laughing, he used his hands to lightly paddle himself toward the shore, while still floating, Natalie keeping pace. When he was close enough, he stood and held out his hand, anchored her shorter body to him, turned her toward the dock. "I could put you in my collar and bring you out here tonight, when it's dark. I could tie you to the posts there, so half of you was in the cold water, and half of you was in the warm air, available to me to touch and tease however I wanted."

He kept one arm around her waist but brought the other up and tugged lightly at the little bit of fabric that stretched between her breasts.

Her pulse was beating wildly. He was pretty sure she knew that what he proposed wasn't technically feasible, but she was certainly getting the picture he painted.

"So, anyway," he said lightly, hauling her toward the shore. "Let's eat, I'm hungry."

She sputtered and planted her feet, so he let go of her, and wasn't at all surprised when she splashed water at his back. Grinning, he turned and threw her over his shoulder and hauled her to the shore. He put her down, then went to get their stuff from the dock. They toweled off and sat on grass to eat. It was a beautiful day. Hot but clear and not terribly muggy. After eating the sandwiches he'd made, they applied sunscreen to each other, then lay back and soaked in the sun.

"I love living in Boston, but it's nice to get out of the city like this once in a while." He'd pillowed his head on his arms, lying on his stomach, face turned toward her. He loved that she'd gotten over her body shyness so quickly, seeming perfectly content to be lying next to him in the sun, the tantalizing white and navy striped suit drying quickly. She'd bunched the coverup under her head and was also turned to face him.

"Did you live in a big city, growing up?"

"A suburb. We went camping every year, though. My parents had an RV. My sister and I would pitch a tent, unless it was raining."

"Are you close with your sister?"

"Fairly close, considering we live on opposite sides of the country. She had gotten married and just found out she was pregnant when Uncle Paul got sick. I was going back every year to see her and her family, and my parents, but now that my parents have moved to Arizona it's a little more complicated. She and her family came out here last year, which was fun. The kids are nine and seven. We had a blast going to historical sites, the water park, that kind of thing. I took them to work with me one day and let them play in the dirt."

She smiled, but it was touched with a hint of sadness, likely due to the thought of the cousin that she'd lost through no fault of her own. But then her smile deepened. "I'm excited to meet the baby. I know Sonya's due date isn't for six more days, but really, the baby could come at any time."

"Yeah. I made it back in time for Deena, my niece's, birth. It was pretty cool being at the hospital when she was born and seeing her when she was less than an hour old."

"Do you want kids?" she asked.

"Probably."

She nodded. "Yeah. Same. I don't think I'll be super upset if I don't meet the right guy, or if it doesn't happen for other reasons, but mostly I expect I'll have them. Two, if possible."

He reached out and ran a hand lightly along her shoulder. Just an easy caress, not to light any fires, but to remind her she wasn't alone.

"Two's a good number," he agreed. "You don't have to get a bigger car for two."

She laughed. "Yes, definitely a consideration to keep in mind."

"And they can share a bathroom without killing each other. Three would push that limit so you'd need a bigger house, more bathrooms."

"I can see you've given this some thought."

He hadn't. Not really. But for the first time in his life, he wondered if he'd met someone he could see a future with. A family with. He'd had long-term partners before, sure, but he'd been young and they'd never really reached that stage. It was seriously jumping the gun to think that he'd gotten there now. They weren't even a couple. They'd only been more than acquaintances for a few weeks. Definitely jumping the gun. For sure.

"A bit," he said.

When they were hot and sweaty, they dove back into the pond, and Natalie did a couple of laps while he encouraged her. He wanted her tired, and sun and exercise were bound to accomplish that.

They went back to the house to shower and watch a movie. She fell asleep within half an hour. Giving her twenty minutes, he turned off the television, then retrieved the rose and used it to tickle and tease her nose and cheeks until she woke up.

She blinked awake, her mouth curving on seeing his face above hers. He rewarded that instant response with a soft kiss. She wrapped her arms around his shoulders but he pulled back so he could watch her as he asked his question.

"Do you want to play? Or do you want to do this?" He nodded toward her, to indicate they could make love without playing.

The line between her eyebrows appeared. "Yes."

He pretended to scowl at her. "You have to choose one."

"Can I let you pick?"

"Yes."

"Okay, you decide. Please."

Perfect. He kissed her on the lips, light and quick, then stood from where he'd knelt beside the couch. He was maybe a little bit of a sadist, after all, because he'd wanted her tired from an afternoon in the sun. He'd wanted to see if he could make her cranky and now was the perfect opportunity.

"Robe off, on your knees by the door."

He went to get his bag from the room without checking to see how quickly she complied.

When he returned, she was positioned as ordered.

"Shoulders back." His command was more stern than he'd been using before.

Her spine stiffened and her shoulders straightened.

He locked her collar on and gave her forehead a kiss. He added the wrist and ankle cuffs, but this time he hooked a short strap between the ankle cuffs, hobbling her so she could only take small steps. He hooked the wrists cuffs together.

"Hands and knees."

She dropped down into position and he eased the bigger plug into her butt. Working with him, she accepted it with only a small catch of her breath when it was fully seated.

"How does that feel?" He rubbed his hand along the top of her ass.

"Full, Sir."

"Lucky for you, I'm a nice guy, and I won't make you worry about keeping it in today."

"Thank you, Sir."

He was such a bastard. He pulled out some straps and wrapped a harness around her, which would keep the plug in snuggly. Then he added a butterfly massager to the front, over her clit.

She frowned.

He pulled out his phone and used the app to turn the vibrator on low.

Her eyes widened and he smiled. "No coming."

"Yes, Sir."

He checked his watch. "It's three, and those sandwiches from lunch are long gone, but it's too early for dinner. Think you can make me a peanut butter and jelly sandwich? You can make one for you, too, if you'd like."

"Yes, Sir."

"Great. I want you to make it at the table. Pull out everything you need and set it on the table, to get started."

She took tiny steps at first, then bigger, as she adjusted to the hobble, the harness and the vibrator on her clit. He enjoyed the show. She made several trips to get everything she needed to the table. She surveyed the items, then looked to him.

He came to her, cupped her cheeks in his hand and kissed her softly. "Nicely done." Then he took the clip off her cuffs, and watched her delight change to consternation as he moved her hands behind her back and re-hooked them. He kissed her nose. "Don't make a mess, or I'll have to punish you."

She opened her mouth. Closed it. Glared at him, then looked quickly away when he raised his eyebrow at her. Finally, with her lips in a thin line, she turned her back to the table and picked up the peanut butter. He probably should have warned her to at least open the lids.

He turned a chair around and sat to watch, arms resting against the back. She got both lids open, after a short struggle. She'd set the bread out on two plates, rather than bringing the whole bag from the kitchen, so she didn't have to deal with that. Taking a deep breath, she picked up the butter knife and got to work.

There was definitely a mess. There was peanut butter and jelly on the bread. And her hands, the table, the floor and her ass. He was such a bastard. When she finally moved the plate, with his sandwich, to the spot in front of his chair, he nodded.

"Thank you." He reached out and unhooked her cuffs. "You should clean up before you sit down, or you'll make the chair a mess, too."

Her lips were pinched, but she didn't say anything. She washed her hands, wet a paper towel and wiped her butt, then another for the table. By the time she sat down to eat, he was nearly done. He wasn't a complete ass, so he got up and poured them both glasses of water.

She'd calmed down by the time she was finished. She picked up their plates and took them to the sink.

"Those can wait, let's talk about your punishment first."

The plates clattered into the sink and she whirled. "No fair! You set me up. There was no way I could do that without making a mess."

He raised an eyebrow at her, mostly because he was pretty sure if he opened his mouth, he'd start laughing. He needed a second to make sure he could pull himself together. She was fucking magnificent.

"Don't give me that look. You can't possibly deny that there is no way I could have done that without making a mess."

"There were absolutely things you could have done to not get punished," he said, managing to keep his voice stern. "At least two."

She scowled at him. "And what, pray tell—" Her scowl changed to a frown. "Safe word? Was I supposed to safe word over a sandwich?"

"That was one possibility. Especially since you have a variable safe word. A three or a four, maybe?"

"Damn it." Her anger diminished slightly, and confusion colored her words. "You wanted me to say my safe word?"

"You had one other option to avoid punishment, besides not making a mess."

He could see that defeat was setting in, but she still narrowed her eyes at him. "How?"

"When you cooked the eggs, what did I tell you to do if you were going to get hurt?"

Her shoulders slumped. "Ask you for help." Then she scowled. "But you didn't say that this time, and what's the point in telling me to do something that I can't do without asking you to undo what you did?"

Fucking adorable. He bit his tongue to keep from smiling.

"To show that you were listening, for one. To show that you can come to your Dom for help when you need to. To show that you trust me to take care of you." Her shoulders sagged at each sentence. "Lastly, do you remember discussing punishments when we went over your limits list?"

"Oh, crap," she whispered. They *had* talked about the idea of the pretend punishments that were meant to be for fun and pleasure, not correction.

"You said you might be interested, but you weren't sure that being punished for things that you didn't actually screw up would be something you were okay with."

Natalie swallowed hard at Noah's words. She really hated fucking up. Which is why she'd told him that.

"So, if I'd asked you for help you would have given it?"

"Or asked if you wanted a funishment."

"But since I didn't ask for help, or use my safe word, I'll get the funishment?"

He laughed. "Oh, baby, no. I think you definitely earned a real punishment, don't you?"

She'd known he was going to say that. She thought about how she'd yelled at him, and shivered.

"I'm sorry, Sir." She shuffled over to his chair and knelt down. The damn vibrator was still slowly beating against her clit, but she was super thankful she didn't have to worry about the butt plug coming out. When he put his hand on her head, she felt her eyes get wet, but she swallowed hard to keep the tears back.

On the one hand, yeah, he'd set her up. But on the other hand, she'd hella overreacted. So where she'd thought she'd fucked up, by making a mess, that hadn't actually been a problem. How she'd reacted to it, *oh yeah*, that was the fuck up.

"What would the punishment have been for making a mess?" she asked.

"Oh, you'll still get that. Six spanks."

She sighed. "And what will the punishment be for having a freak-out and yelling at you?"

"Because I'm such a nice guy, and you're still new at this, you'll have three choices. Twenty spanks with my hand, five spanks with a wood paddle and five spanks with my hand, or no spanks, no paddle, and no orgasm for the rest of the day. Be aware that we will still be playing, and *I* will certainly be coming, but none for you."

Well, at least that was easy. "The wood paddle, please, Sir. Thank you for letting me decide." She knew he'd been waiting to use the wood paddle, in case it brought back any memories from that long-ago night, but she really felt like he'd brought her so far past that experience that it wouldn't be an issue. And if it was, it would be over quickly. And he'd help her through it.

"Are you sure?" He cupped her chin in his hand.

She met his gaze. "Yes, Sir. Despite what just happened, I trust myself to use my safe word if there's a problem. And I trust you to help me."

His smile did funny things to her heart. "Good girl. We'll do the six spanks for making a mess now, over my lap. Then we'll clean up the kitchen and you'll do your journal, then we'll do the second punishment."

She'd rather get it all done now, but it wasn't up to her. "Yes, Sir."

He helped her stand and position herself over his lap. Then he turned the vibrator up to full power. "You can come if you want," he told her and smacked her ass. Which is when she remembered that this was the funishment, not the punishment, and she was supposed to enjoy it. This was helped out by his stopping after the second smack to grab the base of the butt plug and ease it in and out of her, then wiggle it around a bit, reawakening all those nerves. She came on the fifth spank and cried out on the sixth.

"There now, that wasn't so bad, was it?" He gently wiped the tears off, then grabbed a napkin from the table and held it to her nose.

Humiliated, she nonetheless blew into the paper and remained still as he wiped her clean. Then she tucked her head under his chin and tried to disappear. She was feeling such a weird mix of relief and pleasure from the orgasm, but confusion from the crying and the upcoming punishment, and from having actually screwed up.

He rubbed his cheek against her hair, apparently in no rush. For some reason, that made things deep inside her break up, and she started crying in earnest.

"That's my Petal, just let it out." He stood up and moved to the couch, settling in, crooning words in her ear the whole time. He handed her a tissue and pulled her in tightly against him.

She couldn't say why she was crying but it poured out of her, and he didn't seem worried, so she just gave into it. Finally, when she'd gone through several tissues, she managed to sniffle her way to silence.

"Deep breath, now. You're fine. You're doing great."

She took several and listened to his heartbeat under her ear. The whole point of this weekend was to see if she wanted to move forward in this lifestyle, and how that might look. It was *not* to fall for Noah Tucker. But while it was getting easier and easier to imagine playing these kinds of games with him, it was getting harder and harder to imagine them with anyone else.

Her hand clenched in his shirt at the idea. Intellectually she knew that she'd get over that, if she had to. But she wasn't sure she wanted to. Even if he stuck to their arrangement and waved goodbye on Monday with no plans to see her this way in the future, she wasn't sure she wanted to explore with anyone else. Probably she'd get over that. She owned her body, not him, and if this is what gave her pleasure, she'd take charge of that and find someone to give it to her. Eventually. Probably she wouldn't wait another five years this time.

He smoothed her hair back from her face and she raised her eyes to his. He searched her face, then kissed the corner of her eye, which was probably gross and crusty.

"Why don't you climb into bed and do your journal there. Then you can take a nap when you're done. I'll make dinner."

"Yes, Sir. Thank you, Sir."

He helped her sit up. Only then did she realize he'd turned off the vibrator at some point. "Leave the toys in the bathroom, you can clean them after your nap," he told her as he released her from all her bonds.

"Okay, Sir."

He kissed her temple and she went to do as she'd been told.

When she put the journal down and snuggled into the bed, she wasn't sure anything she'd written would make sense later. Or how long she'd been at it. The bedroom door was open and she could see that Noah had taken a seat on the couch where he could keep an eye on her. She tucked her hands under her cheek and watched him reading until her eyes got too heavy and she dropped into sleep.

When she woke, the cabin smelled delicious. Noah was back in his seat and when she raised her head to rest on her elbow, he put his ereader down. Then he crooked his finger at her. She'd been warm and comfy in the bed, didn't want to move, but that little finger wiggle gave her some motivation. Of course, she wasn't wearing his collar, and they weren't in scene, so...*fuck it*, he was still hot as hell.

She rolled out of bed, pulling on her robe as she approached him.

"Smells good out here," she managed before he snatched her off her feet and into his lap. Giggling, she burrowed into him.

"How are you feeling?" he asked.

"Good. Rested. Not weepy. Hungry."

He checked his watch. "Ten more minutes."

"You're handy."

"I have my moments. Tell me what you think about earlier."

She sighed. She'd been hopeful that the talking-about-it portion was already done. Not *very* hopeful, mind, but slightly. "I think I'm not a fan of funishments."

"What if I'd told you I was going to cuff your hands behind your back, make you fix us sandwiches, and then punish you for the mess you were sure to make?"

"I guess that would have been okay, but if the point of it was to get to a fun spanking with orgasm, I feel like we could have just done that without me getting jelly on my ass."

"You could have asked me to lick the jelly off your ass," he pointed out.

She huffed out a laugh. "Maybe. I guess I can see it as a valid form of play. But I would definitely want it to be negotiated beforehand. I don't like feeling like I screwed up. And apparently it's apt to make me actually screw up."

"It also would have felt differently if I'd done the real punishment before the play one."

"Yes, that would have been a little less confusing, now that you say it. Why didn't you?"

She was tracing her finger over the freckles on his arm, but she looked up to meet his gaze.

"Timing. Logistics. Order of operations."

She laughed.

The timer on his phone beeped. "You hit the bathroom, I'll get this plated up."

She came out to a pork chop, mashed potatoes and roasted Brussels sprouts on her plate. It was delicious, and she felt fully back to normal by the time she pushed the plate away. They'd discussed their favorite video games over dinner, as well as the blockbuster action movie that had released that weekend. He was skeptical, but she thought it looked like fun.

They cleaned up together, then she got dressed and they headed out for a walk. The clouds had come in, and the humidity had risen, but it wasn't too bad.

"Tell me about your job," he said when they were walking through the woods.

"Ah, it's boring. I like most of the people in my office, I like that it's not customer service or sales, and that I have some room for advancement, but I'm not on like a corporate track or anything. I guess I could be, if I wanted to, but I don't. If I do have kids, I *think* I'd like to stay home with them until they're in school."

He laughed. "That was a lot of emphasis on the word think."

"Sometimes I see stay-at-home parents and they look so stressed, I don't know." She smiled up at him. "But I think it could be fun."

"It was fun having my niece and nephew for a few days, but it was a little bit of a relief when they left, too."

She laughed. "I bet."

"What about knitting then, why do you enjoy it?"

"Oh, boy, I don't know if you want to get me started on that. I love the mix of creativity and rules. Like, if you follow the pattern exactly as it is, you'll end up with this cool thing. But you can be creative with all the choices in patterns and yarns. I mean, the colors are so much fun, but also there are blankets and sweaters and hats and scarves and baby Yoda."

"I liked that sweater you made for Alec's mom for Christmas, it's such a great color for her."

She beamed up at him. "Isn't it, though? As soon as I saw that yarn, I knew it was for her. I love picking out the right colors and patterns for people. And I've started playing around with altering the patterns, customizing them a bit."

"It's relaxing watching you do it. Peaceful. Except for when you cuss."

"Hey! Okay, well, yeah. But, to be fair, my attention hasn't been as good here, with you, as it normally is."

He puffed out his chest. "Are you saying I'm distracting?"

She smacked him. "Noah, a little bit. Sir, more than a little bit."

He smirked. "I'll take it."

"Are you…enjoying this weekend?" she asked.

CHAPTER THIRTEEN

The tentative sound to Natalie's question had him pulling her to a stop and facing her. "I am. Very much. Isn't it obvious?"

"I guess I'm not sure how much you're doing to help me out, and how much you're doing because you want to."

"I'm not doing anything that I don't want to."

She frowned, and he put a finger on the line between her eyebrows. Her eyes crossed, looking at it.

"I'm enjoying topping you very, very much. And I'm enjoying talking to you, hanging out with you, very, very much."

She relaxed. "Okay."

He considered saying more. Telling her he'd been thinking of things beyond the weekend, but he didn't want to change her mindset. He'd promised her this time, and didn't think it was fair to add the pressure of even the idea of more, not when her mind, and emotions, were focused on this. But he was definitely starting to think that walking away on Monday wasn't what he wanted. Not even close.

She told him more about her knitting and how she sold some of her projects online. He enjoyed hearing her talk about her passion. Her whole face lit up and her words spilled out in a steady stream.

They stopped and sat on a rock for a while so she could use her hands to show him the shapes she was describing, drawing them for him, in the air. Fucking adorable.

When they headed back, she grew quiet.

"Are you worried?" he asked.

"Mm. Sort of. But not really. I know that doesn't make sense."

"It's all right, as long as it's honest."

She snorted. "My confused and contradictory statements are honest, absolutely."

"Nobody claimed this would all make sense."

She pulled up short and looked at him, her mouth hanging open in outrage. He tried not to laugh. He really, really did. But he failed. She smacked him on the chest, then giggled.

"Well. I guess no one did make that claim," she said when he managed to get himself under control.

"Sorry, baby. Even worse, when you *think* you've got a handle on your needs, your desires, then they do fucked up things like go and change on you."

"That's just cruel."

"That's being human."

"Hmph."

When they were within sight of the cabin, he pulled her into his arms. Hers came up to encircle his neck. "Tell me what you'll do if you get overwhelmed," he demanded, pressing a kiss to her temple.

"I'll use my numbers."

"And if you get scared?"

"Use my numbers and ask you for help."

His arms squeezed her tighter at that. "And if you get horny?"

"Uh, beg you as nicely as I can to let me come."

"That's my girl." He leaned down and kissed her. Slowly, sliding his tongue between her lips, one hand on her hip, the other on her rib cage so he could just feel the swell of her breast with his thumb. And so he could keep himself from pushing the kiss into more. He wanted to savor this, just this.

She moaned into his mouth and tried to step into him, but he didn't let her. Her body softened under his hands. They kissed, and kissed some more, until a bird nearly dive bombed them. He broke away, enjoying the dazed look in her eyes.

"Let's go inside," he whispered.

She took a deep breath, and preceded him up the drive and into the cabin.

He closed and locked the door while she disrobed. When she went to her knees, he pulled his gear bag from where he'd left it nearby. Her eyes were on the collar when he brought it up, then closed as he snapped the little lock into place. He teased a finger along the collar's edge, watched goose bumps pebble on her neck.

Moving slow and easy, he put the wrist cuffs on, then told her to stand so he could do her ankles. He added the same type of cuffs, but bigger, to her thighs. "Go stand behind the couch and lean over so that your torso is resting on the back. Your breasts hanging over the cushions. You can put your hands at the small of your back."

She took a deep breath and then did as he asked. When she was in place, he reached under her and pulled her lip from between her teeth. "The only biting will be what I approve of."

"Yes, Sir."

He took her wrists and clipped them to the thigh cuffs, then nudged her feet farther apart. After checking that she was properly supported, he rubbed his hand along her back, butt and thighs. He hadn't been hitting her hard enough to leave redness, and he wouldn't this time, but…soon.

With one hand spanning the middle of her back, he gave her the five spanks, harder than he previously had. He spaced them out slightly, but didn't pause, giving them all in a row. Her breath was hitching when he finished, but she wasn't crying.

From his bag, he pulled a basic wood paddle. He'd asked her what kind had been used on her in the club that last day, and this was a close match. She'd sworn she was fine with that, but he wanted to be sure it wouldn't trigger her before she went off to play with any other Doms.

Well, that had been the original idea, anyway.

Putting thoughts of the future aside, he rubbed the wood against her abused bottom.

"What's your number, Petal?"

"One, Sir."

"I want you to thank me, and then tell me your status number, for each paddle strike. Do you understand?"

"Yes, Sir."

He reached over and fingered her nipples, tweaking them until she gave a low moan. Then he used the paddle. Not full force. He judged it to be medium-hard.

"Thank you, Sir. One, Sir."

"Good job."

The next hit was the same strength.

"Thank you, Sir. One, Sir."

He could feel the heat coming from her skin now, when he rested his palm on her ass. She pushed into his hand, ever so slightly.

Another paddle.

"Thank you, Sir. One, Sir."

He didn't wait, as soon as she finished speaking, he gave her a harder hit.

She cried out, then gasped the words. "Thank you, Sir. Two, Sir."

Tears were falling, now, but she held her ass out for him without hesitation.

One more strike.

Her head dropped down, but he could still hear her clearly. "Thank you, Sir. Two, Sir."

He dropped the paddle on the couch and left his hand on her back to show her she shouldn't move. He bent over and rubbed his whiskered cheek along her heated ass. She gasped and pushed into him.

"Maybe next time I'll give you a hickey on each cheek. Something to aim for."

She giggled.

Unlatching her wrists from the thigh cuffs, he eased her to

standing. Examined her face carefully. Her tears had stopped and her eyes were dilated. He moved his gear bag to the sofa and led her around so they could sit.

"My lap or the seat, it's up to you, but go gingerly," he suggested.

She bit her lip and eased herself onto his lap. He wrapped an arm around her and dug into his bag with the other hand, bringing out a chocolate bar.

"Ooh, my favorite."

He knew. He'd checked. "Why don't you open that since my hands are full?" He handed it over.

When she'd torn open the wrapper, she started to bring it to her lips. He opened his mouth, and her hands froze. Then she put the bar between his teeth, and he took a bite. He nodded for her to take the next.

They sat quietly, alternating their way through the candy until she offered him the last bite. He took a tiny one so that she could still have half. Beaming at him, she popped it into her mouth.

"Do you know why you thanked me for doing that?" he asked, when she'd stopped chewing.

"I—not really, Sir."

"Because it was a punishment, so that we could move on from the mistake and not worry about it. But it took time and energy and effort from what we would both rather be doing."

"Oh. Yes. I see. I'm s—"

He put his finger over her lips. "No more apologies. You took your punishment, beautifully, and it's over now."

"Okay."

He traced her lips with his finger, since it was right there, then pushed it between. Her warm heat welcomed him in, her tongue delicately swirling around his finger.

"I had planned for us to do some impact play this evening. But we can switch to something else if you think it would be too much. Think carefully, it's not a problem. I'm giving you this choice, so make sure you give it consideration."

He pulled his finger free, and since it was nice and wet, moved it to her nipples.

"I would like to keep to your plan, Sir. I feel fine, I promise."

"The wood paddle didn't scare you?"

"No, Sir. I mean, no more than anything else harder than your hand would have. Honestly, I have to make an effort to think back to that day, now. It's hard to even equate it with what we've done here."

"All right. I think we'll make you come first, just for funsies, if that's all right with you."

Another giggle. "Whatever you like, Sir. But I can't believe you said funsies."

He leaned down and kissed her nose. "I've gotta keep you on your toes."

Her hand came up to caress his beard. "So soft." Her whisper did things to his insides.

"Even on your abused ass?"

"Well, maybe not so much then."

Natalie had liked all her time here at the cabin, with Noah. Well, the sitting at his feet thing hadn't been the best, but whatever. Sitting in his lap, sharing a chocolate bar, him teasing her, that had to be her favorite, though. At least, her favorite non-orgasm time.

Her butt was hot and tender but she'd sit here the rest of the night if he asked her to. She was a little nervous about what he had planned for tonight, but only in the sense of the unknown. She wasn't the least worried he'd hurt her or go too far.

He picked her up and set her on her feet. "Go into the bedroom and kneel for me at the foot of the bed. Hands interlaced and behind your neck, elbows out straight. Facing the door. Eyes watching the floor. Go."

She went, forcing in a deep breath, ears straining to hear what he might be doing behind her. She heard him get off the couch and turn out the lights, but then she was in the bedroom and getting into position. She wondered how long she'd be able to keep her arms like this. It seemed easy enough, but she suspected they would get tired pretty quickly.

Picking a spot on the floor, she trained her gaze on it, refusing her instinct to glance toward the door when she heard him approaching. His bare feet came into her view and his hand settled on her head, softly playing with her hair before he tucked it behind her ear.

After a moment he let go, and then she only had time to blink at the dark shape in front of her eyes, before the blindfold settled over them. He adjusted the strap until it was snug. It was soft against her lids and when she tried peeking, she found it was completely successful at eliminating all light and vision.

She clenched her fingers tightly together because for one wild second, she wanted to reach out and touch...something. Anything to anchor her in the darkness. But Noah's warm hand came to the middle of her back. He didn't rub or caress or do anything, but it was enough. When he let go, she didn't react. She focused on her knees and feet, pressing into the wood floor. Her elbows, making sure they were straight out. Her breathing, trying to keep it even. And her ears, attuned to any sound that would tell her where Noah was.

The sounds of him taking off his clothes made her smile. She smelled the rose before she felt it, it's satin caress along her spine, down to her feet, then along her legs and dipping between her thighs. Should she widen them? No, he would tell her what he wanted. She didn't have to guess. The soft touch played along her stomach for a moment, then up to her breasts and the hollow of her neck. Then he pushed her breasts together, trapping the thorny stem between them. Little pricks of pain washed through her as the scent of her rose combined with the scent of him.

He was right there. Naked. She was positive if she moved her elbow she'd find his leg, but she held still. And he rewarded her by bumping his cock against her cheek. Her lips parted and it took all of her discipline not to turn or lean forward.

Her arms were beginning to ache, but it was easy to forget about that as she focused on the smell of the rose, the smell of *him*, the hope that he might slip inside…and he did. She almost sobbed her thanks, doing her best to show him with her mouth and tongue, instead. He eased up on her breasts, letting the rose fall into her lap.

When he pulled free from her mouth, despite her best intentions, she found herself leaning forward, trying to keep him inside. She got a smart smack to her ass to remind her of her place. Breathing deeply, she pulled her lip between her teeth and tried not to think about how tired her arms were getting. Should she give him a number? She thought she might be approaching a three, or maybe she was already there. Now that she had nothing else to focus on, they were almost shaking.

As if he knew her thoughts, he took her wrists in his hand. "How are your arms doing, Petal?"

"They're getting tired, Sir."

"Let me fix that for you. Stand up."

He brought her arms down, and helped her stand, then bent her over the bed. He removed the cuffs she'd been wearing. She heard him rummaging in one of his bags and then felt him encase her left arm in something stiff and unyielding. He tightened it, starting at her wrists and working up to the top, just below her elbow. He moved her arm to the middle of her back, then brought the other to join it, lacing it into the binder as well.

"That should be easier on your shoulders."

"Thank you, Sir."

"You look lovely. Now crawl up onto the bed and put your back to the pillows. There you go, scoot back farther." He arranged her so she was leaning back on her arms, into a mound of pillows, then pushed her knees up to her chest. A click and clank and she found her legs attached to the headboard from the thigh cuffs.

She couldn't decide if it was better or worse that she couldn't see. Running around the cabin naked, bending over for him, all of that had been one thing, but having her knees open and spread, pulled back so her pussy was just...out there, was a visual she was having a hard time coming to terms with. And she really didn't want to think about how much her stomach was rolling and bulging, either.

"What are you thinking about, Petal?"

Uh oh. "Um. Wondering what I must look like right now, Sir."

"And what do you think you look like?"

"I—it's—um, I think I look...exactly how you want me to look."

"That's exactly right. Are you comfortable?"

"Yes, Sir."

"Well, let's see what we can do to change that."

Oh dear. She heard what she thought was a lid and figured the lube and butt plug were next. Would it be bigger than before? She'd felt so freaking full. She couldn't stop herself from jerking a little when his oiled finger touched not her anus, but her clit. He rubbed her for a couple of seconds, then stopped.

"I'll be right back, don't move," he teased.

She would have rolled her eyes if she could. As it was, she strained her ears and heard him walking away, and then the rattle of the ice dispenser. Apparently he was thirsty. Then he was back, and she returned her focus to herself. And realized something was happening. Her clit was getting warm. Like, really warm. And it kind of felt like he'd put a clamp on it, like he'd done to her nipples yesterday, but she was sure he hadn't.

He blew on her cunt and she tensed her muscles at the sensation, but then forced herself to relax. Some kind of heated lube, she realized. He kissed her ankle, his hand on her flank. Then slowly, oh so very slowly, worked his kisses up to her middle as her clit pulsed in its heat. She needed his mouth on her. On there. Needed *something*. She scried out when instead of his tongue, something cold and wet met her heated folds.

It took her a second to identify the cold drips of water and the slick, hard ice cube that he was rubbing around her opening, then up to her hot clit. She gasped at the touch, but it was only fleeting, and then the cube was moving again. He teased it into her opening, pushing against her natural muscle movements, but then holding on when those same muscles tried to grab the slick ice and pull it inside of herself.

Inside her channel, she could barely feel the cold, but the opening was apparently full of nerve endings that were feeling quite confused about whether to push the offending item away, or suck it inside. Confusion turned to overwhelming sensation when his mouth clamped around her clit and sucked.

The tight bead of her clit shot electricity through her whole body. Her hips tried to rise up, but she was held fast by the tether holding her thighs to the headboard. The clinking of the metal clasps rang in her ears as she tossed her head from side to side. The ice cube had already heated to a tiny size and he dropped it, letting the nearly liquified piece slide down to her butt crack. His mouth lifted from her clit when she was *so close* and she bit back a wail.

A new ice cube settled at her opening, and his mouth returned, but now it was cold, and she realized he'd suckled the ice.

As his mouth cooled her clit, and her flesh warmed his tongue, her body nearly gave into the conflicting sensations and she wasn't sure if she was allowed to come or not. Had he told her? She couldn't think, could only beg.

"May I come, please, Sir? Please, I need— Ah!"

He worked the cube all around her hot folds, once, twice, before lifting his tongue from her. "You asked so nicely. Come for me, Petal. I want to taste you."

She arched back against her bound arms. He thrust his tongue into her pussy and she felt the cold ice at her lips. Sucking at it eagerly, she tasted her own juices from the ice. His cold fingers held it firmly against her mouth while his tongue fucked in and out of her. She exploded into sensation, vaguely aware of the cold drips along her chin or the slow licks and nibbles he gave her cunt.

Her ears were roaring and her heart racing. The darkness surrounded her, made her lose track of herself, so she focused on him, instead. His shoulders between her legs, his hand resting on her chin, his whiskered cheek against the crease of her thigh.

"Noah. Noah."

She didn't realize she'd been speaking until his own words penetrated the buzz in her ears. "I'm here, Petal. I'm right here, I'm not going anywhere."

His actions seemed to bely his words as his body moved away from her. She held back a cry, but his hands were on her head, easing the blindfold away. She blinked against the light. His expression was soft and pleased.

"I hope you're feeling okay because I have something I think you can help me with." He glanced down at his cock. It was hard and jutting toward her, as if eager for her attention. A bead of pre-come glistened at the head and she wanted to taste and touch. He unhooked the clasps holding her thighs, and eased her legs down, then swung over so he was straddling her stomach.

He rubbed his finger lightly, barely there, over the tiny pink spots in her cleavage from the rose thorns. "So pretty," he murmured.

"Yes, Sir," she agreed.

Leaning up on his knees, he braced one hand beside her head and thrust his fingers into her hair with the other, holding her head tight and fast in a way he hadn't done before. She gasped, and he took the opportunity to slide his cock between her lips. She accepted him, encouraged him, unable to move against the pull of her hair, only able to take what he gave her.

She moaned her appreciation, her gaze fixed on his. The heat in his eyes, the hunger in his face, made her want more, but he slid in only so far. She licked and sucked as much as she could, urging him forward.

"Get me wet, Petal. Nice and wet so I can slide between your tits."

She redoubled her efforts, wanting everything he had to give. She wished she could touch him, but she felt wrapped up in his hold, even as her arms were behind her back. She arched her neck the very tiny bit that she was able to, just to feel his hold on her hair and his collar around her neck.

He fed her more of himself, and she concentrated on making him feel good, getting him wet, pleasing him. She hummed around his cock and he grunted.

When he backed out of her mouth, she wanted to whine in protest, but she also wanted to give him what he'd asked for, to see his cock sliding between her breasts. He let go of her head and dribbled lube along her breasts. Her skin was so hot, so ready, that the lube felt cold, though nothing compared to the ice cube from before. He pushed her breasts together and slowly pushed his cock between them.

His fingers kneaded and pressed against her flesh, his look of concentration intense and erotic. She'd never had anyone fuck her boobs before, wouldn't have imagined she'd find it pleasurable, but *oh yeah*, with this man, in this moment, it was amazing.

She opened her mouth and he let her lick the head, then pulled back.

"You feel incredible," he told her, his voice rough. "I want to stay here an hour and just work my way in and out of your lusciousness. But I also want to watch my come splash across your face and chest."

"Oh, please, Sir."

"You like that?" he asked as picked up his pace. "You want that?"

"Y-yes, Sir, please." She'd never wanted any such thing before, but she wanted it now. He brought the head back to her lips, and she sucked as much as she could before he slid back again. He sped up, and she just left her tongue out so that he could slide against it when he wanted. He was panting hard, his knees pressed tight against her sides, his hands manipulating her breasts how he needed them for his pleasure.

His back straightened and his gaze fixed on hers as he froze, then jetted a stream onto her mouth and chest. She lapped up what she could reach and he let go of her breasts, braced his hands on either side of her head and swooped down to invade her mouth with his kiss.

Her legs were pulling against the strap holding her to the headboard, her core empty and begging, her hands useless behind her back, but she gave him everything she could with her mouth. Eventually he slowed down, one hand drifting back into her hair. Not the tight hold from earlier, but a gentle anchoring. Finally he released her and sat back on his heels, only a fraction of his weight on her.

His eyes swept up and down, taking her in. She could only imagine how wild her hair must be, how red and puffy her lips, the remnants of his release on her chin and chest, her breasts slick and mottled from his grip. It was very clear that what he saw pleased the hell out of him.

"Now. I think that was a nice little transition, don't you? Warm us both up a bit before we start with the impact play?"

She'd forgotten all about his intentions for the night. A shiver that she couldn't define as either need or nerves raced through her. He smiled.

CHAPTER FOURTEEN

Noah watched the shiver run through Nat and smiled. She was ready. He helped her sit up and unlaced the arm binder, massaging her shoulders for a minute, then pushed all the pillows off the bed.

"How do your shoulders feel?" he asked.

"Good, Sir." She rolled them under his hands.

"Turn over and lay down on your stomach, put your arms over your head like a Y."

He grabbed the bright red bondage tape he'd brought, and safety scissors. Putting the scissor down near her head, he used the tape to wrap her wrists and secure them to the metal part of the headboard.

"Give them a pull," he told her.

She tried, and he nodded, satisfied with the hold and that the tape wasn't pinching or pulling on her. Then he did the same to her legs, angling them so that her feet stuck through the bars of the footboard and he could tape her ankles to it.

Her hair had fallen over her face and she was trying to jerk it away, but wasn't having much success. He grabbed a hair band she'd left on the bedside table and pulled her hair back into a little tail.

Stepping back, he looked her over. She was watching him

closely, lip between her teeth, ass still a little bit red, the orange collar bright against her skin. Fucking gorgeous.

He kept his gaze connected with hers when he reached into the bag and pulled out a crop. It was a standard crop, simple in its devastation. It had a loop of leather for the end, about three inches that tapered out from the shaft. Her expression was worried, but not scared. He ran the tip lightly over her instep and she tried to jerk away, then settled. He touched it to the inside of her knee, just barely.

"Make as much noise as you like," he told her. "I'm pretty sure everyone is off the pond and safely involved in their own home activities at this point."

The one eye he could see went a bit wide at that implication.

"If you want to come, ask me nicely. You do that very well."

She blushed, which was kind of hilarious and kind of adorable.

"You'll use your numbers, even if I don't ask."

"Yes, Sir."

He played the tip over her toes, then pressed the rod along her thigh. "Are you ready, Petal? What's your number?"

"Yes, Sir. Just nervous. One, Sir."

He cracked the tip against his own thigh and she jumped, then let out a nervous laugh. He leaned over and kissed the corner of her mouth. Her lips curved up in response, and he tapped the crop onto the fleshiest part of her leg. Not hard enough to sting. Not yet.

Her breath shuddered out and her whole body relaxed a tiny bit. She'd been braced for pain. He peppered more smacks like that, up her legs, over her shoulders, very light taps on her ribs and arms. When she'd fully relaxed, he started to make some of the hits a little harder, building up the intensity. Every few minutes he used his hand to run along some part of her skin, feel the warmth for himself and remind her that he was the one giving her the strokes.

She was squirming now.

He gave the reddest spot on her butt a good smack and she let out a little cry, but her hips tilted up as much as she was able, asking for more. Her eyes were closed, but not scrunched tight. He used the tip of the crop between her legs, gathering the wetness there. Her eye popped open. She watched his face as he pushed the tip into her opening, then pulled it out and brought it to his lips.

He sucked her cream from the leather, enjoying the way her gaze went needy and her lips parted.

"How are you doing, Petal?"

"Good, Sir. One."

"You look amazing. Do you want more?"

"Yes, please, Sir."

He increased the level, making most of the hits hard enough to sting, and a few of them hard enough to make her flinch and gasp and moan. He stayed on the same side of the bed, so that she could see him at all times. After a few more minutes, he leaned in close and touched her face. A light sheen of sweat had her hair sticking to her forehead. She opened her eye slightly, but it was unfocused. Perfect.

He used the scissors to cut the tape off wrists and ankles. She whimpered.

"Turn over now, Petal."

It took her a second to understand what he was saying, but then she rolled over with his help. "I think you're enjoying this," he murmured as he rebound her to the headboard and footboard. "Tell me what you think."

She was clearly not in a talkative mood. He grinned at her and she came back to herself a little more with her annoyance. He raised an eyebrow and her face flushed. "I like it, Sir. I was feeling…floaty."

The line appeared between her eyebrows and he kissed it away. "Good. Are you ready for more?"

"Yes, Sir."

"You have some interesting targets when you're turned up like this," he pointed out, drawing the tip of the crop down her chin and then circling one of her breasts. Her eyes went wide again.

"Still ready to continue?" he asked.

She swallowed and he watched her throat work under his collar.

"Y-yes, Sir. One, Sir."

"Good girl."

He gave her a stinging slap to her upper thigh, then a light one to her belly. Working in a random pattern, he peppered her legs and the side of her breasts with alternating levels of force. When her eyes had closed again and she was squirming unconsciously, he gave her nipples a firm slap, one immediately after the other. She cried out with the first, extending it with the second, her eyes opening, dazed and unfocused.

Bending over, he drew one offended nipple between his lips, resting his hand along her pubic bone, pressing the rod of the crop into her so that she would feel it as he soothed first one nipple, then the other. When she was moaning again, hips pressing up, he let go and resumed cropping her.

With one hand, he soothed her matted hair from her forehead, while the other rained heavy stings across her thighs and stomach, earning a tight cry when he chose high up on her inner thigh. He walked around to the other side of the bed, giving the blows to her arms and breasts while his free hand soothed lightly across her stomach and settled on her pubic bone. He pressed firmly and she pulled at her ankles.

He eased one finger down, across her clit and into her wet, welcoming heat. He hit her nipples again as she clutched tighter on his finger.

"Sir, please, Sir."

"What would you like?" he asked, as he kept his finger still and gave a light tap to her armpit. She jerked and squealed.

"I—I don't know, Sir."

"Then you'll leave it to me to decide?"

"Please, Sir."

She made him smile, his Petal. Her eyes were still closed, her head tossing about, her body straining toward him even as he offered little bites of pain in random spots across her needy body.

"Open your mouth, Petal."

Her eyes slitted open as she followed his order. He placed the crop between her lips.

"Hold that for me, for a moment. You can still use your numbers."

He used his now free hand to pluck and tease her sensitized nipples while he added a second, then a third finger in her pussy. Her keening cry of need made him even harder than he already was. He pushed his thumb into her clit and she came quickly, but her body didn't ease, didn't stop straining for him.

He rolled on a condom, knelt up onto the bed, and slid into her. Pausing inside her, he pressed his body into her warmed, sensitized skin, scratching it with the hair on his chest. Her eyes begged him for more, for him. He kissed her, the crop still between her lips, drawing her tongue into his mouth around the thin rod.

She whined at the obstruction. Or maybe at the roughness he was bringing to her tender skin. Or maybe trying to get him to move inside her. He broke the kiss and picked up the crop, setting it aside. Then he kissed her for real, deep thrusts with his tongue that mimicked as he began to fuck her. He loved the feel of her, imagined her without the barrier of the condom.

The idea had him groaning, and her eyes opened, watching his face with avid hunger as he worked over her. She was pulling on the tape, trying to get her arms around him, but could do nothing but take him. He knew she was close to coming again. He gave another thrust, then pulled out completely.

Her wail of frustration almost had him smiling, but he managed to make his face stern.

"Did you want to come?"

"Yes, Sir!"

"Did you ask?"

NATALIE'S HEART stuttered at Noah's question. *Shit.* She hadn't asked, and she'd already come once. Maybe he wouldn't punish her for the first one, it hadn't been a *real* orgasm. Kind of.

"Please, Sir, I'm so sorry, I need you."

"What do you need?"

"I need *you*! I want to come, please, Sir."

He palmed her breast and flicked her nipple with his thumb. It was sore from being hit earlier, and somehow that soreness, his touch, had her fighting to keep from coming. *Why is that so fucking good?* It didn't make sense, nothing made sense right now when she couldn't think about anything other than getting his thick cock back inside her and letting her come.

"Please," she drew the word out on a long moan that lasted several seconds. He studied her, that stern expression giving her no hint as to what he might do. Then his face softened and he leaned down, brushed his lips with hers, spoke so that his breath entered her open and eager mouth.

"You can come when you stop kissing me," he invited, and lowered his mouth to hers.

She lifted her head as much as she could to take him in, but that wasn't necessary. He gave himself to her, letting her pull his tongue into her mouth even as he slid his cock into her channel. She sucked and tasted while he kept a steady rhythm. Her body was on fire, but now she was torn between making the kiss last forever and holding back the electric need that arced through her.

Tears tickled their way down her temples as she held back, his body rubbing on her clit, the hair on his chest scratching at her, his silky tongue kissing her like he was content to stay there forever. When the electricity built into a lightning bolt of need, she tore her mouth free and came. She screamed when he bit her upper arm, a place he'd bruised with his crop. Her orgasm redoubled and she grayed out.

When she came back to full awareness, he'd lowered her hands to her sides and wiped her face, chest and pussy with a warm washcloth. He returned to her side and she curled into his body. He wrapped his arms around her and held her close.

Her mind was emptier than she ever remembered it being and she had no idea how much time passed before she began to think again. She knew she wasn't a masochist, or at least, she didn't think so. She'd honestly thought tonight would be about showing him she could endure something if it made her top happy.

He smoothed her hair back from her face and remade her ponytail. "Back with me?"

She found it harder than she could understand to open her mouth and form words. "Yes, Sir."

His lips twitched as if he understood she hadn't lied but hadn't exactly told the truth, either.

Pulling in a deep breath, she concentrated on the feel of his skin touching hers, the little aches and pains on her body, the smell of him. "I'm good."

Now he grinned. "You are that." He produced a candy bar and shared it with her, then sat her up so he could get the pillows from the floor. He tucked her into himself and settled them against the headboard, then offered her a glass of water. They sat quietly, eating a second bar and sharing the water.

"I don't really know what I was expecting, but I never even imagined that," she blurted out into the silence.

"I remember thinking exactly that."

She looked at him. "I forget that you've tried this stuff. Do you ever...*want* it?"

"Would you ever want to spend an hour cropping someone, like I just did?"

She couldn't help it, she wrinkled her nose at the idea. "I think I could, if someone I loved wanted to try it, but it wouldn't be on my list of things to do just for fun."

"That's pretty much how I feel about being on the other side of it."

"Oh. That makes sense. Sorry, my brain is still fuzzy."

"Don't apologize. I like knowing what you're thinking. But you'll still want to write a journal entry before we go to sleep."

She yawned, then laughed. "Your powers of persuasion are impressive if you can make me sleepy just by saying that word."

He grinned. "I'd like to take credit, but that's your third yawn in two minutes."

Oh. She hadn't noticed. Now that she was aware of it, the tiredness was pulling at her bones. But she didn't want to move. She reached up and rubbed her fingers on his soft whiskers. She liked him like this. But she'd also liked him clean-shaven. Hell, she just liked him. He didn't react as she explored his face, traced his lips.

When she yawned again, he smiled and moved, carefully disentangling himself despite the pout she offered. He got off the bed.

"Come here, I want to show you something."

Sighing, she took his hand. Her legs were shaky when she made it off the bed, but he held her steady and brought her to the bathroom. She stared at herself. He stood behind her, one arm around her waist for support, the other lightly caressing the marks on her body. And there were a lot of marks. Most were fairly light, but there was a good peppering of red, and a few that were still pretty dark.

He tickled lightly at one on her upper arm, the one he'd bitten. "Most of these will be gone by morning, but this one will bruise."

Her gaze was stuck on the spot, on his fingers circling it, on the satisfied tone of his voice. She'd read about such things, about characters who wanted to be marked. When he'd asked her about it, in their talks about her limits, she hadn't really understood, but she'd agreed to it within strict limits.

Now she got it. It was like seeing a visual representation of the pleasure he'd given her. And, if she read him right, the pleasure he'd taken in giving them to her. She scanned the rest of her body and he pointed out a couple more. One on her inner thigh, that he caressed lightly, his chin on her shoulder.

"Thank you, Sir," she whispered, watching his face in the mirror.

His gaze came to hers and the look of satisfied pleasure at what he saw on her body made her insides melt. She'd thought he'd already turned her to goo, but that look...*whew.*

Once again she had to remind herself that this wasn't a relationship. Not a romantic one, at least. He was being a good guy. An amazing one. Giving her this gift. She would *not* repay him by expecting more from him than he'd promised. But damn, he made it hard not to want him.

He took off her collar and she cleaned up and went back to the bedroom to write in her journal. Again, she wasn't sure what she managed to get down, as she tried to make sense of the tangle of thoughts and emotions. She didn't remember consciously deciding that was enough, and sliding into sleep.

CHAPTER FIFTEEN

Noah sat on the couch to give Natalie space as she wrote in her journal, but kept an eye on her. When she dropped the pen onto the sheets, he went in and helped her put it and the book on the table, slid the hair tie out of her hair, and kissed her as she snuggled down into the blankets.

"Thank you," she whispered.

He watched her for a minute, her face slack in sleep, her hand curled under her cheek. In some ways it was hard to believe it was only Saturday night. They'd been at the cabin a day and a half. They had one full day left, and then they'd leave Monday morning. His head was filling with ideas of all the things he wanted to do with her. And to her.

And not all of them were scenes. He wanted to see how she'd react if he took her to Apex, not to play, but to just see everyone else sceneing. And he wanted to sit beside her at the next Weber-Crawford get-together, so he could hear her opinions and reactions to the action around them. Or watch from a distance as she knit a blanket while charming Uncle Leon and the family.

Shit.

He checked his watch, then grabbed his phone and sent a text to Alec.

Got a minute? It's ok if it's too late.

His phone range thirty seconds later.

"How's it going out there?" Alec asked, not bothering with a hello.

"Good. Really good. How's Sonya? Baby coming?"

"She's tired and wants to hold the baby. We had an appointment today, and the doctor thinks any day. But probably not a Fourth of July baby. Tell me about 'really good'."

Noah leaned back into the couch, his eyes trained on Natalie. "I —might have a problem. I promised her, and you, that this was a one-weekend thing. Help her get past the issue from before and explore with someone she trusts. Decide if she wants to consider adopting the lifestyle."

"Right. And?"

"And…I'm not sure I want it to be over on Monday."

"And you don't think she's on that page with you? Or that you could woo her into being on that page with you?"

Noah squinted at his phone before bringing it back to his ear. "Did you just say woo?"

Alec sighed. "Sonya has me reading historical romances out loud to her when she's trying to get to sleep. It's hard for her to get comfortable and rest right now, okay? Don't bust my balls."

"Hey, whatever makes Sonya happy is good by me." He glanced at the bed, took a deep breath. "I don't want to confuse her. Or fuck up the friendship she and I are developing. Or my relationship with you and your family. She considers your family hers, and I'd understand if you don't want me going there."

Alec scoffed. "Unless you treat her like shit, do you think I'd have a problem with her dating you? My best friend? You think Sonya and I haven't spent the last couple of days stressing out about who might be good enough for her and wishing you would get your head out of your ass about relationships and realize that she would be great for *you?*"

Noah was rocked. "My head out of my ass?" he managed to ask, while trying to wrap his brain around the rest of what Alec had said.

"You've been convinced you don't want a long-term relationship since Britt. And she was, what, four years ago?"

"I was with Janey after Britt. For more than six months," he reminded Alec.

"Not the same. Janey needed a 24/7 Master and convinced you that you were the Dom for the job. You didn't, and don't, want a 24/7 slave. But she needed saving and managed to convince you, or you managed to convince yourself—I'm not sure which, actually— that you were the only one who could save her. You have a bit of a hero complex, my friend. It's probably why you make such a good mentor at the club, but also maybe why you're afraid to get too involved with someone. It takes *a lot* of work to be someone's savior."

"That's...a take."

"It's part of what makes you a good Dom, a good son, a good nephew, brother, best friend."

That sparked a memory in him, from the second month he'd been in Boston. Uncle Leon had sat him down after Uncle Paul had gone to bed one night. "You're not here to be a martyr, Noah. I wish I could say otherwise, but nothing you—or I—do to help is going to save Paul's life. He will live or die because of the cancer, the doctors, and his own will to fight. We won't change that. We'll encourage him and make his time better, and we'll fight like hell to do that. But not to *your* detriment."

Earlier that evening, he'd let it slip that the young couple who'd moved into the condo next door had invited him to come over for their big housewarming party. Of course he'd said no. He needed to be there, doing his part to save Paul.

Leon had wrapped his thin hand around Noah's big shoulder and shook him, making him meet his uncle's gaze. "You will not save him. And he doesn't want you to give up your life to help him. We're so grateful to have you here to help, never doubt that for a second. But you can't help if you burn out, or start to resent or hate Paul."

Noah had reacted to that, denied that it was possible. The ignorance of youth, he could see now. But Leon had convinced him to start *living* in Boston, not just existing in their apartment. He'd encouraged Noah to start hanging out with Leon's nephew and even set him up on a date with a woman from his office. It hadn't taken, but Noah had given in and started to understand.

He'd still been there for Paul, given his uncle a great deal of help, love and support, until the very end. He hadn't been a martyr. But only because Leon had been a good guy, who'd paid attention and understood that Noah's instincts were leading him there.

"You've enjoyed yourself the last few years, I'm sure," Alec said when Noah hadn't replied. "And there's nothing wrong with not being interested in a relationship. But it's been a while, and I see the way you look at Sonya when she's got her hand wrapped around her belly. Or the way you look at Mom and Dad when they're all lovey-dovey planning their big anniversary party. I think part of you, a big part of you, is ready to be thinking long-term. And Natalie's pretty awesome. I think she'd be good for you."

He'd been worried Alec wouldn't think he was the right guy for his sister's best friend. It hadn't occurred to him that *his* best friend was worried about who the right woman for Noah was.

"She is pretty awesome," he agreed. "But this weekend…it's not real life."

"The Natalie I know is smart enough to tell the difference between a vacation and real life. I didn't get the sense that she was interested in a 24/7 type of relationship, if that's what you're worried about. Besides, I doubt you're actually doing full-time at the cabin, anyway."

He hadn't been worried about that. Well, maybe sort of. His experience with Janey had proved to him that wasn't a life he was interested in. Natalie hadn't been wearing his collar the whole time they'd been here, but it was a lot more than would normally be the case for him with a partner.

"Yeah. You're right. And she might not even be interested. She's really thrown herself into experiencing this weekend. I'm proud of her, but her feelings are going to be caught up in that, and she might think—"

"Again," Alec interrupted. "She's smart. Don't think you know her feelings better than she does. You're good enough to find the line between coercing her while her emotions are a jumble and she's vulnerable, and leaving her hanging out of a sense of justice, if she's as caught up in you as you must be to be making this phone call."

Noah let out a low bark of laughter at that. "Yeah. Fair. Thanks, man."

"I'm here. Always. It just may take me longer to get back to you, once there's a baby in the mix."

The joy in Alec's voice brought a smile to Noah's face. "I can't wait to meet the little one."

"Soon. Better be soon, or Sonya's going to make me pay, somehow, some way."

"Well, it is your fault."

"Of course it is."

When he hung up, Noah turned off the lamp and walked back to the bedroom. Natalie hadn't moved an inch. He'd definitely tired her out. He brushed a strand of her hair back off her cheek. He hadn't been looking for a relationship. He'd been enjoying his time at the club, mentoring new subs and Doms, taking on monitoring duties, playing with those who weren't interested in a relationship. He'd even gone on a few dates here and there. But no one had stuck, no one had given him this…almost itchy feeling.

Yeah, he'd wanted to give her this weekend, to help erase the injustice done to her five years ago. But if he was honest with himself, it had gone beyond that before they'd ever even made it to the cabin. He enjoyed their time out of the collar as much as their time in it. Well, almost as much. But sexcapades could only take you so far. And having a partner for the rest of the time was something he'd sort of given up on.

He'd tried dating outside the lifestyle. He'd tried having a vanilla girlfriend who knew about his time at the club. He'd tried all sorts of situations, and maybe some of them would have worked...with the right woman. None of that seemed to matter as he watched Natalie breathe. Those situations were totally irrelevant. Now he just needed to convince Natalie that whatever her plans for the future had been a week ago, now it was time to make some room for him to be by her side.

NATALIE HAD WOKEN up rested and happy on the Fourth of July. She'd rolled over into Noah and he immediately pulled her closer. She'd lain there thinking about the previous night and feeling his cock harden against her leg as he slowly woke up. She grabbed a condom from the table and when he blinked his eyes open, she held it between their faces. His smile was more than answer enough.

He'd slid into her and rocked her into a slow, sweet release that had kept her smiling through her shower. Then he'd suggested they head into town for breakfast.

It was only as they were in the car that her happy high started to wane, and she had no clue as to why. Noah was holding her hand as he drove, and was clearly in an excellent mood. He'd obviously enjoyed last night. So had she. *A lot.*

Looking at the marks that had lasted through the night had given her a bizarre sense of pride and accomplishment. She'd pressed on one and winced. The mind was a funny thing. She didn't like pain, but she'd loved what they'd done. It was weird to think that maybe, over time, she'd have increased tolerance.

The thought had her frowning as she let Noah lead the way to the restaurant he said was his favorite in town for breakfast. Luckily he was holding her hand, walking in front of her as they worked their way through the crowded sidewalk, and didn't see her expression.

Was he hoping she'd take more? He'd obviously enjoyed it so much, was it just a precursor to wanting to push her into higher levels of pain? A feeling close to despair swept through her as they took their seats and she pulled her menu in front of her face and pretended to read it, thankful that though the restaurant was crowded and noisy, they'd had a table for two open.

She was thinking stupid thoughts, because the weekend was almost over, anyway. There wasn't time for things to get scarier, even if she thought that Noah would push her past her comfort levels. Which she knew he wouldn't. She *knew* he wouldn't, so why was her heart racing?

None of it mattered because he'd been very clear that he was doing this whole thing as a favor to her, to make sure she had a good experience to balance out the crappy one she'd caught herself up in when she'd tried this out on her own. He would walk her through this, then stick around long enough to be sure that the next person she chose wasn't a total dumbass. Again.

"Do you know what you want?" he asked, and he sounded so happy and carefree.

She was very much afraid that if she looked, if she saw his smile, she would burst into tears. *What the fuck is wrong with me?* She concentrated on keeping her breathing relatively smooth, because it felt like her heart wanted to beat its way out of her chest and drop itself in front of him in a horrific display of need and want and—

The menu in front of her lowered, with Noah's finger pushing it down. He took one look at her and cursed softly. He stood up and caught the waitresses attention as she passed by.

"Sorry, we have an emergency and have to leave."

Natalie was afraid to move an inch. She didn't know what she was supposed to do. Sit, stand, cry, pretend to smile, assure him everything was fine and they should just eat their food? So she just didn't move a muscle until Noah took her hand, put his other around her shoulder, and urged her up.

She let him lead her out of the restaurant and kept moving. She didn't know where. She didn't really care. She'd fucked it all up, ruined the weekend. He was a good guy, though, so he'd probably still help her make sure the next Dom she tried wasn't abusive. And

Alec and Sonya would help. But maybe she should stop with this whole thing. Maybe it just wasn't right for her.

Her head was down and she just watched their shoes, not caring where they went. She watched as the sidewalk changed to dirt and then sunny grass and then shady grass and then he was pulling her into his arms and wrapping himself around her, holding her tight, holding her in when her body felt like it was going to shake apart into a million pieces.

"Shh, baby, it's okay, you're fine, it will be fine, I promise."

She wasn't making any noise, but then again, maybe she was and was having an out-of-body experience. It sort of felt that way. She concentrated on the feel of his arms, the words he murmured into her ear, the warm air swirling around them in a gentle breeze.

Eventually he smoothed her hair back from her face, and she met his eyes.

"And that was sub drop," he said with a gentle smile. "Not fun, huh?"

She swallowed and shook her head. Sub drop? She'd heard about it. Read about it. But…really?

"Want to tell me what was running through your head?"

"No?" she ventured.

His body shook, but he managed to keep his laugh inside. He kissed her nose. "Fucking adorable. You don't have to right this minute. But it'll probably be easier now, than later."

She felt her lips pull into a pout.

He rested his forehead against hers. "You're fine, Nattie. If you don't want to talk yet, if you want to just sit here a while, we can do that."

And damnit, why did that have tears leaking out of her eyes and her throat closing up? "I'm fine," she choked out, though it took a couple of tries, making her a liar.

"Yes, you are. You will be. We talked about what sub drop could be like, but it's different for every person, and impossible to understand until you experience it. You were doing good this morning and after your shower. Maybe leaving the cabin this morning was a mistake. We could have had breakfast there. I'm sorry."

Gah, how could he think this was his fault? "No, no, it wasn't that. I just, when we were driving I started thinking about how great last night was, and how surprising it was that I liked it like that and wondering if I would eventually like more pain, which seemed scary, and then I--" She broke off. She didn't want to tell him what she'd been thinking, but he sat there patiently, not rushing her, and communication was *so* important in BDSM, and she knew that and believed that but *fuck* she still didn't want to continue.

"You what? Can you tell me?"

His voice was so calm and patient that she started speaking again before her brain could remind her that she didn't want to admit these things out loud. "I started wondering if you were so happy because we'd finally done something you liked and you would want more of that, harder than that, which was scary, even though I knew you wouldn't push me to do anything I didn't want to do, but maybe I would want to do it even though I don't want to do it, and then I remembered it doesn't matter, because the weekend is almost over and you would be done and anyway, I don't want more pain than what we did last night."

She had to pull in a deep breath at that point because she'd run out of air. She closed her eyes to try to hide, but he held her chin and silently encouraged her to look at him, so she sighed and did so.

His warm expression and calm care almost had her crying a-*fucking*-gain but she swallowed it down.

"Thank you, baby. I know that wasn't easy to say, and I'm so proud of you. First, in case it matters, everything you said and felt is totally normal. That doesn't make it easier to feel, but hopefully it's one less thing for you to worry about. Why don't we sit down?"

She finally took in their environment. He'd brought them to a small park. She could see the bustling sidewalk and busy shops on one side, and some lovely homes on the other. A scattering of people were enjoying the park, as well, but not many yet. A man and young boy were throwing a Frisbee, a couple were walking two little dogs, and some kids were chasing a soccer ball, but he'd found them a spot of shade away from the action and prying eyes.

They sat down, and he pulled her into his lap immediately. She snuggled in. "I'm sorry."

"That's your last freebie, I'll punish you if you apologize again," he said, with no heat in his voice.

"That's not fair. I'm not wearing your collar."

"Some things transcend collar time."

"Hmph."

"Now, where was I? Oh, yeah. Second, what we did last night was amazing. It was what was right for you, and me, at that time. Who knows what will be right in five years? Maybe exactly the same thing, maybe something totally different. Traditionally, the crop isn't even my favorite tool, but after last night, with you, it sure as hell holds a higher ranking for me."

He reached up and smoothed the skin between her eyebrows. He seemed to like doing that. She relaxed her frown. "Okay."

"Third, what you and I have had this weekend has been pretty incredible, to me. I'm not sure now is the right time to say this, when you've had such an emotional morning and are super vulnerable, but it feels like a lie *not* to say it."

She felt her body brace.

"I'm hopeful that when we finish our original terms, we can negotiate something new. I would like to see you again. And not just for play."

Well, that wasn't the blow she'd been braced for. She smiled up at him. "I would really, really like that."

"But, I'm worried that your emotions about being with a Dom who treats you well and gives you a lot of pleasure will get caught up with your heart. I agreed to be your mentor, and that's a position of responsibility that I take seriously, and I'm afraid of abusing that gift you've given me when you're in a vulnerable place."

She narrowed her eyes at him. "So…*because* it's been so great we can't continue? If it hadn't been so great, I might not be so emotional, and then it would be okay to take it to the next step?" There *might* have been a bite to her words.

"No, but we need to be careful. Communicate, negotiate, be honest. I want to ask you out, and take you to the club. We just have to—"

"So," she interrupted. "You want us to see each other so that you can prove to me that you're not an abusive ass, and I can prove to you that I'm not a naive nitwit." She didn't make it a question.

"Uh, well, when you put it like that, it sounds fairly asinine."

"How about we just keep seeing each other, keep negotiating scenes to make sure that we're both getting what we want and need out of them, and we keep communicating about where we are with each other? And if things change for either of us, we walk away friends."

He kissed her, long and hard. She lost herself in it and didn't want to stop when he pulled back. "You're very smart. I really fucking like that about you."

The last of her fears and anxieties melted away. "Well, to be totally fair, I didn't want to say any of that at the start, so then we wouldn't have gotten to the good stuff at the end, so thank you for helping me do that. Helping me this morning."

"Since I plan on taking half of the responsibility for how great last night was, I'll take half the responsibility for the crash this morning."

She laughed. "Fair enough, although I'm not sure either was really a fifty-fifty split."

"Close enough for me."

CHAPTER SIXTEEN

Noah tried not to be *too* obvious that he was keeping a close eye on Natalie as they stopped at a different restaurant for breakfast, made a quick stop at the store to beef up the supplies for the cabin, and returned home. He prided himself on his awareness of his subs, and though he knew he wasn't infallible, it still bothered him that she'd been dropping and he hadn't even noticed. He'd thought she was quiet because it was the first time they were going out in public in days and it could be a bit of a culture shock after the intensity of their cabin experience.

It was the reason he'd wanted to do it, actually, rather than drop her off at home on Monday and expect that she'd feel "normal" again. He forced himself to shrug off the guilt and focus on the right things. She was in a good place now, she wanted more, and, as Alec had put it, they were definitely on the same page about being together past the weekend.

For now, he wanted her to know he was there, but not feel like he was hovering, waiting for her to have a breakdown. It wasn't fun, but it was normal, and not a breakdown, though he suspected she felt that way.

When they got back to the cabin, he pulled the canoe out of the shed and dug out the oars. They paddled together, having no trouble syncing their strokes. He took them around the entire perimeter of the pond, pausing to point out some fun things along the way. She told him about her experience white water rafting in college with Felicity, and he remembered that she hadn't just lost her boyfriend and Dom, but her best friend of several years.

They made BLTs for lunch and he watched her go from easy calm to excited expectation. She'd asked if they could still play today, and he'd assured her that he had plans for her for after lunch. Now, as they cleaned up from the meal, he could see that her excitement was tinged with nerves, but that had always been the case for her.

He hoped the scene he had planned for this afternoon would be light and fun for her, but not too boring. When they finished cleaning, she hung up the drying towel and turned to him.

"Are you ready?" he asked, though it was more than clear that she was.

"Yes, Sir."

"All right. Get undressed and wait for me by the door. Close your eyes once you're in position."

He retrieved the supply bag he'd saved for today from the bedroom, along with her collar. When she was in position, eyes closed, he waited and watched. Unlike the first day, she took several deep breaths, and then seemed to settle into the wait with quiet patience. He gave it five minutes, but she didn't fidget, even though she was on the hardwood floor.

He shucked his shoes and shirt, but made enough noise that she would hear him coming. Buckling her collar on first, he loved the way her chin lifted, giving him easy access to making her his. He was glad he'd gone out and gotten the collar for her, in her favorite color. Originally he'd planned to give it to her so she could use it as a play collar if she wanted, but now he thought he'd rather keep it in his own possession. And get matching ankle and wrist cuffs.

But that was for the future, and for now, he had plans that involved some different accessories.

"Keep your eyes closed," he reminded her and brought the lace hood over her face, being very careful as he cinched the ties in back to not snag her hair. He smoothed the lace into place over her face, making sure it wasn't bunched or pinching along the eye holes or where the edge lay across her cheekbones.

Satisfied, he put her wrist cuffs on, then ordered her to her hands and knees and added the ankle cuffs. He wasn't going to attach her to anything, so he took the clips off.

"Bend over now, cheek on your hands, butt in the air," he told her, pulling the lube from his bag. He ran his hand over her back, butt and thighs, giving gentle attention to the few dark spots that remained from last night's fun. When he flicked the cap on the lube open, she gave a very tiny little butt wiggle in anticipation.

He worked one finger in, then two, before easing the new butt plug in. He wiggled it in and out and around a bit, so she could get used to the feeling, then grabbed the nipple clamps from the bag, and a mitt.

"Keep your eyes closed, and stand up." He put a hand on her arm to help her. "Come with me, eyes closed. I won't let you hit anything."

He dropped the mitt onto the couch for later, then led her into the bathroom and positioned her in front of the mirror. Taking his time so they wouldn't make noise, he put the clamps on. They were the loop style again, so he adjusted the bead to a firm hold, but not enough to pinch, so that she could wear them for a while.

"All right, open your eyes."

She blinked them open and stared at their reflection. The lace hood with pointed ears. The nipple clamps with tiny bells that he gave a little flick to, making them tinkle. He turned her a bit to the side so that she could see the long tail coming from her butt.

"Kitten," he said. "Kittens don't talk. They can make noise, but not words. If you forget, I'll give you a gag to remind you."

She pulled her lip between her teeth and he pulled it back out.

"Kittens can pretty much do whatever they want, besides speaking, so no orders for how you'll spend the next couple of hours, beyond not taking off anything I've put on, not speaking, and not walking on two legs once we leave this room."

Her eyes darted around as she observed her mask, her tail, his face, the room.

"Though kittens can't use hands, they do love yarn, so that will be the one exception. If you want to work on your knitting, you can. If you need to use your numbers, of course you can say them out loud, but I would prefer you get my attention and you can show me with your fingers. Unless it's a four or a five, then you should speak them as soon as you need to. All right?"

She looked like her brain was going a million miles a minute, but she nodded.

"All right then." He kissed her on the temple, feeling the lace against his lips. "Down you go. Unfortunately for me, kittens don't do well with leashes."

She gave him one last look, then dropped to the floor.

***

Natalie remembered telling Noah that she was curious about what the puppies and ponies and kittens got out of their play, but she hadn't really expected him to go there for the weekend. She'd also been clear that she was unsure of the dehumanizing aspects of the role. Like humiliation and degradation, it was something she didn't understand, though she didn't judge others for it.

Noah headed to the living room and sat in what had become his spot, then pulled over his laptop from where he'd left it on the side table. Crawling around on the floor wasn't her favorite thing ever, but at least now she understood and appreciated why Noah had decided they should use the Swiffer before they ate lunch.

The wood floor was hard under her knees, and the soft furry tail bumped against her thighs as she slowly made her way to the couch. The little bells hanging from her breasts let Noah know she was approaching, and he looked up and gave her a little smile, then returned his attention to the computer.

Her knitting bag was on the floor next to the couch, so she curled up into her spot and got to work. Normally it was easy to lose herself in the rhythm of the pattern, but she also normally listened to her books or the TV while she did it. And she was having a hard time concentrating with the tail pushing into her ass.

She kept glancing over at Noah, but he seemed fully absorbed in what he was doing. Focusing on the sweater she was working on, again, she managed a few rows before she acknowledged to herself that she was bored.

Would he let her put on her earbuds to listen to a book? Cats had active ears, didn't they? It was less unlikely than knitting, that was for sure. But probably using her phone to turn on and play the book was pushing things. He'd said she could do almost anything, though. She needed to think like a cat, she decided.

Hm.

Putting her project back into the bag, she looked over and caught Noah watching her from the corner of his eyes, but he immediately looked back at his screen. *Well.*

Rising up on her knees, little bells tinkling, she crawled over to Noah and plopped down—gently—on top of his hands and keyboard, just like Missy P would do.

He huffed out a laugh but didn't say anything, he just lifted her up and to the side. But then he moved the computer off his lap and patted his legs. Smiling, she curled into him. He'd taken his shirt off and she rubbed her lace-covered forehead against him, imagining the roughness of the lace against his nipples.

His shifting should have alerted her that he was making a move, but she was surprised to feel soft fur sliding over her naked skin. She tore her gaze from his chest and found that he'd put on a furry mitt and was using it to pet her.

Oh. She abandoned trying to torture him and melted against him instead. He increased the pressure, sliding the softness over every part of her that he could reach without moving their positions.

Nice. She enjoyed the sensation for a while, and when he paused, she dug her nails into his stomach just a bit, without conscious thought. He grunted and resumed petting her. Amused, she considered what else she could do.

When he was mid-stroke, she abruptly sat up and moved back to the other end of the couch and pretended to ignore him. She snuck a peek, though, and he appeared to be fighting a grin.

She gave it a few minutes, then made her way back over to him and rubbed her head against his shoulder. He scritched the small of her back, absentmindedly, though he hadn't brought back his computer or anything else to grab his attention. This was all part of the play, she realized.

Turning, she tried to smack him in the face with her tail, and probably succeeded if the light sputtering was a good indicator. He flicked her rump. Okay, she couldn't fault him for that, though she assumed he wouldn't actually do the same to a pet.

"Feeling a little feisty, kitten?" he asked.

She turned back around and moved her hands to his thigh, kneading her nails into his shorts, moving them close and closer to his cock. He grinned and lifted her back into his arms, banding them around her so that she couldn't get at her goal.

Huffing a breath, she tried to wriggle free, but he held tight. Giving up—for now—she relaxed back into him. He put the mitt back on and pet her some more. With the way she was sitting now, he was petting mostly her front. Her breasts. She squeezed her butt around the plug, bigger than the one from yesterday, which was a lot, but also felt like it wasn't about to squirt out of her at any moment, so that was good.

It all felt good, the soft fur, the firm strokes that made her bells tinkle. But…she wasn't sure she liked it. It felt weird to get turned on but she couldn't deny it was happening. It was supposed to happen, right? That was the point of the scene. She bit her lip and realized she'd stopped watching him when his finger slid under her collar.

"I need to get some work done, kitten. No more pets. You're probably hungry though, I'll put your food out."

Hmph. He nudged her with the glove and she rolled off him and sat on the couch, watching as he headed to the kitchen. She supposed she was expected to crawl after him. Honestly, though, did people really crawl around their houses all day? Although, if this were something she found intriguing, she'd be able to negotiate the rules a little better next time, and maybe include kneepads. Or just do away with the crawling except for certain circumstances.

It was interesting to think about the different negotiation options as she headed toward the kitchen, but she couldn't keep from scowling when he set a saucer on the floor.

Really?

"Come on, it's good, you'll like it," he encouraged, squatting down next to the small plate.

Grumbling, she took the last couple steps and he pet from her head to her tail in approval, giving the tail a little tweak. She looked down at the plate. There was a scattering of crackers, cheese and grapes. She wasn't really even hungry, but now she wanted cheese.

Bending her head, while Noah kept his hand on the small of her back, she tongued up a piece of cheese, then a cracker, and sat back and chewed. He kissed her on the top of her head and went back to the couch.

The food was good and she was kind of bored, so she kept with it, and ate the rest. She didn't feel like crawling back to the couch right away, but sitting on the floor with the plug up her ass wasn't really fun, so she went back.

She didn't want to knit, so she climbed onto the couch and lay down with her head on Noah's lap. She could take a nap and be super rested for whatever he had planned for the night. She could pull out a yarn ball and throw it at Noah. But then he'd throw it and she would have to chase it, which wasn't happening on hands and knees. She could scratch him. She could nuzzle his cock. The idea was enticing but...weird. She just kept getting trapped between the act-like-an-animal thing and the have-sex thing, and even though she knew lots of people made it work and enjoyed the hell out of it, somehow her brain was not letting those two acts come together.

She sighed and glanced up to find Noah watching her. She showed him three fingers.

"Not loving it, huh?"

She shook her head.

CHAPTER SEVENTEEN

Noah wasn't surprised Natalie was ready to stop the kitten play. When she'd shied away from him petting her breasts, he'd guessed sexing up the kitty wasn't going to work for her. He just had to decide if she was okay to move to another scene, or if she needed a break.

"All right. I'm proud of you, you gave it good effort, but you let me know it wasn't working. Lift your head up." He unlaced the hood and pulled it over her face.

She rubbed her hands over her cheeks and forehead.

He slid the beads on the nipple clamps down and pulled them off. When he unbuckled her collar, her face fell. He leaned over and kissed her nose. "Go to the bathroom, take off your tail and clean it, do whatever else you need to do, then take your position by the door."

"Yes, Sir."

She sprang up off the couch and headed for the bathroom.

He went to the bedroom and considered his supplies, then switched between bags until he had what he wanted readily accessible. He used the bathroom himself and checked that she'd cleaned everything up. Of course she had.

He knelt in front of her and put on the collar with chest harness. He used clips to attach the wrist cuffs to the front loop on the collar, so that her hands were clasped under her chin. He smoothed her hair back into a ponytail and studied her.

Her eyes were bright and eager, her breaths even. Ready and waiting, but excited with just a touch of nerves. He'd almost brought the leash, but it wasn't really his thing and hadn't seemed to excite her, either. "Come with me, Petal."

He waited until she was standing, then led the way to the bedroom. "Up on the bed. Sideways so your head is on one side and your feet are hanging over the other," he ordered. It took her a minute to sit and scoot herself into place without the use of her hands.

She lay back and looked around until she could see where he stood at the foot of the bed. He had a strap in his hand, but she didn't look past his face.

"Good girl." He went behind her head, slid his arms under her shoulders and pulled her toward him a little more so that her neck was at the edge of the bed. She drew in a breath but didn't make a sound.

"For this scene, you can speak however you like," he decided. "Although there are definitely people out on the lake, so I'd go easy on the screams if I were you." He winked at her.

"Thank you, Sir."

He grabbed two straps out of his bag and moved to her feet. Taking one, he bent her knee so that her foot was flat on the mattress, at the edge of the bed. He widened her leg out until it was maybe just a touch beyond comfortable for her. Then he attached a clip and brought the end of the strap to the headboard. Adjusting the length, he attached it and checked the tension. He attached her other leg to the footboard. He stood between her legs and watched the flush rise up her neck, but she didn't say anything.

He went back to his bag and retrieved the thigh cuffs, put them on her, and attached them to the headboard and footboard with additional tethers. He hadn't planned it, but adaptation was key and her breathing was getting more shallow with every piece of bondage. Good thing he'd brought a lot of straps. And that the headboard and footboard had the iron pattern for lots of attachment options.

He got his longest strap and found the middle, then eased it under her hips, crossed it over her front and attached each end to the bed frame. Then he tightened them until the strap was snug. Her eyes were dilated now, though he'd only touched her perfunctorily. Beautiful.

Two more straps were left so he looped one around the leg of the footboard, down at the floor, and brought the clip to the ring on the back of her collar. Then did the same around the headboard leg. Her mouth was open with her panting now, her head secured over the side of the bed, with very little movement available to her.

He double-checked the collar against her throat, ran his fingers along her arms and breasts, checking her temperature and the tightness of all the straps.

Going back to the bag, he pulled out a vibrating dildo. It was silicone and rainbow colored, which he'd found amusing. It had both a clit stimulator and a thrusting action on the main shaft, which he was pretty sure Natalie would appreciate.

His grin might have been a bit evil as he brought it around for her to see. "Open wide, Petal." He brought the toy to her lips. "Get it nice and wet for me."

She put her tongue out and he ran the head over her tongue, then the first part of the shaft. He eased it between her lips. She sucked it in eagerly, and he let her play with it while he watched her carefully. Her color was good and her neck was supported, but he wouldn't keep her like this for too long.

He eased the dildo in farther, twisted it around to let her get it nice and wet, then pulled it free. He moved to the other side of the bed and teased her clit while he thumbed open the cap on the lube. He drizzled the gel over the head and shaft, twirling it to get it covered. Maybe overkill after her careful attention, but better safe than sorry.

He turned on the vibrating function of the shaft and teased it around her opening. Her hips and legs tried to move, but there was no give in the straps. He heard a rattle and saw she was trying to lift her head to see, but quickly gave up. He eased the vibrator into her an inch and stopped.

She moaned. He took his time, easing it in and out, until it was fully seated, which brought the clit stimulator to the perfect spot. Her hips were twitching but he positioned the little tickler into place and pushed the button.

"Oh, crap," she said.

He laughed. "Indeed."

He had the bondage tape at the ready, but the device seemed secure where it was. Of course, he hadn't hit the last button yet. Couldn't hurt, he decided, and used some tape to secure the toy in place. Then he turned on the thrusting motion.

"Ahhhhh."

He walked back around to her head. Her eyes were wide, but got even wider when she saw him unbutton his shorts. She licked her lips and shuddered.

"Is this too much?" he teased. "Will you be too full?"

"No, Sir. Please fill my mouth. Please, Sir."

He eased his shaft between her begging lips and had to fight back a shudder of his own.

NATALIE COULDN'T THINK. She was just a mess of sensations as the little beast between her legs vibrated and thrust inside her, and covered her clit with tingles. She was fully trapped, unable to move an inch, could only stay where Noah had put her, do what Noah allowed her to do. She was just thankful he'd allowed her to suck him.

He was hard and smooth and filled her up in this position, sliding to the back of her throat. She managed to swallow and wanted to shout in triumph when he groaned. She couldn't do much, could barely pulse her tongue against him, but he moved in and out of her, taking what he wanted. Taking *her*.

The action at her pussy and clit suddenly overtook her and she screamed around his cock, thankful he'd already given her permission to come because she was absolutely certain she wouldn't have been able to stop it, no matter how much she may have wanted to.

He didn't stop, didn't hesitate, just let her scream around his cock as he fucked her throat. What he *did* do was lean over her and pinch her nipples. Not super hard, but in combination with everything else, she screamed again.

"Ah, that's nice," he said, though his voice sounded strained to her ears.

He slowed his movements, a pace that was in contrast to the quiet frenzy happening at her pussy. His fingers traced her cheekbones, her chin, her ears.

She fluttered her tongue against him as best she could, so fucking happy when his fingers tightened on her earlobe in reaction. His thrusts got a little jerky and sped up. Her toes tightened as she tried, this time, to fight another orgasm. Somehow he knew, and he squeezed her breasts.

"Come for me again, Petal. I want to watch one more time, like this."

She had no choice, with those words. Could only do as he commanded and let the fire burst through her whole body as he continued to fuck in and out of her mouth. She screamed, but it was more hoarse this time. He pulled from between her lips and she tried to hold on, suck him in. She wanted to taste his release. But he clearly had other plans.

He reached under her and unclipped the straps holding the ring at the back of her neck. He unclipped the strap that went around her hips as he made his way around to the other side of the bed and put his hands on her hips, slid her up slowly so that her head was fully supported, her knees more bent than before.

He unwrapped the tape holding the toy inside her, and turned it off. A minute ago, all she'd wanted was to feel him ejaculate down her throat, but now she could barely stand to wait as he rolled a condom on, knelt up on the bed and slid into her in a single hard thrust. She lifted her hips to meet him, the tiny bit she was able.

Although he didn't vibrate, he felt so much better than the silicone. He braced his hands beside her face, so that the only point of contact between them was his dick and her pussy. Her fingers reached for him, but it was impossible with her wrists locked to her throat.

He slid in and out, watching her. She watched him back, his half-lidded eyes, his strong shoulders, the hair on his chest, which came so close to touching her breasts.

"I want to touch you, Sir. Feel you."

"Are you not feeling me?" he asked, sliding in again. "I feel you. Hot and wet and holding me tight."

She pulled her feet against the straps, trying to close her legs against his hips, but there wasn't nearly enough give.

"I want to feel more of you." Her fingers stretched toward his chest.

"Don't you feel me?" he asked again, his voice starting to sound strained. "Don't you feel me holding your ankles tight, right where I want them? Holding your wrists secure? Wrapped around your throat so I can feel your every breath?"

Her mind simply grayed out at his words, as the points of contact he described seared into her skin and she felt them anew, felt his hold on her in all those places. "Yesss."

"I like being able to touch so many places at once. I like holding your wrists even if I'm on the other side of the room."

God, how did his words make her clit pulse like that? "Yes, Sir. Thank you, Sir. You feel so good."

His continued thrusts picked up speed, just a bit. He swiveled his hips, and she gasped. He lowered his mouth and teased his lips just above hers, almost but not quite touching. Finally he kissed her, light and teasing, flicking his tongue inside her and lifting his head if she tried to chase him. She held herself still and he returned, playing with her lips and mouth like he had all the time in the world to enjoy this.

Part of her agreed, she wanted to stay like this all night. But part of her wanted to see him come, see him lose himself inside her.

His breathing was getting harsher, his thrusts a little less smooth. She squeezed her inner muscles and his breath hitched. His eyes were closed now and one hand moved into her hair, gripping it with just a hint of pain. She watched his neck arch, his lips part. His hips froze and he came with a long groan.

He lowered his body to hers, his heavy warmth enveloping her. She sighed, content to lay there all night if he wanted. Well, okay, that was a lie, she'd rather be able to wrap her arms around him.

He rested for a few minutes, then pulled free from her and knelt up. He unhooked the straps from her ankles and thighs and dropped back down beside her, wrapping his arms around her and rolling so that he was on his back and she was lying on top of him. He unhooked her wrist cuffs from her collar, and unbuckled the collar and the strap under her breasts, pulling it out from between them. Left with only the wrist, ankle and thigh cuffs, that weren't attached to anything, she snuggled down into him, her fingers playing with his soft hair.

CHAPTER EIGHTEEN

They roused after a bit of a doze and she put on her robe and went to get a glass of ice water, which he promptly stole from her, downing nearly half. She figured he'd earned it and got another glass.

"Want to play cards?" he asked. "Or watch a movie? Or would you like to get some knitting done?"

"I love card games." She narrowed her eyes at him. "How competitive are you?"

He laughed. "I see you've played with Alec before. I'm not like that, I promise. I enjoy playing, and I enjoy winning, but I'm not invested in the game."

"It suddenly occurred to me that not wanting to lose was a Dom kind of thing," she said as she grabbed the deck of cards from the bookshelf that held several games. "I've only played with him a few times, and it can get intense."

He smirked. "If you're not wearing my collar, I won't order you to lose to me. Or act like a prat if you win."

"All right. How about crazy eights to start?"

She dealt the first round and was pleased that they both stuck to light-hearted teasing and grumbling. After a couple of rounds, they switched to speed, which had them laughing as their adrenaline spiked, causing her to accidentally fling a card three feet in the air. When they switched to poker, she watched him, but couldn't figure out any of his tells. Hm, she'd have to study him a bit more.

When they got up to make dinner, he held a hand out and hauled her up from the floor, then twirled her in a circle.

"I remember watching you dancing at Alec's wedding," she told him as they moved into the kitchen. "Have you had lessons?"

"Just my mom teaching me enough not to embarrass myself at prom. You?"

"No. Annalise and I practiced before that wedding, and I danced with her dad and Alec and I was concentrating so hard. Alec made me laugh so I'd forget to be nervous."

"We should take a class. Could be fun."

Pleasure washed through her, and she shot him a grin as she handed him the meat and veggies from the fridge. "Could be."

She spiced the ground beef and formed patties while he sliced onion and tomato. When the burgers were ready, she put on shorts and a t-shirt and they took the food out to the porch to sit in the Adirondack chairs. The burgers were slightly overcooked, but the view, the atmosphere and the company couldn't be beat.

"Tell me what you think about the weekend."

She glanced over and found he'd put his plate down on the ground and turned slightly to watch her.

"I think it will be wild to go back and read the journal from Friday. In some ways it feels like we've been here for ages, and I'm not the person I was when I got in your car. But I also wonder how much it will seem like a weird dream when I get home, and you're gone again."

She'd opened her mouth and blurted it out without real thought, but it was true.

He nodded. "This was not real life, so it's kind of hard to reconcile what real life will be like again."

"Yes. Because now I know I do want to be a sub, but also because

I know I want to be with you, and it's been a while since I've been in a relationship."

"How long?"

"About two years. I was seeing a guy in the spring, but it didn't even last two months."

"Annalise was not impressed with him," he told her with a grin.

"Ha, no, she wasn't. She told you that?"

"She did. Come sit with me?"

She'd finished eating, so she put her plate down and joined him in the big chair. They put their feet up on the railing and watched birds swoop down into the water for their meals.

"Do you want to go to Apex?" he asked after a while.

That was the BDSM club he went to, as did Alec and Sonya. "I'd like to check it out. I don't know if I want to start going on a regular basis."

He nodded against her hair.

"Noah, I know some people go to clubs to play without their—"

"I'm a one-woman guy, Nat. If we play, we play. If we don't, we don't. If that stops working for both of us, then we go our separate ways. But I'm going to consider us exclusive from this weekend forward, unless we specifically agree to another arrangement. Does that work for you?"

She turned her head so that she could see him. "Yeah, that works for me." He kissed her. When he stopped, she faced forward again. "It'll be weird to see Alec and Sonya that way."

"We can go a night they're not there the first time, if you like. Or wait until they've finished playing for the evening, so they can be there with us, but not sceneing in front of you. We won't try anything the first time, we just want to see if it's something you might get comfortable with, later."

"That sounds perfect."

The loud report of firecrackers reached them from not too far away, and she shook her head. "It's not even six, they've still got a ways." She pulled out her phone and checked. "Sunset isn't until eight twenty-nine."

"The kids are probably too excited to wait. Plus, those weren't even legal. I should have gotten some sparklers, but I was too busy packing things to torment you with."

"I can see you put a lot of thought and effort in that direction."

He squeezed his arm around her. "Oh yeah."

She smiled. The air was heavy with heat and humidity, so they went back inside to play cards some more. He kicked her butt in gin rummy and she returned the favor with double solitaire. It was still warm when they went for a walk, but not as bad as it had been. They climbed up to the tree house and necked.

"Why does this feel naughty?" she asked. It was sort of ridiculous, considering the things they'd been up to all weekend.

He laughed. "It does, doesn't it?" He backed her up so that her butt was on the little window sill. She wrapped her legs around his hips and sank into the pleasure of him.

When firecrackers sounded again, he ducked his head to look out behind her. "Sun will be down soon, let's head back."

They tromped through the trees and back around to the front of the cabin. He stopped her and pointed at the big windows that faced the pond. "See how the sun is reflecting off the windows and you can't see in?"

She nodded. "We can keep the curtains open as long as the lights are off, and no one will see in. Does that mean I'll be naked while we watch the fireworks?"

"That's exactly what it means."

She pretended to sigh. "If that's what Sir wants."

He bit the curve of her shoulder, through her shirt in response.

Despite the teasing, when Noah opened the door to the cabin, he didn't give Natalie a chance to get naked and kneel. "Help me move the couch." He went to one end and she went to the other, and they moved it a couple feet closer to the windows.

He went to her, cupping her bottom in his hands to urge her up a bit, then leaning down to meet her for a kiss. She opened for him, as always, so sweet and welcoming. He could lose himself in her. Wanted to lose himself in her. Except, more, he wanted to show her all the pleasures she could endure, and that took concentration.

But now was for simple pleasures. He squeezed his hands on her butt, then moved them up her back, snagging the hem of her shirt and lifting it up. He broke the kiss and pulled the shirt over her head.

He looked at her, not surprised when she blushed. She'd spent most of the weekend naked, but blushed while wearing shorts and a bra. He slipped a finger of each hand under the straps and ran them up and down, watching her chest rise and fall, her lip disappear between her teeth.

The peach bra was lacy and delicate and didn't really seem like it could support her ample breasts, though the straps were wide. Slight red marks showed where he'd lifted them. He reached behind her and unhooked the clasps, drew the lace down and away from her tempting flesh.

He rubbed lightly at the redness on her shoulders, then more firmly, drawing his thumb under her breasts, where the skin was slightly indented. She reached for his shoulders and drew her hands down his back.

"I get to touch," she whispered.

"You do," he agreed. "Let's see how much I can distract you, though."

Her mouth went mutinous and he kissed it. She melted under him and he smiled against her lips. Her fingers dug into his biceps. He kept kissing her as he massaged her breasts, thumbing her nipples into tight points.

Her hips pressed into his and her nails drew light scratches down his back. She brought her hands around to his front and worked his belt open. Good to know that his woman could multitask. Seeing her bound for him that afternoon had pleased him very, very much. But so did having her eager and willing hands jerking open his shorts and trying to shove them and his boxers off his hips without breaking their kiss.

Luckily, her shorts were just elastic at the top, so it took little effort to slide them down, along with her panties. They broke their kiss so they could step clear of the clothes. She offered him a wicked grin he'd never seen on her before, and gave him a shove. Not a hard one, he could have resisted, but…why? He went down on the couch and reached for her as she kneeled up onto it, straddling his legs.

She threaded her fingers into his hair and joined their lips again. Nice of her to have parted her legs so neatly. He snuck a hand between them and tested her entrance. Wet and slick. She moaned into his mouth when he eased his finger inside. He broke the kiss and brought his fingers to her lips. She sucked it in eagerly, her eyes bright and needy.

"You make me so fucking hot," he told her.

Her cheeks flushed in surprise and pleasure and she glanced down at his cock—curving up to hit his stomach—as if to check the evidence for herself. The gleam in her eye warned him he better move fast. He lifted her up and turned, so that they were both laying on their sides, facing the windows, his back against the back of the couch, hers against his chest. She immediately put her top leg up over his and he slid inside her.

She reached behind him and grabbed a handful of his ass. Barking a laugh into her ear, he circled her clit, lightly at first, then more firmly.

The sun had dipped below the tree line, casting the room in deep shadows. But he didn't need to see anything when he had his arms full of Natalie. She rotated her hips and worked with him, her fingers flexing on his ass in time with his thrusts.

He licked the shell of her ear and she shuddered. "When you're ready, *if* you're ready, I'll make you come at the club in front of whoever feels like paying attention. I don't know if you'll be naked, or fully clothed, but I do know that you'll come so sweetly, because you do, every time. For now, though, I like knowing that they're all for me. Only for me to hear the little sounds you make. Definitely

I'll be the only one feeling your nails digging in as you try to hold off from coming."

"Noah," she breathed.

"Oh, yeah, that's a good sound, there." He nuzzled the hollow behind her ear. "Say it again."

"Noah!" Her voice was higher this time as his fingers pulsed around her clit.

"Don't come yet," he warned her, even though she wasn't wearing his collar. "Wait for me."

She tightened around him, moved her hand from his butt to his head, holding on to his hair. He moved the hand that was under her, having just enough leeway to offer his thumb to her lips. She latched on and sucked him in, bit down.

Fuuuuck. He wasn't sure how much longer he could last. His heart was pounding in his ears like they'd been running a marathon, but he could still hear her moans and gasps. His balls tightened and he had to close his eyes. He pushed into her and held, pinched her clit. "Come now, with me."

He managed to wait for her muscles to spasm around his, and then the electric currents overtook him and he came, hard.

Two seconds later, the night exploded in color. Natalie gasped as the boom of the fireworks chased the lights. Grinning against her ear, he held her tight as the fireworks show lit up the sky and she giggled.

"Okay, that was impressive, Mr. Tucker."

"You're supposed to say explosive."

She convulsed into laughter.

More and more fireworks burst into the night, their reflections rippling over the pond. The show went on for a good fifteen minutes while they watched. Different explosions sounded in the distance behind them. If they'd been outside, they probably could have stood in a way they could see several shows at once. But this was enough. This was more than enough.

CHAPTER NINETEEN

Natalie had felt sad when, after breakfast, Noah put the magnetic collar on instead of her locking collar. The weekend at the cabin had been amazing and part of her never wanted to leave. She hadn't loved everything they'd done, but that had been part of the fun, trying new and different things. Maybe they could come back for another long weekend, when they'd settled in on what kind of play they liked to do together. Then again, she hoped there'd always be room for trying new things.

They'd watched a movie last night, after he'd drawn the curtains, with the occasional boom of fireworks continuing long into the night. This whole weekend she'd slept surprisingly well for being in a strange bed, and sharing it with someone else. She'd cooked their eggs wearing his cuffs and collar while he started the laundry, then he'd packed all his gear away and they'd cleaned the cabin.

The drive home had been easy and when she'd asked him to swing through a drive-through to get a shake, she'd had the odd sensation of wearing the collar while someone else was talking to him. She'd walked into a club wearing a man's collar before, but that seemed like a completely different Natalie. A girl who'd had no clue who she was and what she was capable of.

She'd be proud, she decided, to walk into a club wearing Noah's collar.

She told him she wanted to go to Apex with him, whenever he was ready. The grin of anticipation he shot her made her giddy. When they reached her apartment building, he lucked into a parking space half a block away.

"Hard to believe we left only," he paused and squinted as he calculated "less than seventy hours ago."

"I remember wondering if this was weekend was going to be a waste of both our times, and feeling guilty that it might be. That I would quickly decide that my kinky side was just a phase and not anything I wanted to resurrect. Feels so silly now, to have thought that. And I thought, 'don't get caught up in Noah, he's doing you this favor, don't repay him by hoping for something else.'"

"I thought I was being this magnanimous mentor, donating my time and attention for a good cause. Okay, not really…I thought I'd have a fun weekend of helping you to explore, and that later I'd give you all kinds of advice about who was right for you and who wasn't."

She smirked. "I'm sure I would have been happy for your advice."

He growled. "Oh, I'll be giving you advice all right. Plenty of it."

She smacked a kiss on his lips. "It's a little weird. I've never started a relationship with a nearly seventy-hour sex-a-thon before."

"Think of what we can tell our grandkids," he teased.

She burst out laughing, then sobered when he put his hand on her neck and fiddled with the collar.

"Even though we're starting something new, we haven't really talked about it, or negotiated, and now isn't the time. Our weekend of you following my orders is over when I take this off, so I'm going to ask this of you as a favor."

"All right?"

"I want you to keep in mind what happened yesterday morning. You had sub drop. You could get it again this week. And it might feel like that morning, or totally different. If you start feeling sad or confused for no good reason, call me. Doesn't matter what time. If your brain starts spinning in different directions, call me. If you really don't want to call me, or text me, call Annalise."

"Oh. Okay. I can do that."

"Good. I'll be in touch, too, but I don't want to be a creepy stalker." He leered at her.

She laughed, but it only lasted a minute because he gently pulled the collar off and tucked it into his pocket.

"I'm sorry you have to go to work today," she said, focusing on the fact that he wasn't walking away, he would be putting a collar on her again, in the future.

"It'll be fine. Give me something to concentrate on rather than thoughts of you, naked and willing and ready."

They got out of the car and he grabbed her bag. He walked her to her apartment and put the bag on her couch, then pulled her into a hug. "Thank you for an amazing weekend." His voice was rough, his arms tight around her.

"Stupendous," she said, her throat tight. She didn't want to let him go. She was afraid it would all turn out to be a really intricate dream and next time she saw him, he'd just be Alec's best friend who'd give her a friendly smile.

"I'll call you after I get home tonight." He cupped her face in his hands and kissed her. "But you promised, so I'll expect a call or text if you start to feel droppy."

"Yes, Noah."

He grinned and left. She locked the door behind him and dropped to the couch. Then she called Annalise.

"Oh. My. God," she began when her friend answered. And gave her a highly edited version of events. Annalise teased her about having been right about Natalie and Noah all along, and she could only grin into the phone.

When she finally hung up, she looked around her apartment, feeling a little out of touch with the life she'd led before getting in his car. Not only was she now a woman with a kinky side, she was a woman starting a new relationship. It had been a while.

The apartment felt stuffy from being closed up, so she opened all the windows, put an audio book on and her earbuds in, and started to clean. When she took a break for lunch, she sent Noah a text with the number one and a smiley face. He responded with a thumbs up and a kissy face.

When she finished with the bathroom, she unpacked and dropped onto the couch, falling into a nap almost instantly. She dreamt that she and Noah were on the public swings on the Lawn on D. The public park had installed giant adult-sized swings, wide circles that lit up at night and could fit more than one person at a time. She was naked and Noah was making love to her while other —fully clothed—people went about their evening, paying them no attention.

She woke up with a start when her phone rang.

"Sonya and Alec are at the hospital," Annalise told her when she answered. "She's in labor, but it's probably going to be a while."

"Do they want people there, or do they want privacy?"

"They don't mind if we come by, but only her mom will be in the room with them once things progress. There's a restaurant across the street. We were thinking of going to the hospital for a quick hello, then going to dinner to get out of the way, but still be close if it goes faster than they expect. I'll pick you up in fifteen?"

"I'll be ready."

She loved that it was assumed she would be there. But that if she had a reason not to be, that would be understood, as well. After her dad had died and her aunt and uncle had moved away, it had just been her mom and her grandparents. It was fine, she'd been loved, in a quiet sort of way. It had taken time to get used to the boisterous and insistent version of love and family in the Weber-Crawford clan.

Annalise was grinning from ear to ear when Natalie hopped into her car. "I'm gonna be an auntie!"

Natalie laughed. "You are, it's going to be awesome."

They chatted on the way to the hospital, Annalise practically bouncing with her excitement. They stuck their heads into Sonya's room and were waved inside.

Sonya looked tired but excited. Alec looked excited but nervous.

"The nurses say it will be several hours at least," Alec said. "I hear you guys are going out to dinner." He kept talking as Sonya started a contraction. She gripped his hand, and he rubbed her shoulder and kissed her temple.

"I'm jealous," Sonya panted. "I don't get to eat. Doesn't seem fair."

"Can we sneak you in something?" Annalise asked. Her eyes were wide and she looked a little green.

The contraction ended and Annalise relaxed and grinned. "No, I'm just whining. I have an endless supply of ice chips, I'll be fine. But when it's over, I'd really love something sweet. And chocolate."

"Ooh, have you tried the pastries from that new place?" Annalise grabbed her phone and pulled up the website to show her sister-in-law.

Alec pulled Natalie to the side and scrutinized her face. "You had a good weekend?"

She smiled, loving that he cared. "Yes, it was awesome." She hesitated. She wasn't sure if Noah had said anything to Alec yet. It had only been a few hours, and he might want to be the one to tell his best friend that they were starting something together.

Alec's lips quirked. "Noah's needed someone like you for a long time. I'm glad he recognized that."

"Someone like me?" she teased.

"Someone kind and giving but with plenty of backbone."

Curious, she cocked her head. "And how do you know I have that?"

"Who waded in and got Uncle Harvey to back down from fighting that umpire at his son's baseball game? And who convinced Grandma that giving up her driver's license meant she would get to see her grandkids and great grandkids *more*, not less, ending the battle that had raged for two weeks? I could go on."

"Huh."

He laughed and slung an arm around her shoulders, dragging

her back to the bed to hold Sonya's hand through the next contraction.

"Are you sure it's going to be hours?" Natalie asked. "Maybe we should stay at the hospital, the contractions are a lot."

"Apparently this is nothing and it's going to get a lot worse." Sonya grimaced then patted her husband's arm when sweat popped out on his forehead. "It will be worth it, though."

"Suddenly adoption seems like a really worthy goal," Annalise muttered. Natalie couldn't disagree.

Sonya's mom came back, so Natalie and Annalise headed out to grab chocolate pastries from the bakery, then over to the restaurant. The family already had a table and they squeezed in, Natalie ending up next to Ophelia, Alec and Annalise's mom. She was beaming and chattering with excitement. Although she had grand nieces and nephews, this would be her first grandbaby.

"And what about you, my lovely?" she asked Natalie as they gathered up their leftovers. "When are you going to give me more babies to spoil?"

Nat laughed. "You haven't even had a chance to spoil this one yet. Wait, that's not true, I've seen the nursery."

"There will be plenty to go around. Cousins are a blessing, and this one will—" She broke off, then wrapped Natalie in a hug. "Oh, sweetheart, I'm sorry."

"Don't be. Cousins *are* important, and I hope I'll add to the brood. Nothing would make me happier than for my children to grow up part of this family."

Ophelia kissed her forehead. "You know, in this day and age, you don't even really need a man if you want to get started now."

"Ophelia Crawford-Weber, I thought you'd be on my side in this." Noah's strong voice wrapped around Natalie's senses as his arms wrapped around her waist.

NOAH HADN'T EXPECTED to see Natalie less than ten hours after he'd dropped her off at home, but he was pleased that he was. And very pleased when she leaned back into him and raised her head up to smile at him. He dropped a kiss on her lips.

Ophelia's eyes went wide with delight. She brought her hands up in front of her mouth. "Yes? Really? Two of my favorite people, together like this?"

"No promises for babies, as this is very, very new," Natalie said. "But I'm going to need your recipe for chicken noodle stir fry. If I remember right, that's one of Noah's favorites. I'm going to invite him for dinner this week and I need to wow him. We'll see how things go from there."

He liked that she'd noticed what his favorite meal was. "She could probably wow me with burnt toast," he told Ophelia.

The older woman clapped her hands, but was distracted by half a dozen phones beeping in unison. A group message from Alec was letting them know that the baby was on its way.

They headed over to the hospital, Noah holding Natalie's hand and getting a thumbs up in approval from Annalise. He hoped things worked out with Natalie, not only because he liked her a hell of a lot, but because he was pretty sure he'd get shit for it if things went south. He wasn't worried they'd kick him to the curb, but it would probably suck for a while.

When Alec brought out Matthew Isaac Weber to meet them, Noah felt a little kick in his gut. The instant, intense love was almost staggering, and for the first time in his life, he could truly imagine being a father. As Annalise held her nephew, Noah and Natalie crowded in close. He rubbed his finger along the downy head while Natalie caressed the round cheek.

"Wow," Annalise whispered. "These things come out of us. That's just so crazy."

They laughed and passed the baby around, then went in to say goodbye to the beaming but exhausted parents, and offer up the pastries to a thankful Sonya. Noah pulled Natalie aside while Annalise was hugging her brother.

"You can come home with me," he offered.

"Tempting. Very tempting. But I have to be at work at eight, on the opposite side of town. And I suspect we wouldn't get a ton of sleep."

It was nearly midnight and she was right. "All right. But I'll drive you home."

"Annalise lives three blocks from me. You live three neighborhoods from me."

He sighed dramatically and lowered his forehead to hers. "If you don't want to see me anymore, just say so."

Her giggle made him smile.

"I mean, I still plan to use your body quite a bit, you're not getting out of this *that* easily."

"Good to know." He kissed her and watched as she and Annalise walked to the car, arm in arm.

When he got home, he was both wired and exhausted. He sent a picture of the baby to his family chat and wasn't at all surprised when his mother called.

"He's beautiful, you tell Alec and Sonya we send our love."

"I will, Mom. How was your Fourth?"

She told him about the barbecue block party with her neighbors and the mostly friendly potato salad contest that had developed.

"I didn't feel the need to get involved," she told him. "I just sat back and got to taste all the effort. What about you, did you go to Leon's?"

"No, he went to someone's beach house with Cedric, so I took advantage of Cedric's cabin being empty and went out there with a friend for the weekend."

"What kind of friend?" He could practically here her waggling her eyebrows.

He laughed and leaned back into the couch, the tiredness starting to pull at him. "Well, we didn't fish, but we did use the canoe once."

"I see. A whole weekend at the cabin and you only went out on the water once, and didn't fish. Interesting."

His mom prided herself on not being the kind of mother who tried to push her children into anything, though she always had their backs. Her own mother had made it very clear she expected her daughter to get married at a young age and start producing babies, which had driven her crazy. She'd sworn not to do the same.

"Her name is Natalie, and I like her. A lot."

He grinned at the pleased sigh that traveled through the phone. "Then I hope it works out. I want you to be happy."

"I know. It's early days yet, but I can see myself being happy with Natalie. She's Alec's sister's best friend, so we've sort of known each other for a while, but now…now it's different. Everything's different with her."

He didn't know how to explain it. He just felt it, knew it to be true.

A suspicious sniffling reached his ears, and he grinned. His mother was a sap. "How's the garden doing?" He'd planted it on his last trip out there. It was the second time he'd done it for them since they'd moved to Arizona. His mother blamed the change in climate for their lack of success, but she hadn't been much of a gardener in Oregon, either. He didn't mind.

"I'll send you proof of life tomorrow."

His father got on the phone to ask him what he thought about them renting an RV and driving up to his sister's, then out to Boston. They discussed possibilities for a while, until he was yawning every time he opened his mouth.

The garden center had been busy and he'd been on the floor, helping customers, from the moment he'd arrived. He hung up with his parents and took a quick shower. When he climbed into bed, it felt big and empty. Despite that, he fell asleep quickly and dreamed very good dreams about his blonde temptress.

CHAPTER TWENTY

Natalie fended off teasing coworkers as she walked out of the office with the Chess pie she'd removed from the fridge. She'd made two, sharing one with the appreciative staff, and threatening bodily harm if they touched the second.

"Let me guess," Edgar asked, holding the door open for her. "This is for the same guy who sent you flowers last week?"

She grinned. Noah had sent a small but beautiful arrangement of mostly orange flowers last week, after she'd made him dinner at her place. Tonight, he was making dinner, and she'd promised to bring the pie.

"You're so smart, Ed," she ribbed as he followed her to her car. She clicked the remote and he opened that door, too, so she could set the pie safely on the passenger seat.

"He's a lucky guy. I hope he knows it."

"He acts like he knows it." And it was true. Noah treated her like he was lucky and thankful whenever he saw her. Like he was still chasing her, even though she was well and truly caught. "He's making dinner tonight." And after, they'd be making their debut trip to Apex. She shivered as she got into her seat, waving Edgar off.

Noah had helped her pick out an outfit from an online store, one that would make her feel like she wasn't naked but was risqué enough she wouldn't wear it anywhere else. He'd promised her she could wear jeans and a tank top and be just fine, but she wanted to feel sexy and submissive and not like they were just out on a regular date.

She'd had the dress shipped to his house and had modeled it for him to make sure it fit and was appropriate. They'd been late to meet up with Annalise and visit Alec, Sonya and the baby after that, but she'd been assured that the dress would do just fine.

Tonight, they'd be going to the club after dinner. Sonya and Alec had planned to go, but her friend had texted her at lunch time to say she just wasn't ready to leave the baby with a sitter yet—even though the sitter was her mom. Natalie reassured her that she understood one hundred percent. Little Matty was only three weeks old, and his parents were thoroughly besotted with him. So was Natalie.

When she pulled up in front of Noah's house, he came to meet her before she managed to get her purse and bag and the pie and get out of the car. He took the pie and her bag and gave her a deep kiss. It was still kind of hard to believe that they were together. *Freaking* Noah Tucker. *Gorgeous* Noah Tucker.

They'd spent most of their nights together these last few weeks, and he'd done an excellent job of convincing her that they were, in fact, together. He was sweet and kind and dominating and patient and giving and fucking hell, she already loved him so much. She tried to tell herself it was too fast, too soon, too easy, too much. But she didn't listen. If it fell apart, she was just going to have to deal with the fallout later. For now, she was going to enjoy every minute of their time together, and work hard to make it last.

They'd fallen into a routine of weeknights that were "normal", going out to dinner or cooking, watching television or playing games. And weekends that included her wearing his collar, and everything that entailed. Not the whole time. Last weekend they'd spent Saturday afternoon with her in bonds and him wielding a flogger. It had been incredible. Then they'd gone to the museum on Sunday and out to dinner with Uncle Leon.

The weekend before, he'd told her their destination was a surprise, and they'd ended up at the swings on the Lawn on D. She'd told him about her dream, and he'd held her as they swung, whispering naughty fantasies about slipping his fingers inside her pussy, or bending her over the swing and taking her from behind as everyone enjoyed the show.

She'd been hot as hell by the time they'd made it home and then he'd tied her up and masturbated in front of her, which had made her scream in frustration. He'd made it up to her by licking and sucking her until she was mindless with need and had come twice before he fucked her with the dildo he'd found in her bedside table.

"Dinner will be ready in ten minutes," he promised as he led her to the kitchen and put the pie in the fridge. "Come here." He turned and leaned against the counter and beckoned her with a finger.

She pretended to consider the idea. "Or what?"

"Or I won't spank you later?" he asked.

Laughing, she went to him and wrapped her arms around his neck. His phone rang, and he let out an aggrieved sigh. She leaned back so he could fish it out of his back pocket.

"It's my mom, and she wants to do video call." He rolled his eyes. "She knew you were coming over for dinner. Do you mind?"

She turned around in his arms and leaned against his chest so that he could hold the phone up and they were both visible. Helen Tucker appeared on the screen, Oliver peering over her shoulder. She grinned broadly when she saw that Noah wasn't alone.

"Hi Mom, Dad. Meet Natalie."

"It's so nice to meet you, dear. Leon told me you all had a lovely dinner last weekend for Noah's birthday."

"We did, he's such a nice man." Noah's uncle had insisted that she join them for the belated celebration of Noah's late-June birthday. Since they hadn't been together for his birthday, she didn't think she should get him a real present, but she had ordered some bondage cuffs that had a big bow on them, and surprised him with them later that night. He'd expressed joyful appreciation for the gift.

Natalie found Helen to be easy to talk to, with Oliver and Noah interjecting on occasion. When the timer on the stove went off, Noah handed her the phone and she continued the conversation until he'd made up their plates and brought them to the table.

"They're nice," she said as she took a look at her plate. "Oh, you made our first dinner." Baked chicken thighs, roasted squash and rice. "But you didn't do it naked."

"There are several perks to being the Dom," he noted.

"I see that."

They ate in silence for a few minutes until he leaned over and pulled her lip from between her teeth. "You're chewing on the wrong thing. What's wrong?"

"Nothing's wrong, I'm just nervous."

"About going to the club tonight."

"Yes."

"We've already agreed we're not going to do a scene, so what's making you nervous. Seeing something that will upset you? Or just memories of the last time you were at a club?"

"No." She didn't really want to say but she couldn't lie and knew he'd get it out of her anyway. She got up and dished them pie to give herself some time, but then told him. "About making a good impression on your friends."

He burst out laughing, and she glared at him. "Noah!"

"I'm sorry, Nattie, but that's just ridiculous. Unless you suddenly turn into an entirely different person when we walk through the doors, there's no way you could make a bad impression."

Well, that sort of made her feel better. She took a bite of pie. "The thing is, it's not like you're just a regular member. You're a monitor and a mentor. The members respect you and some of them look up to you. They'll be checking to see if I'm good enough for you. And I haven't got a single doubt that there are some submissives there who are going to be upset you're no longer available."

He'd gone to the club twice to pull monitoring duty, and had been worried she'd be upset about that. She loved that he was there to keep people safe and secure while they played. She trusted him to not cheat on her. He'd been very clear about what kind of touching he might do while there, and she was fine with what he'd described.

"Would you rather go to a different club?" he asked. "I can tell you that my friends will welcome you, and I don't really care what anyone else thinks, and will have words with anyone who tries to treat you badly, but if it's something you're really worried about, we can have your first experience somewhere else. I know a few other clubs I'd be willing to go to with you."

She sighed. "No, it's fine. I'll be fine. But thank you, I appreciate that you made the offer."

"Let me know if you change your mind." He checked his watch. "You better get dressed. I'll put away the dishes."

She blinked and looked at her own watch. "I thought you said you wanted to leave at eight-thirty?" It was only just after seven.

"Yes, but I'm pretty sure I'm going to need to fuck you once I see you in your dress again, and I don't mean a quickie."

She stared at him, jaw open. He picked up their plates and headed for the kitchen.

⁂

NOAH HELD Natalie's hand as they entered Apex. The club was its usual Saturday night full, music loud enough to feel, but not so loud it impeded on conversations too much.

He'd fucked a lot of the nerves out of her before they'd left, which had been his plan. Then he'd had her kneel so he could put his collar on her, while she was still naked, her lips swollen from his kisses and her inner thighs still red from his beard.

"Whose job is it to make sure that things go all right tonight, Petal?" he'd asked as he clicked the lock into place.

She'd licked her lips. "Yours, Sir."

It hadn't been the most emphatic statement.

"And how am I going to do that, since I'm not a mind reader?"

The little line had appeared between her eyebrows, then it had cleared. "I'll tell you if I start to feel uncomfortable. Or worried. Or scared."

"That's my girl." He interlaced their fingers, holding her hand in the normal way. "You have my permission to hold my hand at any time while we're at Apex." He let go and wrapped her hand around one of his fingers. "If you do this, I'll know you're at one." He moved her fingers so that she was holding two of his fingers. "Two. Like that. You can grip my whole hand if you get to five. It's different than when we're holding hands and our fingers are interlaced. All right?"

She'd nodded and practiced grabbing his fingers. Then she'd kissed him. "Thank you, Sir."

He'd ordered wrist and ankle cuffs to match her orange collar, but they hadn't come in yet. If she decided she was ready to play at the club soon, he'd save them for that night, as a special treat.

Now she held his hand tightly, but he could see her begin to relax as the club was presented. They'd entered a large room, with a hallway on the opposite side, which led to individual rooms for play. A bar took the space to their left and a stage to their right, with conversation areas dotted between them and several play stations on either side of the stage. A small retail area next to the bar sold some toys, clothes and essentials like condoms and lube.

A Saint Andrew's Cross had been set up on one end of the stage and a set of stocks on the other. Both were being used, giving those in the conversation areas a good show, if they chose to watch.

The dress varied widely. Some wore jeans and shirts, like him. Some wore nothing but collars and cuffs. There was leather, latex, and lace aplenty. A lot of corsets, some with nipples showing, some without. Natalie's black mini dress fit right in. It had wide lace panels up both sides, allowing a tantalizing view of thigh and breasts, and a vinyl-like center that barely covered her nipples and was only inches below her pussy. A lace V at both of those positions allowed for a peek at those points, less than her sides, but enough to fire the imagination.

He brought her to the bar and introduced her to Marcos, one of the club managers, who was currently offering drinks. He requested waters and let her take a seat on the stool, then stood between her legs. It meant that her dress was stretched wide, but no one could see since he was covering her. She narrowed her eyes at him but didn't say anything. The stool was high enough that she could see over his shoulder, it also meant she could watch the room from around him, get a sense of it, without everyone seeing her.

He put his hand on her thigh and she wrapped her fingers around his index finger. Good to go.

Marcos gave him a rundown of the few interesting things that had happened since he'd last been there, and they both pretended not to notice as Natalie's nerves waned and her curiosity rose. She'd moved her hand to his biceps and was leaning forward, trying to get a better look at the action.

After a few minutes, he put his water down next to her untouched glass. "Ready to get closer, Petal?"

"Yes, Sir."

She snapped her legs together the second he stepped free of them, and used his offered hand to hop down from the stool. Her ankle booties were higher than she normally wore, so he tucked her hand into his arm and made sure she was steady before walking across the room.

His friend Eric was on monitoring duties, so he headed there first. Eric was keeping an eye on the whole play area on this side of the stage, but clearly had most of his attention focused on the two ladies working in the giant web. The Domme had her submissive wrapped up in the straps and was teasing her with a whip.

Eric didn't take his eyes off the scene when he greeted Noah, until he introduced Natalie.

"Great to meet you, Natalie. Let me know if you have any questions about any of this. I'm here to help." He gave her a genuine smile, then returned his gaze to the ladies. "Are you two going to play today?"

"No, just giving Nat a feel for the place. They look like they're having a good time."

"Yeah, Penny asked me to keep an eye out since it's her first time using the web, but she's got it all under control. I don't think Ayla has any complaints." The bound woman was screaming in pleasure.

Natalie chuckled next to him. "We'll leave you to it," Noah said, and maneuvered Natalie to a seat where she could watch a couple of scenes at the same time. He'd recognized a Daddy Dom and his little girl exploring the play areas, and kept an eye on them, but they settled in a spot too far away for Natalie to hear them over the music.

Noah brought Natalie into his lap in the wide chair and wrapped his arms around her. "See those three?" He indicated the trio in front of them. "The one holding the flogger is Grant. The one chained to the frame is Jesse. And the blonde with the green streak in her hair, kneeling at Grant's feet...and oh, unzipping his pants... is Stephanie. They're friends of mine, so we'll probably chat with them if they don't leave after they're done."

She watched as Stephanie drew Grant's cock into her mouth, his hand firm in her hair, directing her. The cat o' nine tails he was holding swished at his side, then gently caressed Stephanie's ass, before he suddenly flicked it across Jesse's thighs.

"Are they just playing together, or are they partners?" Natalie asked, after jumping slightly in his arms.

"They're all together."

"That must be a lot of work for Grant," she mused.

"That's what I said." He grinned in appreciation as Grant continued to flog Jesse while Stephanie worked him. After a few minutes, Grant gave Stephanie a command and she tucked him back into his pants and went to Jesse. She latched onto his nipples as Grant stalked behind Jesse's back.

The scene continued, and Grant directed Stephanie and flogged Jesse until both of the submissives were squirming and begging. Grant smashed Stephanie between his body and Jesse's and worked them both in ways the audience couldn't quite see, until they cried out in release.

"Wow," Natalie whispered. "That was really hot."

"Are you imagining yourself up there, with two men?"

She ducked her head. "No, Sir, just with one person."

"Is it Jesse?" he teased.

Her laughter was sweet music. "No, Sir, Stephanie."

"She is pretty hot, but I don't think she can give you what you need."

Her fingers wrapped themselves up into his shirt. "Only you, Sir."

"Good girl. Are you wet, imagining yourself up there with me?"

"Yes, Sir."

"Maybe next time I'll strap a butterfly vibe to your clit when we come. Of course, if I've got you strapped up, I might as well put a plug in your ass, too. So you can feel me from the inside. How would that be?"

"I—I—if that's what you want, Sir."

He smiled at her dilated eyes. "I don't think you could come from that alone, but I wonder if I sat you in my lap like this and we watched some of the scenes, if that would do it. What do you think?"

"Probably, Sir. Especially if you talked to me the whole time."

While they'd been chatting, the trio had cleaned up the area and moved away for aftercare. A new couple was getting set up to use the frame. He looked around to see what else she might find interesting, but spotted a sub he recognized with their sights set on him.

The lithe subbie had short, spiky hair, lots of eyeliner and an infectious laugh that never failed to make Noah smile. They knelt at the side of the chair he was sitting in and waited to be addressed.

"Natalie, this is Faryn. They've been a member here for several years and would most likely be happy to answer any questions you have when I'm not around, or it's not my opinion you're looking for. Faryn, this is my Natalie, she has some experience in the scene, but not a lot."

"Thank you, Mister Noah, that's a great compliment. It's nice to meet you, Natalie."

Natalie squirmed around in his arms so she'd have a better angle to talk with Faryn. "It's nice to meet you, too. Your top is amazing, I love it so much. Your whole outfit, really, but the top especially."

Faryn grinned at her, but turned their attention to Noah. "Mister Noah, I'm sorry to interrupt. Mister Shawn asked me to see if you had a few minutes to show him that hold you were telling him about last week. He understands if now's not a good time."

Noah looked around to find Shawn in the direction Faryn indicated. The top was on the far side of the stage, fairly close to where the Daddy and his little were playing. He looked down to Natalie. "I'd rather you didn't go over there right now. If you don't mind staying right here, it should only take about fifteen minutes. But if you're not comfortable with that, I'll stay here and work with Shawn another time."

CHAPTER TWENTY-ONE

Natalie reassured Noah that she was fine and he should go help his friend. She grabbed his finger to reassure him that she was good with it. He kissed her—a soul-deep kiss that left her wide-eyed and breathless when he stood—turned to deposit her back into the chair, and strode away.

"Wow," Faryn said.

"Right? Whew." Natalie fanned her face, then dragged her attention from watching Noah to the person still kneeling at her feet. "Don't feel like you have to stay and keep me company, but if you want to, then you *have* to tell me where you got that top."

Faryn laughed and got up, dragged a nearby chair closer and sprawled into it like a teenager. "I made it." The top appeared to be black pleather, a simple band that went around the back and tied in the front with a big bow. "But I bought the boy shorts."

"I don't think I could hold something like that up, but it looks fantastic on you."

"Well, you're working that dress just fine. How are you liking things here? Is it as you expected?"

Natalie nodded. "Yes and no. It's been years since I've been to a club like this, and this is nicer than where I'd gone. But the energy, the atmosphere, it's great. I was so young and nervous when I went before, I found it kind of scary." A loud scream rent the air in perfect timing, and she and Faryn grinned at each other.

"It's been ages since I've seen Mister Noah with someone, it's awesome to see him happy."

"He's amazing. I've known him for a while, but only from a distance. And I didn't know about this." She waved her hand at the club in general. "I'm not sure how long it will take me to be comfortable playing in public like the screamer, there, but it's certainly fun to get some ideas." She gestured to the group that had formed nearby. They seemed to be doing yoga poses. Naked yoga poses. With a lot of inserting of body parts into other body parts. "Not that Noah lacks in ideas."

"The exhibitionism can be fun for the right people, but there's also the theme rooms in back. Plus, you don't have to worry about your neighbors calling the cops when you scream."

"That is a definite benefit. He took me to a cabin out in the woods where the neighbors were far away, but we still had to be careful of people wandering by on the lake."

"Ooh, a weekend in the woods, sounds like you passed the test." Faryn's grin was mischievous as they waggled their eyebrows at her.

Natalie had the oddest sensation of feeling her lips go numb. She sort of froze and waited for the feeling to go away as her brain kept hearing Faryn's voice saying "test" over and over.

"Test?" she managed to squeak out.

"Too see if you're into a 24/7 relationship, right? It's not for everyone, having your Dom be in charge of things outside the bedroom." Faryn's grin faded away into a look of distress. "Oh. I've said something wrong, I'm so sorry. Don't listen to me, I was just making assumptions. I shouldn't have done that, it wasn't on purpose. I barely knew Mister Noah or his slave Janey when they were together, I don't know what I'm talking about. I was trying to make you feel comfortable, and I've screwed it up and I'm babbling and I'll shut up, I'm so sorry, I'll go get him."

"No! No, it's fine, sit down, you're fine. I'm fine. I just...I—well, that's not really where we are with things, so it just threw me off." Noah wasn't testing her, that wasn't what the weekend had been about. She *knew* that. But was he hoping to lead her into a 24/7 dynamic? It didn't feel like that. They'd talked about where they were and had agreed on the level of play, and he'd seemed to be on the same page with her. Was he grooming her to want more and more time in the collar? Was that something she could live with?

"Please let me help you," Faryn said with earnest eyes. "I screwed up, let me help. What's wrong?"

Natalie pulled her focus back to the other sub and took a deep breath. "It's okay, it really is. I guess you could say test is a trigger word for me. I had an asshole Dom who screwed me up years ago. But I know, one hundred percent, that Noah wasn't testing me, *and* I know you didn't really mean it like a real test, anyway."

"I didn't. It was a stupid way to be excited that you got to spend a whole weekend locked away with him, and then he brought you here. You should tell him about this. And tell him that if I deserve a punishment, I'll absolutely own up to it."

Natalie glared at them. "You did nothing wrong, and if you keep thinking you did, I'll have to paddle your ass myself."

"Well, I leave for fifteen minutes and come back to my sub threatening to beat you. Well done, Faryn." Noah rounded the chair and scooped Natalie up and resumed his seat.

Natalie burst out laughing, which finally seemed to do the trick of reassuring Faryn that they hadn't screwed up.

"If you're actively trying to earn a spanking, you're going to have to set your sights elsewhere," Natalie told them.

Faryn pretended to pout, despite the twinkle in their eye. "A person has to work so hard to get spanked around here."

A big bear of a man had been walking past them and he stopped to palm the back of Faryn's neck. "Is that right, little Faryn?"

Natalie tensed, but Noah put a calming hand on her thigh. Faryn's eyes went wide, but not with distress, as far as Natalie could tell. They twisted their head to meet the Dom's gaze. Something unspoken passed between them, and then Faryn twisted around and put their feet down, sitting primly in the chair, hands on their knees.

"Hello, Master Owen, it's nice to see you again."

Owen walked around to the front of the chair and squatted down in front of the sub. Natalie felt like she was watching an intimate moment, and Noah must have agreed. Without saying anything to the other two, he stood and walked several steps before lowering her legs.

Natalie rested her head against Noah's shoulder, suddenly exhausted. They'd only been at the club a couple of hours, but the music, the visuals, the nerves, the stress, the excitement, the emotions…it was all adding up to a lot, and she kind of wanted to be home. She looked up to tell Noah, but he cupped her face in his hands and kissed her. She gave herself to it, willing her body and mind to rally for whatever he wanted of her.

When he broke the kiss, he watched her face for several seconds. "Let's go home."

She smiled and nodded.

On the drive home, she considered how she wanted to tell him about the conversation with Faryn. There was no question that she should tell him. But now that she was out of the club, she was trying to analyze her upset.

The idea that Noah would test her like that was absurd, it had just taken her brain a minute to get past its initial freak-out over the word. Had the mention of Noah's ex-girlfriend been part of the problem, as well? She wanted to ask him, *would* ask him, if it had been a Master/slave relationship, as Faryn had indicated.

But what would it mean, for her? He'd never indicated he might be interested in that, for them. And it had been clear to her, after the weekend of experimentation, that *she* wasn't interested in it.

Maybe he'd planned to negotiate more control over her daily life? It wouldn't suck to have someone, say…decide what she was going to wear every day. But that was just because she wasn't a morning person, yet never remembered to pick her outfits out before bed. Besides, she had no idea if he had good taste in women's clothing. Regardless, the idea didn't sit well with her. Not at all.

And…this was all a ridiculous train of thought. They'd discuss it later. Mm, maybe over pie.

They pulled up in front of his house, and she couldn't believe they were already home. He distracted her from her disjointed thoughts by pulling her into the house, undressing her, tying her to his headboard and proceeding to torment her with long kisses all over her body and slow movements designed to make her insane. He ordered her to come whenever she wanted, as long as she said his name first. And then he drove her to peak after peak, whispering her name as he worshiped her body. A tiny voice at the back of her head whispered to her that maybe this was worth giving herself to him—in all ways—if that's what he wanted. She pushed the thought away, concentrated on his amber eyes as they seemed to stare into her very soul. He was *already* giving her this, and all she'd needed to do was give him her heart.

They lay in a sweaty heap for several minutes before he pulled her into his lap. "I love you, Natalie."

Her heart nearly burst, pulling her out of the exhausted stupor. She flung her arms around him and hugged him tight. Tears were leaking from her eyes, but she couldn't stop smiling. "I love you too, Noah."

He removed her collar and they went into the bathroom to clean up. When they'd finished and she was ready to collapse into a coma, he turned her toward the bathroom mirror. "Close your eyes."

She did, startled to feel something light touch her throat.

"Open them."

Her reflection showed a delicate rose, in full bloom, nestled in the hollow of her throat. It was dark orange, two delicate leaves flanking either side. From the rose, a double row of pewter chains wrapped around her neck. Tiny triangular thorns were spaced every few inches along the chains. Her eyes were huge in the mirror as he leaned down and kissed the little thorn closest to him.

Her brain stuttered to a stop. A choker. A collar. A day collar?

Isn't that what this was? A collar to be worn 24/7, to show she was owned by him? He'd told her he loved her, and she'd done the same, so maybe, in his mind, this was what followed?

She clamped down on her frantic thoughts. That didn't make sense. It wasn't what they'd discussed. She just needed to talk to him. Ask him what it meant.

"Is it—does it lock?" she managed.

"It does." He gave her a wicked grin and held up a little tool. "It c—"

Something shot through her and she didn't even know what the hell it was. Not fear. Not panic, exactly. *Maybe?* But it was heavy and hot and real and she couldn't think, not with Noah's warm body behind her and his grinning face reflected in the mirror in front of her. She should have talked him into pie before sex, so they could talk when her brain wasn't...whatever the hell it was right now, because all she could think was *wrong*, this was wrong, this wasn't what they'd talked about, wasn't what they'd agreed on.

She knew what to do when a scene went past what she'd agreed to. What she could handle.

"Four. Five. No, four. I don't know. Can you please take it off?"

His hands had frozen on her shoulders when she'd interrupted him, and he just stared at her in the mirror for several seconds.

Her heart was beating out of her throat and she knew she *was* panicking and it was crazy, this was all crazy, this was Noah, he wouldn't hurt her, he wouldn't push her into something she didn't want, but it was Noah and she wanted to give him whatever made him happy, but she couldn't—

"Natalie," he barked, and her eyes flew open.

He'd unhooked the collar and was holding it out toward the mirror to show her.

"I have to go." She pulled in a shuddering breath and turned to the door, pulling away from him.

"Natalie, no, we need to talk about whatever this is." He reached out for her and she jerked back.

They did need to talk, but she couldn't, not right now. Not until she could stop her brain from spinning in a hundred different directions. And not where he surrounded her, where just being touched by him made her body want to surrender to him, completely.

"I can't. I need to go." Tomorrow, they could talk tomorrow. Pull out the fucking pie. She forced back a sob. Right now, while it felt like everything was falling apart, wasn't the right time to talk. Which wasn't fair to him. She wasn't being fair to him. Maybe she wasn't right for him, she wasn't right for any of this, she just didn't understand how it all worked, obviously. She kept fucking it up, misconstruing what was happening and turning it all around in her head until she thought she understood...

She shook her head and threw on her clothes.

"Natalie. This isn't okay. You can't just run off like this. Regardless of anything else, it's not safe to drive."

She was so tired, so numb.

"I need you to trust me, Natalie. I need you to stay so we can figure this out."

She was the last thing he needed. Why didn't he see that? No, no, that wasn't right. She just needed to get her head clear. To be alone, so she could get her head clear. So she could *think*.

"I'm sorry. I'm so sorry. I have to go." She brushed past him, unable to look at him, her bag overflowing with everything she could cram into it.

"You can't drive." His voice had gone cold.

"I'll call for a ride." She pulled out her phone and clicked the app open. "There's one four minutes away." She forced herself to look up at his face, but only lasted a second. It had gone carefully blank, showing her nothing. "I'm sorry."

She turned and walked out the door.

***

WHEN NATALIE WOKE UP, she felt as though she was hungover. She'd been incredibly exhausted when she'd gotten home, but she'd been unable to sleep, had simply cried for hours. At some point, she must have drifted off, because now she was awake, blinking against the late-morning light streaming through the windows, and she hurt. Head, body, heart.

What had she done?

Her hand went to her throat. It was bare, but in her mind she could see the beautiful necklace that had seemed so dark and sinister to her muddled brain. It had seemed so clear that she'd misunderstood the relationship Noah wanted with her. That she'd made it into what she wanted it to be, when all along it was something else.

But now…now that seemed really fucking ridiculous.

Noah was not the type to pretend. But the thing was, everything they'd done, since that day at Alec and Sonya's, had been about what she wanted. Or what she needed. She'd asked Noah what he'd wanted, that weekend at the cabin, and he'd said it was about her, finding out what worked for her.

But after that, when they'd transitioned into an actual relationship, they *had* talked about what they wanted, what both of them wanted. He wouldn't have strung her along, trying to get her far enough into him that she would just give in to a completely different dynamic when he told her he loved her. That wasn't Noah.

It was hard to even understand how her brain had been spinning last night. The club had been wonderful, but *so* much. And then he'd overwhelmed her senses in amazing ways, and told her he loved her. She'd felt it, believed it. And felt the same.

She groaned and held her head tightly as if she could keep her splitting headache from bursting out of her eyeballs.

*Stupid, stupid…*how could she be so fucking stupid?

She forced herself to get up and take something for her head, drink a glass of water. She made herself take a fast shower, and then ordered a car. She was going to have to beg, and hope Noah could forgive her.

NOAH HEARD the vehicle arrive at his house. He wasn't surprised. Natalie had left her car behind, and a few belongings. The question would be, did she bother to retrieve what was still in the house, or would she just get in her car and leave, without facing him? He figured chances were about even.

So when the knock came on the door, he simply opened it and handed her the bag he'd filled with her things. He'd had all night to gather stuff up, since he hadn't slept, hadn't even bothered to lie down. If he closed his eyes, he'd just see her flinching away from his touch. Over and over again. Filling the bag with her stuff had only taken a few minutes. She hadn't been in his life long enough to leave much behind.

She looked like shit, but he forced the thought away. She was staring at the bag he held out like it was full of spiders.

"Can we talk?" she asked, her voice hitching on the last word. "I came to apologize."

A spark of hope began to worm its way through the ice encasing his heart. He waved her in. She took a seat on the sofa and stared at her hands.

"Last night...I'm so sorry, Noah. I fucked up."

"How?"

She jerked at his voice, but didn't look up. "Because I left without talking to you."

He took a deep breath. She was here. She was apologizing. She was communicating. He sat on the coffee table in front of her, but he didn't touch her. "Can you tell me what happened?"

She nodded. "It was the collar. The necklace. Can you tell me what it meant to you? What you meant it to be, for us?"

He frowned. He wanted to hear what she'd been thinking, not explain himself. She was shaking, though, her hands clasped between her knees, her whole body hunched over. He wanted to pull her into his lap, but he forced himself to stay still.

"It would mean whatever we decided. It has a double clasp. A regular one that you could do up yourself if you wanted to wear it. Maybe if you expected to have a stressful day at work, you'd put it on to know that you had a piece of me with you. Then it also has a locking clasp. The kind I would have to use the tool to open and close it. If we wanted to go somewhere and be on scene, but not somewhere you could wear your leather collar, you could wear this necklace."

"I'm not sure what that means. Where would we go?"

He rubbed a hand through his hair, frustrated, not sure what was going on in her head. "Just like anything else we do, it would be whatever we negotiated. Maybe there's something you know you need to do, but don't want to, and you need extra motivation. Like you talked about wanting to do laps at the pool, but you keep not doing it. We could institute rewards and punishments if you really wanted the motivation. Although, I suppose that necklace and the pool aren't really a great mix."

He stood up and paced in front of her, feeling antsy. "Or, you and I pretty much keep everything in the bedroom, but as with going to the cabin, sometimes it's fun to do things differently. Maybe we go to a restaurant, and like I teased you about last night, use a vibe on you, but this time really in public. I wouldn't want to do play like that without you wearing a collar to know at all times you're under my protection."

"Is that something you would want to do a lot?"

His frustration had eaten away the numbness from last night, and now he was just confused. "Once in a while, I guess, if you found you liked it. If not, no big deal. Maybe you'd wear the neck-lace if we went to a dungeon party but weren't playing. They have Christmas parties and other get-togethers. Whatever we decided. Natalie, I need you to explain to me what happened."

She nodded and twisted her fingers together. "Something happened at the club last night. I was going to tell you, I promise. I had no intention of *not* telling you. I just…you know when we left? Right before? You kissed me and said we should go. Do you remember that?"

"Yes, of course."

"Why did you want to leave?"

"Because I was kissing you and I wanted to do a hell of a lot more than that."

She nodded. "I was about to ask you if we could leave. Tell you I was at four."

He sat back, surprised. He hadn't realized she'd been upset, had been too busy kissing her senseless.

"When Faryn and I were talking, I mentioned something about the weekend at the cabin. I don't remember how it came up, exactly, but they made a little quip about how I'd passed your test about being able to live a 24/7 D/s dynamic."

"Excuse me?" He couldn't keep his voice from being harsh, but regretted it when she flinched. "They thought I was testing you? *You* thought that?"

"No, not really. It was just a comment, they didn't mean it like that. But I kind of froze for like, a whole second. But then my brain kicked in and I knew you weren't. That you wouldn't do that. But they said something about your last relationship being that way, and I was confused, and I was thinking how if things kept going the way they were, you could talk me into something like that, eventually, but then I was like, no that's stupid, and then Faryn was upset and I assured them that they hadn't done anything wrong and then you were back and I pushed it aside until we could talk about it, later."

She chanced a look at him, then went back to watching her hands at her knees. "I really enjoyed visiting the club, but it was a lot, you know? The music and the scenes and the screams and the nakedness and the excitement, and it was all good stuff, it was just a *lot*."

He swallowed, trying to wrap his brain around what he was hearing. "All right."

"But then you suggested we leave and that was perfect timing, and I knew I had to tell you, but we were home before I could even figure out what I wanted to ask you, then we were here and you were amazing, and I think you blew every scrap of energy I had left out of my toes, and you said you loved me, and *I love you*, and it was so much and so amazing and it was…you know how when you spanked me, I cried?"

She glanced up again, but this time she held his gaze. "It wasn't because of the pain. I didn't really understand what it was, but somehow it was just this huge emotional ball inside of me dissolved and leaked out of my eyes, but you said the necklace locked and I thought that meant it was a day collar, and that means full-time slave dynamic, and this time it was a huge emotional ball of anxiety that I didn't even know was there and I just kind of lost my mind. All I could think was I needed to be alone so I could get my brain to work right. Like, I *knew* it was fucked up, but that didn't mean I could make sense of it. My brain, I mean." She sighed and scrubbed her hands over her face. "I'm so sorry I had to leave like that."

He understood. Sort of. She probably had barely slept Friday night, with nerves about going to the club. Then they'd had dinner and she'd talked to his folks, which had gone well, but surely was stressful. Then the club, good but overwhelming for someone whose last club experience had been traumatic. He could understand all that. However…

"You didn't trust me," he told her. That was the part that was sticking in his gut and clawing at his heart. "You didn't trust me to talk, even a little bit. You just left."

"I fucked up. I'm so sorry. I do trust you. As soon as I woke up, I knew I'd made a mistake. I knew you weren't trying to, I don't even know…groom me into your slave. I'm sorry."

He believed her. She was sorry. But it wasn't about sorry. It was about the fact that she'd thought he could do any of that, be that person, and then didn't even trust him enough to explain. Had jerked away from his touch. She hadn't even said she was just leaving for the night and would be back when her head had a chance to clear. She'd packed up as much of her shit as she could manage and wouldn't even look at him as she walked away.

"I think you should go now." He didn't want to say the wrong thing. The only words that wanted to spill out of his mouth were "how could you not trust me?" and that wasn't really something she could answer. She just…hadn't.

Her eyes closed and her body rocked back at his words. He had to fist his hands to keep from reaching out. But how could he move forward with someone who claimed to love him, but didn't understand him at all?

"Okay, Noah."

She stood up and once again walked out the door.

CHAPTER TWENTY-TWO

This time, the knock on the door was unexpected. Noah ignored it. He was positive it wasn't Natalie, and he didn't care about talking to anyone else.

When the back door opened, he sighed. He was lying in the grass, staring up at the sky. He didn't need any company for this all-important task. He draped an arm over his eyes.

"Hey," Alec said.

"Hey."

"You really going to ignore Matty?"

Noah moved his arm and blinked his eyes open against the blinding sun. Sure enough, his best friend was holding a baby car seat.

"Shit, Alec, get him out of the sun."

He stood up and they moved to the patio, where there was shade. Alec unbuckled the baby and immediately handed him to Noah. Noah scowled at his friend, but then checked that the baby's eyes were closed, and he wouldn't be scared off.

As if sensing his attention, Matthew scrunched up his whole face, made a tiny noise, then promptly went back to sleep.

Noah took a deep breath. "What the fuck, man?"

"Exactly my question. Natalie called Annalise. Annalise called and yelled at me. So I'm probably here to yell at you, but Annalise kept swearing that Natalie said she'd been the one to fuck up, so Annalise had to promise not to get mad at you. My sister told me I better figure this shit out, and fast, so here I am."

He'd gone numb again, around about the time he'd realized that Natalie hadn't trusted him. He could understand her freaking out. But he couldn't get past that vital aspect. Trust was everything to him. Earning that trust, as a partner, as a mentor, hell, just as a good friend. In his mind, he hadn't given her any reason to not trust him.

Now, as he nudged Matty's hand with his finger, and the baby immediately uncurled his fingers and latched onto Noah's, something deep inside of him threatened to shatter. He thought about how proud he'd been that she'd decided to go to the club with him. He'd known it might be too much. Had absolutely been ready for her to panic and need to leave. And she had. He just hadn't recognized it. And then he'd compounded her panic and instead of figuring out a way to break through, he'd let her leave the safety of his house.

Of course, kidnapping would have been a problem, but surely he could have done something. Instead, he'd been flabbergasted that they'd gone from such an amazing moment of sweetness and love to her walking out on him. He'd ordered the stupid necklace made special for her, and her response had been to walk away. It had hurt. A lot.

But with the baby's fingers gripping his tightly, he remembered the haunted look in her eyes, the one that had kind of pissed him off, because why would she look afraid of *him*?

Fucking hell, it was like he'd decided she was cured of her past traumas and now she needed to react accordingly. He was a bastard. Her last Dom had blindsided her when, as far as she'd known, everything was great between them, and here she'd thought he'd done the same, and instead of reassuring her, he'd let her leave once, and sent her away the second time. He wanted her to turn to him if she was panicked or upset, but when she didn't, his response was to *push her away?*

Had he played the role of mentor, without the emotional entanglements of a relationship, for so long that his ego had taken over and he'd forgotten that being a boyfriend, a lover, a *couple*, was a different thing, entirely?

"I need to go see her," he said, finally looking at his friend.

"I'm glad we've had this talk."

Noah just shook his head, not sure what Alec was on about. "I need to go see Natalie, now."

"That's going to be a problem since you don't know where she is."

Noah narrowed his eyes. "What are you talking about?"

"She told Annalise she was driving to her grandparents'."

"They live in Atlanta."

"Then you see the problem."

"Fuck. Call Annalise."

"You call her." Alec took his boy from Noah and walked back into the house.

WHEN HER CELL PHONE RANG, Natalie sighed and wiped her eyes. As soon as she'd gotten settled into her hotel room, the damn things had started leaking and wouldn't stop. She cleared her throat and picked up the phone, expecting it to be either Annalise or her mom. Both knew she was on the road, and she'd let them know she was stopped for the night. Annalise had demanded her location, even her room number, and then sent up an ice cream sundae through room service. Her best friend was amazing.

But the caller ID showed Noah.

Fuck. She didn't want to talk to him, didn't want to keep apologizing when no apology would make up for what she'd done. But she owed him whatever he'd ask of her, so she answered the phone.

"Hi, Noah." Her voice sounded flat, even to her own ears. She cleared her throat again, determined to not add the burden of her sadness onto his shoulders.

"Open the door, Natalie. Please. I'd like my turn to talk to you."

A frisson of hope sliced through her, and she ruthlessly buried it. "I'm sorry. I would, but I'm not home."

A knock sounded on the hotel room door. "Please open the door, Nat."

Her gaze flew to the door. That wasn't possible. Was it?

She got up. "Noah, I'm in a hotel. In Baltimore."

"I know. I'd like you to let me in."

She looked through the peephole. Noah stood right outside her door. She threw it open and stared at him. "What are you doing here?"

He took his phone away from his ear. "You had your turn to talk. Now it's my turn."

She blinked at him, but he brushed past her and into the room. He sat at the desk chair opposite the bed.

Not sure if she was dreaming, Natalie sat at the end of the bed and waited for this to make some kind of sense.

"I'm sorry, Natalie."

"What? No, Noah! This was all my fault. You have nothing to apologize for."

"The fact that you think so means I have even more to apologize for than I'd thought."

He reached over and smoothed the space between her eyebrows. It was something he'd done countless times before and it had her breath getting choppy. What was happening?

"I fucked up."

She shook her head but couldn't say anything.

"I let my ego get the better of me. 'How can she not trust me,' I thought. But if you didn't trust me, it's because I didn't earn it. Plain and simple."

"Noah, No."

He held up his hand and her mouth clicked shut.

"You were exhausted, physically and emotionally. Mostly from good stuff, but also from stress and fear. Walking into that club was hella brave, and you handled it so well, that I forgot the whole point of being there was to help earn your trust—in me, in the club, even in the lifestyle. The point wasn't to prove I already *had* that trust. It was just another step in getting you there. It wasn't a test for either of us. But I failed it anyway. Not you. *Me.*"

She was crying for real now, not just leaking tears but full-on sobs, and she couldn't seem to do anything but shake her head at him.

"Ah, fuck, Nat, you're killing me. Can I hold you?"

She managed to change direction with her head and nod, and within a second he was on the bed, his arms wrapped securely around her.

"I love you, Natalie, and if you'll give me another chance, I *will* earn your trust."

"I do trust you, I do."

He shook his head. "You don't, but it's okay. We'll get there, I promise."

Heat burned away her tears, finally, and she sat back, glaring at him. "You can't tell me I don't trust you."

The bastard had the nerve to smirk. "Can't I?"

"Do I have to prove it? Let you whip me? Let you…" She trailed off at the sad look in his eyes that replaced that moment of amusement. She stared at him. "Oh."

"Oh?"

"I get it."

"Tell me."

"I trust you, Noah." She brought her hands up to his face. "I trust you enough to say you can't whip me, I'm not ready for that, and probably never will be. I trust you enough to say I won't be your full-time slave, even though sometimes I love the idea of it, I know the reality isn't for me. And I don't think it's for you, and we can talk about it, but it still won't happen. I trust you enough to tell you I won't share you. You can tease me about threesomes or voyeurism out in public, but it won't happen for real. I think we can work up to them at the club—the public orgasms, not the threesomes—but that's about it."

He was smiling at her now, and her heart felt like it was going to burst, all the hope stretching it so tight. "I love you, Noah Tucker. I trust you, and I love you, and I want to be with you, and I want to choose when to lock the necklace, and when to wear it loose."

He scowled at that. "I'm throwing the damn thing away."

"No!" she gasped. "Please don't. Punish me, but don't do that. It's so beautiful, and I love it. While I was driving here, I kept thinking I understood now, what you meant. How if I'd been driving to Atlanta for any other reason, but still upset, it would have given me a lot of comfort to wear it. To have you with me."

"I'd prefer to actually be with you, if you're that upset."

"I know. Me, too. But it's not always possible." She looked up at him. "Would you like something to wear? From me?"

The pleased surprise on his face warmed her up.

"I've never thought about it. I suppose carrying a pair of your underwear in my pocket when I need a bit of you with me is maybe not as elegant as something you could come up with."

She bit his shoulder through his t-shirt. "I'll get you a bracelet. I guess I'll forgo the locking mechanism, but I'll make sure it's something you won't mind wearing in public."

He wiped the fresh tears from her eyes. She imagined she looked a mess. Red, puffy eyes, her hair matted, her rattiest comfort pajamas that had fresh ice cream drips on the top. But none of that seemed to matter to him as he looked at her with love.

"We're going to have to negotiate our punishments."

She frowned. "Our?"

"You are not spanking me."

Her frown deepened, and he traced her lips with his finger.

"What?" he asked. "You don't think I deserve to be punished as much as you do?"

She kind of did think that but suspected he wouldn't appreciate that answer. "Maybe…it can be a wash?"

Now it was his turn to narrow his eyes. "Will you forgive your-self if I do?"

Hm. She wasn't entirely sure. "Maybe we should think about this part tomorrow, when we've had some sleep."

"Excellent idea."

He suddenly seemed as tired as she felt. She smoothed his hair back from his forehead. "Let's go to bed."

He nodded but wrapped his arms around her so tight, neither of them could move. She didn't mind, just held on.

Finally, he stood and pulled her up with him. He lifted her top up over her head and knelt in front of her to bring down her pants. She threaded her fingers through his hair while he undressed her, then waited patiently while he disrobed.

When they climbed between the sheets, he wrapped his arms around her and she was asleep before she could worry about whether or not she'd be *able* to fall asleep.

She woke to his fingers at her pussy and her nipple, soft, teasing touches.

Light danced around the edges of the curtains and she felt a hundred times better than the previous morning.

"Are you awake?" His voice was low and soft.

"Yes." Her whisper was full of need.

Still, he asked, "Do you want this?"

"Yes." Not so much a whisper now, but a demand.

His smile turned wolfish. "Excellent." He kissed her, and she remembered that she wasn't wearing his collar, or cuffs, so she pushed him until he rolled over, still holding the kiss. Landing on his chest, her legs to the side, she reached for his cock, feeling it grow in her hand as she squeezed.

He retaliated by sliding two fingers inside her. The fact that she was wet and ready made it easy.

She gasped and he took advantage, rolling them again. They tumbled and turned, kissed and fondled, fucked and made love, until they were spent and nearly fell asleep again.

"Check-out is in ten minutes," she said, vaguely alarmed but unable to summon any real effort.

"I'll call the front desk and add another day. You text your mom and Annalise."

"You text Annalise," she grumbled.

"Fine."

"Good. I love you."

He flashed her the devastating grin that never failed to melt her insides. "I love you, too."

CHAPTER TWENTY-THREE

One year later

Natalie sat at the bar, one foot propped on the rail, the other swinging freely. She was wearing a prim business outfit, one that her coworkers would be shocked to see her in. But her blouse was unbuttoned to between her breasts and a hint of the starkly red lace bra showed to those close enough to notice.

Her finger played with the necklace at her throat. Or collar, rather, as Noah had engaged the tiny lock before she'd left the hotel room several minutes ago.

They'd come to Atlanta to see her mom and grandparents. It was their second visit, as she and Noah had flown down a couple of months after he'd given her the necklace. Tomorrow was her grandparents' fiftieth wedding anniversary, and she and Noah had come to take them, and her mom, out to dinner.

The celebration was nothing like the anniversary party that Annalise's family had thrown for her Crawford grandparents a couple of years before, but that was fine. The Handels loved each other, and that was what mattered. And they'd welcomed Noah with reserved, but open, arms.

She sipped the appletini when it arrived, only to discover that she did not, in fact, like appletinis. Well, it had looked good on the menu and she'd figured it was more sophisticated than the wine or apple cider she normally ordered at a bar.

She felt him behind her, then. Her Noah. It was hard to remember what not having him in her life was like.

"Is this seat taken?" he asked, coming around to the stool next to her.

Looking him up and down, she gave a nonchalant shrug though it took every bit of her meager acting skills. "I don't believe so."

She'd expected him to wear the suit he'd brought for tomorrow's dinner, to line up with her upper-management look. Instead he was wearing black leather pants and a burnt-orange shirt that fit him very, very well. He'd put on the brown leather bracelet with the infinity knot that she'd bought him to wear when he wanted a reminder that he belonged to her.

Picking up her full glass, she took a tiny sip just so that she could eye him over the rim as he asked the bartender for a beer. He'd ordered her not to wear panties, and now she was wishing she'd negotiated that a bit better, because she was definitely going to get her skirt wet.

"Buy you a drink?" he asked, his voice a little rougher than usual.

Sparks of electricity shot through her. They hadn't done this before, and she'd had no idea he could role play this well. He was always surprising her.

She tried for haughty as she pointedly looked at her hand holding the full drink, and the engagement ring on her finger.

He shrugged. "Doesn't look like you're enjoying the drink, and that's not a wedding ring."

She had to bite her tongue not to laugh. They'd started talking about their long-term future not long after being together. She'd moved in pretty quickly, because it had become ridiculous switching things between his house and her dinky apartment. Just over three months ago, he'd taken her to Cedric's cabin in New Hampshire for her birthday. He'd spent the day ordering her into sexual bliss, then taken her out to dinner. He'd brought her back to the cabin and asked her, beside the pond, under a blanket of stars, to be his wife. They hadn't set a date yet, that was on their agenda for next week.

Without waiting for a response, he ordered her a bottle of cider. She didn't comment, but pushed the martini glass out of her way and ignored his almost smirk.

"You in town for long?" she asked when the bartender left.

"Sod convention."

She laughed, but turned it into a not-so-delicate cough.

"Ah. I'm here for the funeral service professionals convention. It's at the hotel next door, but I wanted a break from my colleagues for a little bit."

The corner of his mouth turned up. "I didn't realize you folks had a convention."

"Oh, sure. It's important to stay current on the latest technologies."

"I bet. Is your fiancé in the business, as well?"

"Well, he's more on the dirt and flowers side of things."

He had to cover his mouth at that, but he rallied. "Sounds boring."

"Oh, no, he keeps things quite…lively. I promise."

"Well, if that's the case, maybe he'd be interested in," he looked her up and down very obviously, "sharing."

She felt her eyes widen and her mouth open at that. "Oh. I'm not sure he's…prepared for that." She was thinking of his promise to buy toys and fill her up as if she were with two men, like Jesse and Grant at Apex. They'd gone to dinner with the guys and Stephanie a couple of times, and had enjoyed their company very much, but she'd forgotten about her tease to Noah about a threesome. Until now.

"Oh, I think he sounds like the kind of guy who's very prepared."

"Hm, you're not wrong." She moved her hand a few inches so that she could trace her finger over his bracelet.

He put his hand on the small of her back, letting his palm warm her through the silk of her blouse, his fingers pressing into hard little points at her waist. He'd come off the stool, crowding in closer to her, so her whole side was enveloped in his heat. She took her hand off his wrist and moved it below the bar, touched his leather-clad thigh.

His muscles flexed under her hand and she drew it toward his cock.

"Be very sure about what you want." His warning, growled into her ear with his lips just touching the sensitive skin, had her shivering.

"Maybe you won't like him," she warned, hearing the breathiness in her voice.

"You'll be what I'm focused on." His fingers pressed even harder into her side.

She gulped down some cider, her throat suddenly dry.

He placed his free hand over hers on his thigh and dragged it to his cock. "Do you like it rough, blondie?"

She swallowed hard, enjoying the feel of the leather over his hardening bulge.

"I'm a good girl." She tried for a touch of outrage.

"I'll just bet you are." He pressed her hand harder. "Would you still be a good girl if I put you on the back of my bike and drove you around until you were making my seat wet?"

"I—um, I don't think we'd make it out of the parking lot."

He tried to smother his laugh, but failed. "So you're a naughty girl, too."

"I guess so."

"You need someone to take you in hand."

"I don't know, I think I might be a handful."

He smiled, Noah's smile. "Without question."

He drained his beer and eyed her full appletini and nearly full cider, but ignored them and slapped some cash on the bar for a tip. He leaned in close to her ear again. "I've heard enough sass out of you. You're going to close your mouth and come up to my room with me, or I'm going to go next door and tell your mortuary colleagues that you're running around in this tight-ass skirt with no underwear, leaving wet spots on the furniture."

She was glad his face was at her side so he couldn't see as she struggled to get her laughter under control. Finally, she managed to speak. "Oh, please, don't get me into trouble. I need this job."

"Then you'll do as I say. Not another word."

"Yes, Sir."

"That was two words. I'm going to have to punish you now."

"Oh, no, Sir. Please, I'm so sorry."

"I don't know if I can count that high."

There was no containing the laughter that burst out of her. Several heads turned their way and Noah buried his face in her neck, but she felt his chest shaking against her.

Finally she cleared her throat and very pointedly said nothing. He grabbed her hand and helped her off the stool, then dragged her to the elevators.

When they got to the room, he closed the door and shoved her up against the wall, her wrists gripped in his hand, held above her head, his mouth taking full possession of hers.

She kicked off her shoes and wrapped one foot around his leg, but she couldn't manage much because the damn pencil skirt was too tight. Whether he was aware of that or not, she didn't know, but he yanked her skirt up her thighs and growled when he found her slick and wet. She wrapped her leg more firmly around him.

But not firmly enough, because he was suddenly gone, leaving her to lock her knees to avoid sliding to the floor. Her arms fell to her side but she didn't move farther as she watched him rip his belt off. Then he moved. He spun her around, pressing her hard into the door again. He wrapped the belt around her wrists several times before buckling it securely. Spinning her again, he ripped—actually ripped—her blouse free.

Natalie stared at him in wide-eyed shock and excitement. He shoved his knee under her skirt and felt her wetness as he unhooked her bra and dragged it down. Fuck, he'd already tied her hands. Trying not to laugh, he grabbed her blouse and rolled it into a gag, held it up to her lips.

Her eyes lit with mischief and she turned her head away, dramatically. He shoved his knee harder against her core and she gasped. He slid the silk between her lips and knotted it behind her head. It was already ruined, so cutting it free wouldn't be a problem. Speaking of cutting.

He propelled her backwards until she hit the bed and fell back onto it. He'd left his bag of supplies at the foot, ready for their return to the room. He grabbed the safety scissors and used them to cut her bra straps free. Damn, he was going to owe her a shopping trip after this. Totally worth it.

He yanked the red fabric free of her breasts and tossed it aside. He'd meant to use *it* as the gag, but being adaptable was important.

She kept him on his toes, his Natalie. Just by being her. He wanted to always be able to surprise and delight her. He hauled her farther up on the bed and turned her over onto her stomach. She turned her head so she could see him and he pushed the hair out of her way.

"Someone earned some spanks," he reminded her.

She spoke and he was pretty sure she asked, "How many?" but he chose not to answer because he was positive he couldn't do so without laughing. Instead, he slapped her ass, not bothering to take off her skirt. Her sass turned into a moan as he peppered her with spanks.

When she was wiggling in anticipation and pressing up into his hand, he stopped. He kept his hand pressed into her back so she wouldn't move and felt around in his bag.

"Since you only invited two of us, I'm going to have to fill one of your holes before your fiancé gets here." He held the silicone butt plug up so she could see it. Her body convulsed into laughter at the sight of the red silicone rose. He brought it to his mouth and bit one of the outer petals and tears began to leak out of her eyes.

"Don't worry, it will only hurt a little," he warned as he slathered the plug with lube.

She tilted her hips, pushing into the plug, letting it slide fully into her in one easy push. He rubbed her flank in praise. "On your back now."

He helped her roll over, then pulled the next item out of the bag. The dildo was fairly realistic looking, it even had balls, but had taken him a fair bit of internet searching to find the right color.

"Your fiancé is kind of...orange," he said, holding the brightly colored silicone up.

Her eyes squeezed tight and she tried to close her lips around the silk as much as possible to hold in the laughter, but it was impossible. He tickled her ribs and she shrieked, but got ahold of herself. He cut the blouse free and slid it from beneath her head.

"Get any action with your teeth out of the way now, because once he's good and wet, you'll have my cock, and there better not be any biting."

She licked her lips and kept her face on his, rather than the ridiculous toy. He slid it between her lips, and she licked and sucked as if it were him. Soon, it would be him. He gripped her hair, directing her head. Her eyes went glassy.

"You can talk now," he told her, though he'd filled her mouth. "But try not to get security called on us."

When he slid the phallus out, she locked her eyes on his. "Sir." It was a whisper, but it said so much.

He kissed her, softly, gently. "My girl."

"Yours. All yours."

He sat up and took off his clothes, enjoying the way she eyed him hungrily. He dripped lube onto the dildo and eased it into her, her hips bucking up to receive it. Him. He worked it in and out, watching her folds stretch to envelope the toy.

"Please, Sir," she begged.

He climbed back onto the bed and straddled her, facing her

hungry cunt. He fed her his cock and watched her suck him down. He had to close his eyes, because the sight was too fucking erotic. She hummed around him and he almost lost control. Almost. He faced forward and lowered his mouth to her clit, teasing it with his tongue, lightly at first. All the while he kept the dildo pumping, in and out, twisting and turning so she could feel the ridges, angling it to hit that spot inside her that made her hips jump.

He moved his knees back, letting her take more of him. At the same time, he took her clit between his teeth, biting *oh so* carefully. She screamed. He felt it more than heard it. Fuck, he wasn't going to be able to last much longer. He sucked on her clit and began to truly fuck her with the toy. She was trying to lift her hips, but he held her down and kept to his own pace.

She worked her tongue and cheeks around him. He knew her, knew her sounds and rhythm and signs. He'd planned on letting her come this way, but changed his mind. He wanted to see her. Feel her. He lifted his hips and pulled free from her mouth. He eased the toy out and tossed it on the bed, then climbed off her. Helping her sit up, he unbuckled the belt and freed her hands.

"Lay back now, Petal" he told her, all the play gone from his tone. This was his Natalie, and all he wanted to be was everything she needed.

"Noah. Sir." She lay back and lifted her hands, wrapping them around him when he covered her and slid into her slick folds. Her nails dug into his shoulders but she didn't rush him. He closed his eyes tight for a minute to get past the slick feel of her holding him, then opened to find her gaze on his.

Her blue eyes held tight to his as he brought them closer and closer to release.

"I love you, Sir," she whispered, and he nearly lost it.

"I love you, too, Petal. You've taken my soul. I need you to keep it safe."

"Yes, Sir. All mine."

He angled his hips and she gasped. She was back to the edge, ready to go, waiting for him. "Come for me, Natalie."

She cried out, and he let the spasms of her muscles take him over. Shockwaves raced through his body. He slammed his mouth shut over the shout that tried to escape. He dropped and rolled so they were on their sides, still wrapped around each other, his cock still buried inside her.

He couldn't wait to marry her, but it almost didn't matter. She was his, just as he was hers. From the moment he'd wrapped the cheap magnetic collar around her throat, that day in his car, the deed was done.

Still, giving her the locking collar, then the rose choker, those had been excellent steps. As had the diamond ring. And he was looking forward to adding his wedding ring to her collection. But when she'd wrapped the leather bracelet she'd bought for him around his wrist, the infinity knot subtle but unmistakable, he'd determined he wasn't going let her go, not if he could help it. And soon she'd slide the ring she'd bought for him onto his left hand, and he'd move heaven and earth to make sure it stayed there.

But he didn't have to move planets. He just had to be the person she needed. Luckily, that was no job at all.

"I love you, Noah." She told him.

He kissed her. "My Natalie. I love you."

EXCERPT

Bound by Sunlight
By KB Alan
(Available Now)

Kyriana Price has spent nearly a year trapped at her evil day job. And she does mean evil. Her boss is a mage bent on power and lets nothing stand in the way of his quest to gain more of it. When she sees Connul Graysn wielding a flogger at a BDSM club, she formulates an escape plan that will require his considerable skills—as a mage and as a Dom. Going to another mage for help might not be the best plan, but it's the only one she's got, and at this point, she's willing to try just about anything.

The last thing Connul expects when he finds an intruder in his house is that he'll soon have her chained in his bedroom, her lovely body marked by his paddle. But she's begging for his help—how can a gentleman refuse? As they learn to trust each other, he begins to realize that the only thing he's not willing to do for her is let her go.

CHAPTER ONE

A shiver raced down Kyriana's spine. She wanted to blame it on the cold, rather than nerves, but the study she waited in wasn't really chilly. Still, she pulled her feet up to rest in front of her on the chair's wide leather seat, her toes curling over its edge, her arms wrapping around her legs. She studied her bare feet. Damn. *Damn, damn, damn.* What had she been thinking to wear the simple sleep pants and tank top? She had an assortment of seductive outfits to choose from, all of them including four-to-five-inch fuck-me heels. But here she sat, feet bare, toes not even painted, sans makeup.

Despite her self-chastisement, she made no move to get up and go change. There was no question in her mind that if she left the room she wouldn't be coming back. Breaking into the study had taken all of her meager skills as a mole and every bit of her courage. It was one thing to spy on a superior mage such as Connul Graysn. It was another thing entirely to break into his private study and wait for him to find her. If he didn't give her a chance to explain, or worse, didn't agree to her plan, she was dead. At least, she hoped he'd kill her. Because there were worse things in life than death, and if he didn't help her, and he didn't kill her, chances were pretty strong she'd be able to catalog those worse things in intimate detail.

Another shiver raced through her. God, she was such a coward. Which was exactly how she'd gotten herself into this mess in the first place. Dropping her forehead to rest on her knees, she swallowed back the tears that threatened. It was good to remember, actually. Good to remember that her cowardice had gotten her into this mess, so playing it safe wasn't always the smart option. Tonight was an excellent night to keep that in mind.

Connul knew the minute he entered his garage that someone was in his house uninvited. Worse, they were in his private study, which nobody had access to while he was away. The live-in staff should have all retired to their separate wing by now, and certainly wouldn't invade his private room without permission.

He cast his senses throughout the house but found only that one anomaly. He detected no traps, physical or magical. A small spell ensured his entry, as well as his slow progress toward the study, were silent. He could tell the presence was a woman and that she wasn't a mage. If she were intending harm, it would be through more mundane means. The idea that anyone would threaten him or his staff in his own home pissed him off, but he stuffed the anger away. He needed to be clear-headed. Control was key. Being a mage was a heavy responsibility. It wouldn't do to let anger get the better of him and blast an ignorant thief with a spell that would do them lasting damage.

Of course, the chances of an ignorant thief gaining entry into his protected study were just about zero. He would be careful, but he would be ready. He prepared a number of offensive spells as he neared the room's closed door. The obvious first move would be to immobilize the woman so that she couldn't use a weapon against him. She likely had some means to deflect such a spell—a person wouldn't just wait uninvited in a mage's space without expecting the need to defend themselves. Still, he believed in keeping it simple until more complicated means were called for.

Pausing just before the doorway, he closed his eyes and called the room to mind. He wasn't able to project his inner eye just anywhere without serious magical effort, but the room was his private space, where he spent more time than almost any other. He was physically and magically in tune with it, so it took little to no effort to *see* inside, especially since he was so close.

The room appeared empty until he realized that the woman occupied his large reading chair. Turned away from the door, it gave her a view of the fireplace. There was no fire burning and she had her head buried in her arms. She didn't seem familiar to him at all, nor did she appear to be armed. Her hands were wrapped about her legs and clearly empty, so unless she was hiding something in her lap, she was clean. Which made no sense. What the hell was going on?

He wanted to see her face, her reactions, so Connul squared himself in front of the closed door and made a careful noise one instant before he cast the freezing spell. Her head flew up at the sound, but nothing else moved as she was caught by the magic. He'd frozen her vocal cords as a standard precaution, so the only sound in the room was her initial gasp, followed by labored breathing.

The door opened quickly, the locks still disengaged from her entry. He flipped on the lights and hurried to the chair. Once he could see her face-to-face, he let his inner vision go. He hadn't constricted her breathing, but her chest heaved, her lungs working hard. Shit, he hoped she didn't hyperventilate, that would make it harder to get answers. And he *really* wanted answers. She blinked against the light, her face a study in concentration as she clearly tried to bring herself under control. Her vivid green eyes stood out from hair that was a red so soft it was almost gold. It swung in a bob against her chin, inviting fingers to brush it back from her pale skin.

Though he allowed no outward reaction, he mentally chastised himself. What was he doing noticing her quiet beauty at a time like this? He was certain now that he didn't know her. She squeezed her eyes shut and her breath shuddered in and out as his mind whirled, trying to figure out what was going on. While it took some skill to cast the freezing spell as specifically as he had—allowing normal lung function and all facial expressions, but no other bodily move-ment—she should have expected something of the sort. Even if she didn't know his skill level, didn't appreciate the nuances of his spell-work, it was an obvious first move. But she'd simply waited in the chair for him to return to his study? It made no sense.

To make certain she was unarmed, he pulled her hands from around her legs, laying them on top of the chair's wide arms. He stared at her bare feet for a moment. Why did bare feet look so innocent? He grasped her ankles and pulled her legs out, dropping them. Her eyes remained shut as she visibly struggled to bring herself under control. Ignoring the flash of concern that speared through him as her body began to tremble, he took a step back and looked her over. Totally ridiculous. Why in the hell would someone break into his study and wait for him in his own chair, wearing pajamas?

Maybe that was the answer. Maybe she was just crazy. He set his hands at her waist and ran them down her hips and legs, making sure there were no weapons tucked between her body and the chair. At this point, he wasn't really surprised to come up empty. But he was surprised at how tempting her curves were. He was supposed to be focusing on the situation, not the enticing woman. Shaking his head, he brought his hands up to her shoulders. Sometimes, if a spell was subtle enough, he might not detect it on a person without physical touch. He closed his eyes and concentrated hard.

As before, he sensed no spells on her body, nothing that might harm him, nothing she could activate either offensively or defensively. There was...*something*, though. He slid his hands up her shoulders to cup her neck, trying to get a better feel for what he was sensing. A slight lessening of her distress distracted him. Opening his eyes, he watched her face. A single tear tracked from beneath her tightly closed lids, but her breathing was calming and her trembling subsiding.

Once again, he concentrated on what was inside of her instead of her body's reactions. His thumbs traced up and down her neck. Yes. There it was. A powerful spell, trapped in her mind. It was completely foreign to her, he had no doubt. There was a tiny spark of magic that was hers, something distant that he was sure she wasn't even aware of. Probably at least one mage back in her family tree. Interesting. He laid a spell himself, one that ensured her honesty in whatever she said, as well as compelling her to answer his questions. He didn't even try to be subtle, and though she might not know exactly what he'd done, she was sure to know he'd done something.

Releasing her, he stepped back, leaning against the desk, watching as her fear once again overwhelmed her. He withdrew ninety percent of the immobilizing spell. She could move, but not suddenly and not with any strength. It took her only a second to realize she was free. Her feet came back up to rest on the seat and she buried her face in her hands as she struggled to control her breathing.

He probably should have been irritated but he was too curious. The fact that she was terrified but trying to control it was interesting. If she'd just been a sniveling wreck he might not have been patient enough to stand by and wait. As it was, only a minute passed before she wiped her eyes, scrubbed her face with her hands, and looked up at him.

"I'm sorry." She took a deep breath, glancing down at her feet.

He almost laughed out loud at the horrified expression that crossed her face as her legs worked their way down until her ankles were crossed demurely. Could it be that she was embarrassed to be lounging on his chair? While barefoot? And wearing pajamas? After breaking into his study? Maybe he was asleep and this was all a bizarre dream. Her eyes were wide, her gaze fixed firmly on his knees, so he let the smile out, just for a second. Then he drew in a deep breath of his own. Enough of this nonsense, it was time to figure out what the hell was going on.

"What's your name?"

"Kyr. Kyriana Price. I—"

"How did you get in here?" he interrupted. He was in charge here, and the sooner she figured that out, the better for her.

She frowned and answered slowly. "I was hired by Mrs. Tremky."

"Yesterday," she added, when he didn't say anything.

"In this room. How did you get into this room?"

She bit her lip, opened her mouth, grimaced and closed it again. Finally, she tried again, "I...had a thingy." It came out in a rush and her eyes darted up to his before settling on a view of his arms, crossed in front of his chest.

He waited, but she didn't look as if she was feeling compelled to say anything more.

"A thingy."

She gave him a jerky nod.

"You had a thingy, which let you into my office."

Another grimace crossed her face. "Look, I—"

"Ah," he cut her off before she could go off on her own tangent. Then he realized he hadn't actually asked her a follow up question. He'd just made a statement, which she'd been able to ignore. Sometimes magic was annoyingly literal.

"What kind of thingy?"

She fought his compulsion this time. Her stomach clenched and she swallowed hard before gasping out in pain. "It...I...A spell-lock thingy."

She took a shuddering breath and leaned back into the seat, once again daring a brief look at his face. He wasn't sure what she saw there, but he was getting damn curious, as well as concerned. His compulsion spell seemed to be in opposition to the spell already cast on her. And the foreign spell was strong enough to cause physical discomfort.

"Why are you wearing pajamas?"

Her tight features softened.

"I didn't want to wear any of the clothes I had with me."

"Why?"

She squirmed, though he didn't think it was from pain. "They're all...slutty."

Her hands gripped her thighs and he knew she was uncomfortable, wishing she could curl up into the chair. A sitting version of the fetal position. But for now, propriety would keep her sitting erect and he didn't want her too comfortable.

"Why do you only have slutty clothes with you? Surely Mrs. Tremky informed you of the dress code?" He didn't have uniforms for his staff, but there was a certain level of dress expected, and slutty did not qualify.

Another deep breath. "To attract you," she whispered, softly enough that he had to lean forward to hear her.

She was tense, waiting for his next question.

"So that you could...what? Gain my confidence?"

Her stomach muscles contracted as she opened her mouth, but only a soft cry escaped. Sweat broke out on her brow and she began to shudder. This wasn't discomfort, but pain.

He leaned forward and took her wrist in his hand, testing her pulse. It was wild, but her shaking body stilled slightly. He squeezed his fingers around her wrist and she was able to draw in a full breath. She gave the tiniest nod of her head, then collapsed back against the seat, wrapping her free hand tightly around her stomach.

As he watched, her breathing evened out. Goose bumps pebbled across her skin as the sweat dried, and her heartbeat steadied under his fingers. She twisted her arm, just slightly. He knew that motion. She wasn't trying to pull free of his hand, just testing, feeling the hold he had on her. Well, wasn't that interesting?

"How old are you?" he asked as he reached for her other hand. He wrapped his fingers around the delicate wrist and squeezed ever so gently.

Her shoulders relaxed and her expression softened, just a bit.

"Twenty-eight."

"Pull your legs up."

She startled, but complied, pulling her legs up onto the seat, tailor style. He knelt in front of her, his legs flush against the chair's base.

"Look at me."

Her eyes met his for a full minute before blinking rapidly and falling to his chin.

Hope. He'd seen hope in her, as well as fear. His compulsion spell was strictly for words and yet she'd immediately responded to his commands. He almost hated to ask her another question. To bring her pain. But he needed to know what the hell was going on.

"Why are you here?"

Her eyes closed, but not in physical pain. She had an answer ready for this question that wasn't in opposition to the magic that held her captive. But she was still afraid to answer. Afraid of his response?

"I was hoping you could help me."

He rested his arms on her legs, her wrists secured in his grasp. Studied her.

"Do you wish to harm me?"

"No!" Her gaze flew to his, searching his face, desperate for him to believe her. He caressed her arms with his thumbs in an absent, soothing gesture.

"Does someone else mean for you to harm me?"

She looked down, her body tightening, hunching over their arms.

"Stop. Don't answer."

She let out a relieved sigh.

"Can you give me a name?" He hoped that by not being specific she would have some leeway, but her answer was an immediate shake of the head.

"No," she gasped.

"Am I in danger tonight?"

"Not that I know of."

"Will you attempt to harm me, physically or with magic?"

"No." This time her answer was easy and immediate. A spy then, not an assassin. She'd been given some means of entering his study, but had stayed, intending to get caught. Her instructions, her compulsion, obviously hadn't been specific enough to include removing herself before he appeared, and she had taken advantage of that.

He needed to find out what was going on. Whoever was using the girl had strong magic at their disposal and didn't mind hurting others to get to him.

Kyriana opened her mouth, but then closed it without speaking. He smiled and transferred her left wrist into his right hand, easily holding both. He brought his free hand up to her neck, testing, feeling, caressing.

Her pulse sped up but then steadied. Her wrists jerked and she gave a tiny sigh when his fingers cupped her slender neck, his thumb resting against the pulse in her throat. Here was someone who needed to give herself into stronger hands. He had one more test, one he was second-guessing himself about making. But he needed to be sure he was reading her correctly—that she disliked being immobilized by the spell, but her reaction to being restrained by him was completely opposite. Determined, he let go of her wrists and re-enacted the immobilization spell.

Her response was immediate and intense. Similar to the pain reaction she'd shown when he'd asked her a question she couldn't answer—her stomach clenched, her eyes closed and her face drew in tight. He removed the spell, freeing her back to almost full movement. Her arms wrapped around her body and she hunched over herself. A tear fell from her eye but she was already setting her jaw, swallowing hard and forcing her eyes to meet his. She very deliberately returned her arms to her lap, where he'd dropped them.

A test. She didn't know if she'd passed or failed, but she knew she'd just been tested. God, it had sucked. Not painful like the questions had been, but somehow worse. Being forced, magically restrained, horrified her on a basic and primitive level. Something she hadn't been aware of until he'd frozen her when he walked into the office. She'd been concentrating so hard on what she might say to him, what words she could use that would get past the damn block in her head but give him the information he needed, that he'd taken her by surprise. She wasn't a total idiot. She'd considered the fact that when he came in she would have to be careful to make no sudden or threatening motions. She just hadn't thought about a spell that would freeze her. Hell, even if she'd thought about it, she wasn't sure she would have realized how terrifying it would be.

Thankfully, he seemed to be catching on quickly. At the very least he'd realized she'd been forced here and was trying to warn him. He was smart and powerful, and she felt hope that he would figure out what she was trying to do. It was probably a stupid plan, but it was the only one she'd been able to come up with after almost a year. And once he knew what it was, if he didn't think it would work, then maybe he would have other ideas.

"Tell me what you were going to say," he said as he picked up both her wrists in his large hand. She swallowed, just to feel his other hand tighten around her throat.

"Magic." It was so hard to say things that were important without triggering the spell. "Loophole."

His thumb tipped her chin up, prompting her to meet his eyes. The fierce look from earlier had thawed considerably. He'd figured out that she herself was not out to harm him. She had no delusions that he would now go easy on her. She was still a danger to him and they both knew it. But he would be more careful. She hoped.

Holding his stare was hard, but since it was what he wanted, she forced herself to do it. His eyes were a rich brown with warm yellow undertones. His hair was brown too, but with so many highlights from the sun it was hard to pinpoint the final color. He must spend a lot of time outdoors, which was probably normal for mages, who depended on the earth for some of their magic. Her breath caught as she considered one of the other major means of replenishing and practicing magic. Sex. Earthy, elemental, sex. He moved his thumb back down, tacitly giving her permission to drop her gaze, which she did, immediately. She stared straight ahead at the chest covered in a soft-looking sweater. A sweater molding itself lovingly to his—*Focus!* She needed to focus. Yes, she was hoping that his skills as a mage would help her, and was aware of his reputation as a sexual Master, but that didn't mean she was here to stare at his chest.

She started to speak, then thought better of it. Was she still allowed? She dared a quick look up again and he gave her a small nod, his expression serious.

"I saw you." She tried to figure out what else she could say to point him in the right direction.

"You know I'm a mage," he said slowly. "And you know that I visit a sex club." He considered. "Did you see me there?"

"Yes."

Oh, had she seen him. She still wasn't sure what force had prompted her to go to the club that night. She'd known exactly what sort of place it was, exactly the clientele it catered to. Her neighbor was a regular. A submissive who had no steady Dom, Danni had told her all about Loophole. Kyriana had feigned disinterest but Danni had known, had seen, and so had continued to invite her despite her repeated refusals. Until last week, when Kyr had said yes.

Mages rarely identified themselves as such and she might not have recognized him for what he was if she hadn't just seen his picture in her boss's files. But she was positive she still would have been mesmerized. Magic was only a part of who he was and wasn't all that made up the power that surrounded him. He'd been flogging a submissive while the lucky woman's Master watched. The sub was strapped to a Saint Andrew's cross, her bare back to the room while Connul worked her over. Nothing remarkable, a scene that probably played out in the club every night of the week. But somehow, he had made it different. *More.* Every eye in the vicinity had been riveted to them. The girl's moans had sent shivers down Kyr's spine and she'd felt every slap of the flogger like a too-distant echo.

For over an hour he'd worked her, bringing her up then back down before escalating even higher. Her Master had stood by, watching. Finally Connul had brought her to what had to have been an exquisite climax based on the bound woman's cries. Kyriana had sighed with her own small release. And she'd wondered.

She'd always secretly had a desire to be bound. It was this forbidden need that had kept her interested whenever Danni had told her about the club. Spankings and whippings, though. She'd heard about them, of course, but never really given it much thought. Pain was pain and didn't have any place with pleasure. Not that she had much experience with pleasure. What she'd seen at the club told her that just because she hadn't understood the pleasure of pain, didn't mean it didn't exist. Didn't mean it didn't work. Didn't mean it couldn't work...on her.

"When?"

She licked her lips. "Last week. Thursday."

"What was I doing?"

"Flogging a girl. On the cross." It came out kind of breathy, so she cleared her throat.

Both of his thumbs started moving, one caressing her wrist, the other her neck. How could she feel so vulnerable and yet so safe at the same time? He leaned in close, rested his forehead against hers. Though he was barely touching her, she felt as if his whole body was covering hers. She grew damp between her legs.

"Did you like what you saw?"

So much for damp, she was full-on wet now. She tried not to squirm and mostly succeeded. "Y-yes."

"What part did you like best?"

"Uh—" she stuttered. Irritated, she closed her eyes briefly. He must think she was such an imbecile. The need to answer him was strong, but she hadn't thought about it before. The whole thing had been so amazing. The woman's cries, his careful precision, the intense orgasm. Oh, yes, now she knew.

"The end."

"The orgasm?"

She swallowed hard. "No, after that."

His long fingers around her throat tightened just a tiny bit. Why did that feel so good? It should scare the crap out of her. But it didn't—not by a long shot.

"Is anyone going to come looking for you tonight?"

"No."

He stood up, stepped back, and her body cried out at the loss. What was wrong with her? He'd put a spell on her to make her talk. Had he done something to make her need him too?

"No magic tonight. No more spells."

She blinked up at him. No, he wasn't talking about his spells. He meant the one she wanted him to remove. He wasn't going to help her, he wasn't going to try to remove the spell.

"Not tonight. You have to trust me first."

"I—" She stopped herself. Of course she didn't trust him. She wanted to. She prayed to any god that might listen that he would be able to help her. But she didn't trust him. Hell, she'd just been wondering if he was messing with her.

Since he'd stood, her stare was now directed at his cock, which had made a considerable tent in his pants since he'd first stood before her. Oddly gratified, she relaxed, waited to see what he would do.

"I need you to let me earn your trust."

Closing her eyes, she took a deep breath. He understood—knew what she needed. She could do this. She *would* do this. Hell, she wanted this.

"Okay."

"You understand, I can't remove the truth spell, either. Or the compulsion spell."

She hadn't even considered it, would never have asked it of him. Which didn't mean she didn't hate it immensely, but there were other things at the top of her hate list right now that held much higher priority.

"I understand." She wished he'd come back and hold her again.

"Stand up."

She untucked her legs and rose, irritated at how unsteady she felt.

"What experience do you have?"

Oh crap. She ducked her head and whispered, "Not much."

"Don't hide from me."

Damn. She lifted her head. "Not much."

He began to move. He walked around, pushed the chair back and circled her, but touched her only with his look.

"Not much BDSM? Or not much sex."

"Not much sex."

"Pain?" He was keeping his voice neutral, not giving her any clues.

"No."

"And no BDSM."

"No." Should she feel embarrassed about that? Probably not, but she did. She wouldn't drop her head again, but she couldn't stop the blush from firing across her face and down her neck.

Finally he touched her, trailing a single finger along her collarbone as he circled her again. How could such a simple touch ignite a fire all the way to her sex?

Purchase Bound by Sunlight at kbalan.com/books/bound-by-sunlight

To Join KB Alan's newsletter, visit www.kbalan.com/newsletter

ABOUT THE AUTHOR

KB Alan lives the single life in Southern California. She acknowledges that she should probably turn off the computer and leave the house once in a while in order to find her own happily ever after, but for now she's content to delude herself with the theory that Mr. Right is bound to come knocking at her door through no real effort of her own. Please refrain from pointing out the many flaws in this system. Other comments, however, are happily received.

www.kbalan.com

To join KB's newsletter, visit www.kbalan.com/newsletter

facebook.com/kbalan
twitter.com/KB_Alan
instagram.com/authorkbalan
bookbub.com/authors/kb-alan

www.ingramcontent.com/pod-product-compliance
Lightning Source LLC
Chambersburg PA
CBHW071238190726
48292CB00007B/2342